BEFORE YOU FIND ME

ENDORSEMENTS

In *Before You Find Me*, Sheri Schofield gives us a heart-racing thriller during which I seriously had to force myself to put down my Kindle long enough to prepare dinner. I never read a book that fast, so be aware of you time line because you will face the same dilemma! If I could give more than five stars, I would for this page-turner novel."
—**Peggy Lovelace Ellis**, author, *Silver Shadows: Stories of Life in a Small Town*

I could not put this book down. A heart racing thrill ride from start to finish, this story has it all: danger, excitement and romance.
—**Andrea Chatman**, author, *Beneath the Deep*

BEFORE YOU FIND ME

SHERI SCHOFIELD

A Christian Company
ElkLakePublishingInc.com

COPYRIGHT NOTICE

Cover and Interior Design: Derinda Babcock, Deb Haggerty
Editor(s): Marcie Bridges, Deb Haggerty

PUBLISHED BY: Elk Lake Publishing, Inc., 35 Dogwood Drive, Plymouth, MA 02360, 2022

Library Cataloging Data

Names: Schofield, Sheri (Sheri Schofield)

Before You Find Me / Sheri Schofield

304 p. 23cm × 15cm (9in × 6 in.)

ISBN-13: 978-1-64949-657-7 (paperback) | 978-1-64949-658-4 (trade hardcover) | 978-1-64949-659-1 (trade paperback) | 978-1-64949-660-7 (e-book)

Key Words: Western, Suspense, Romance, Murder, Detective work, Montana, Texas

Library of Congress Control Number: 2022943153 Fiction

DEDICATION

For my girls—Christy, Audrey & Chelsea

ACKNOWLEDGMENTS

I wish to thank the following people for their insights about the land, livestock, plants, and other useful information I used in writing this book.

Thank you to Tana Bignell, a realtor/rancher in the Elliston, Montana area, for your helpful information about the practical aspects of ranch life in that area.

Thanks to Jobe Nelson and Roxanne Allen for your insights and advice, and to Jodi Thomas for your helpfulness.

Thank you to Marcia Fry for your help in editing the content of this book.

Thanks to Leo Dutton, sheriff of Lewis and Clark County, Montana, who offered law enforcement information, which I was able to use in this narrative.

Very special thanks to Whit Hibbard for taking time to provide helpful information about the land his family owns, which forms the location this story is based upon, and for all his helpful information about the area and ranching details.

AUTHOR'S NOTE

The Hibbard property along Dog Creek where it runs along Mullen Pass Road served as an inspiration and a loose model for the fictitious ranch called Ruby Hollow in this book. There is a railroad line through the valley which I chose not to use in this story. Mullen Pass is a thoroughfare route to other locations rather than merely a ranch driveway. There is one other property on Mullen Pass before one reaches the area described in this book. Dog Creek is a pleasant fishing stream running alongside the road through both properties, and the wildflowers in this area are beautiful in the spring and summer months.

This book is a work of fiction. The town of Doran, Texas, does not exist. Ruby Hollow Ranch does not exist. The characters in this book except one, Mariah Swingley, are fictitious. Any other resemblance to people currently living or dead is coincidental. Mariah Swingley, who started the "Niceness Is Priceless" anti-bullying campaign in Helena, puts in a cameo appearance in these pages, though this is fictitious. Mariah is with Jesus now, but she impacted Helena, Montana, with her kindness. I have included her in these pages with permission from her mother, Roxanne Allen. Mariah's influence on the youth of this community should never be forgotten.

CHAPTER 1

My best friend, Jenna, and I had just finished lunch at West Texas A&M when I got the phone call that would take me away from Texas the last Friday in March of my freshman year.

"Gotta go, Jenna," I said pulling the phone out of my pocket. "It's Jess. She never calls during school hours, so I'd better see what's up." I put the phone to my ear, waving at my friend as she turned and headed for class. "Hey, Jess. What's up?"

"Tara!" my twelve-year-old sister sobbed, "Gran is dead!"

"What?" I gasped. Opening the hall door, I stepped outside away from the noisy crowd.

"Charlie killed her! I saw him!"

"Oh, no!" I was stunned into silence, listening to her cry. "Does he know you saw him, honey?"

"No."

"Are you sure?"

"Yes," she sobbed. "Uncle Charlie was here at the ranch yesterday. Liam and I had been out fishing. When we went back to the house, we saw his car. Then I heard Charlie yelling at Gran, so I told Liam to take the fishing poles into the barn and to stay out back with the horses until I told him it was safe to come out. I sneaked up to the living room window and looked through the lilac branches to see what was going on.

"Charlie wanted Gran to give him money or sell something. He'd been gambling and owed somebody a lot of money. But Gran wouldn't listen. She said it was something he would have to work out on his own. He kept yelling at Gran, 'You've gotta give me Sundance. I owe Gino a lot of money, and if I don't pay, I've had it.' But Gran kept saying, 'No. That horse belongs to Tara. You can't have him.'"

"This was about him wanting my *horse?* And who's Gino?"

"I don't know who Gino is. I just know Gran wouldn't let Charlie have Sundance. But he kept arguing with her saying his life was in danger, and he'd promised to give Sundance to Gino. Gran kept saying no. They were right at the top of the stairs. That's when it happened. I could see it from the window. Charlie pushed her down the stairs!"

"Oh, Jess!" A shiver snaked up my spine.

"Then he went down the stairs and felt her neck. When he stood up, he called 9-1-1 and told them he had just come into the house and saw Gran at the bottom of the stairs, and she was dead. He said it must have been an accident." Jesse sobbed loudly. "But he pushed her. I saw it! The weirdest part is, he took her wedding ring off her hand too. I don't know why he did that, but it made me mad!"

"Are you sure she's dead?" I couldn't quite believe it. I found a bench in the shade and quickly sat down.

"Yes! Yes! The ambulance came, and they took her away inside a black bag!"

My stomach churned. "Where is Charlie now?"

"He flew back to Houston this morning. I heard him making a phone call first. I think he was talking to Gino. I heard him say something about Sundance."

"Why didn't you call me sooner, Jess?"

"Charlie took my phone away and locked it in Gran's office, so I couldn't use the office phone, either. Then he called Sylvia, and she came over to watch us."

Sylvia was Charlie's local girlfriend when he was in town. I knew he had another girlfriend in Houston too. Sylvia was blonde, pretty, and about thirty-five, I guessed.

"She's downstairs in the living room now watching TV and drinking something in a tall bottle. I don't think it's beer. Charlie told her to keep us in the house until he got back, and not to let us use the phones in the office or her phone, either. She fed us lunch, then I told her we'd like to go to my room to be alone. She said okay, so we did."

"How'd you get your phone back? I thought you said Charlie locked it in Gran's office."

"Well, you know how Gran always liked to leave her office window open just a little," Jess said, trying to control her sobs. "After lunch, I climbed out my window and walked around the roof to the office window and climbed in. It was easy."

"Good girl," I said, reassured Jesse was not too scared to plot a way out of this mess. "Where are you and Liam now?"

"We're in my bedroom. I locked my door and turned on the TV so Sylvia couldn't hear me. Then I called you. Anyway, with the TV on so loud, even if Sylvia came up to the door, she couldn't hear me." She took a deep breath.

"Is Liam okay?" My little brother was seven.

"He's been crying off and on, and I think he's pretty scared."

"Of course. I'm sure you are taking good care of him, Jess." They must be paralyzed with fear.

"Listen, Jess, I'm coming home. I've got to get you outta there. The trip will take me a couple of hours, maybe a little more. Here's what I want you to do. Get out some jeans and shirts for you and Liam and put them in the duffle bag you use when we go camping. Oh, yeah—and put hoodies, shorts, socks, and underwear in, too. Put an extra pair of shoes and your riding boots in a pillowcase. You'll need your coats. Put them on top of the duffle bag. Then put everything in the closet and close the door so nobody will see it."

"Okay, Tara. I can do that," Jesse said, sounding calmer already.

"I'm gonna drive in the back way and park behind the barn. Sylvia won't be able to hear or see me. Then I'm going to climb up the tree to your window, so leave it open a crack for me."

"Got it."

"And don't tell Liam. He might blab to Sylvia. She would tell Charlie for sure, and then I'd never get you away from there!"

"Right."

"I'll see you soon. Love you! 'Bye."

"Love you, too! 'Bye."

I put the phone back in my pocket and headed for my dorm room. I didn't hesitate. Yes, I had plans for which I'd need a business degree. But sometimes, life takes us down roads we do not expect, and the road I was walking seemed to be taking me down a different path than I'd planned. I'd just have to postpone things for a while. I'd contact the college later and see about making up finals. I knew I had a greater responsibility than college. My family came first, and I must protect them, no matter what. I was the only one who could rescue them now.

Two years ago, Mama and Papa had been cruising in the Gulf of Mexico. They died when their boat foundered during a storm and sank. Losing our parents thrust me into a protective mode with my younger sister and brother.

I was seven when Jesse was born. I thought back to those days. Jess was my precious baby sister, and I helped Mama with her all the time. Jesse was shy, the quietest one in our family, and she followed me around like a shadow during those first few years of her life, at least until she started school. After our parents died, she once again turned to me for comfort and protection.

At age seven, Liam was more independent. Curious and adventuresome, he explored and examined everything around him. He didn't want to be told to be careful, though we'd had to take him to the doctor for stitches more than once. But he was mostly a cooperative, cheerful boy, helping us whenever we asked.

We had gone to live with Gran after the boating accident. But she was in poor health, battling cancer. Our other grandparents lived in southern Mexico, and we didn't know them well. I could only recall visiting twice. So, I stepped up to take care of my siblings that summer. I took the younger children with me to every rodeo in which I performed, giving Gran some breaks from their daily care. Besides, I loved having them with me.

During this past school year, I went home nearly every weekend to help Gran. Jesse helped her when I wasn't there. Someone needed to make sure the horses and small herd of cattle were fed and watered. Sometimes our neighbor, Levi, helped with the heavy lifting when I wasn't there. Together, we managed to keep the ranch going during Gran's prolonged illness.

While my college friends were enjoying weekend parties, I was wondering how to earn money for my younger sister's college expenses and later, for Liam's. Grants and scholarships would help, but they wouldn't cover everything. I grew up faster with these added responsibilities.

My mind reeled in a thousand different directions as I headed back to my dorm room. A late March breeze stirred the crepe myrtle trees. Spring flowers nodded in gardens under the warm sun, turning their faces up to its warmth. But my thoughts were focused on getting Jesse and Liam out of Charlie's reach. I couldn't risk the state assigning him to be their guardian.

Charlie was my grandfather's son from an earlier marriage. When Grandpa remarried, Charlie resented Gran. When my father was born a year into their marriage, Charlie hated him even more than Gran. He deeply resented this new brother who got to stay at the ranch, while Charlie had to go back to Houston to live with his mom.

After Papa and Mama died, and we went to live with Gran, she'd had to sell off our ranch and horses—except for Sundance and Rosie, our prize-winning quarter horses. She couldn't manage our ranch plus her own, and the expense was too much for her. She didn't have room for all the horses either, since she ran cattle on her ranch. But there was room for those two, our personal mounts we used in barrel racing competitions. Besides, the prize money we won with the horses was helpful. Rosie had produced a colt by Sundance that spring, meaning we'd have another source of money when we sold him. Since champion blood flowed through the colt's veins, we would get a decent price for him.

Gran had me put the money from the sale of our ranch and horses into the bank, partly to pay for our education, partly to help me rebuild our business once I'd finished school. Fortunately, I was eligible for a college scholarship, so we were able to hold onto most of the money from the sale.

Charlie didn't live on the ranch. Grandpa had left it to Gran for her lifetime, and there was no friendship between Gran and Charlie, who lived in Houston. But since my father and Gran were gone, the ranch would now go to him.

In my heart, I feared what would happen next. *What if Charlie is appointed to be Jesse and Liam's guardian? He would have access to Jesse's horse, Rosie, and her new colt, and all the money in the children's inheritance. He'd find a way to take Sundance, too. He's an addicted gambler, and I know he would take every penny for himself. And of course, he would abuse the children. He already lashes out at us whenever he comes around. And if he learns Jesse saw him kill Gran—he'll kill her too. I have to get the kids out of there. Now! But where can we go to be safe?*

Just about everyone likes Charlie. But with us, it's different. He's angry and cruel so often. He could destroy our futures. All our lives could be in danger. Nobody will believe he's violent. Nobody except us. And maybe Levi.

I can't go to the sheriff about Charlie murdering Gran, either. The sheriff and Charlie have been friends forever. I know Sheriff Bradshaw will never believe anything bad I say about Charlie. He'd just get indignant and tell my uncle.

If Charlie learns Jesse saw him push Gran—I can't let that happen. I just have to get my family away to someplace safe. We need to go somewhere he won't be able to find us. I'm not waiting around for his buddies in the local government to make him my brother and sister's guardian. But where would we be safe?

I opened the door to my room and walked inside. The mirror across the room reflected my brown eyes, high cheekbones, and long wavy dark hair—my inheritance from Gran, a Native American of the Chippewa Cree tribe, and Mama, who had been part Mexican, part Irish. She'd had fairer skin than Gran, but with the same dark brown hair and eyes. I looked a lot like Mama, but my eyes were golden brown, like Papa's. Nothing of Grandpa's light brown hair or fair skin showed in my features like they did in Charlie, my dad's half-brother. But then, Charlie's mother was blonde, unlike Gran.

I stood in the middle of the room for a moment considering what to take with me. The books? Yes. I needed to study for finals, which I'd arrange to take later. My clothes. Bedding? No. I'd use my sleeping bag. Jenna could take the rest of my stuff home with her. I'll leave a note. Right now, getting my family out of Texas matters most.

Soon everything was gathered and packed.

I looked over my other clothes. I wouldn't need them all, but I'd better take them. I pulled my suitcase out of the back of the closet and plopped it on the bed. Shirts, jeans, socks, underwear, riding boots—I tumbled them into the suitcase, except for the boots, which I put in a pillowcase. I put my schoolbooks into my backpack. I'd have to remember to tell Jesse to bring her books too. And Liam's.

I wrote a quick note for Sonia, my roommate, to pass along to Jenna, and stuck it on the mirror. Sonia had already left for the weekend, but the note would be there when she returned on Monday.

I pressed my ear against the door checking for sounds of anyone still in the hallway. I didn't want to draw any attention to myself as I hauled my luggage out of the dorm. I could hear a couple of girls talking and laughing and waited a few minutes until the dorm was silent before opening my door and surveying the back exit leading to the parking lot where my car was parked in a shady place near the building. Nobody was around as far as I could see.

Lifting my suitcase, I had taken one step into the hallway, when a door opened and a sophomore student dashed out, slamming the door behind her, and running for the stairwell. I froze, my heart beating rapidly.

Closing my door softly, I decided not to emerge quite yet. *Five more minutes. I must be sure nobody sees me leave. Charlie will probably check here to try to find out where I am.*

No more noise sounded in the dorm. Looking both ways, I headed for the exit, unlocked my old Corolla, and tossed my things into the back seat. Moments later, I cautiously pulled away from the university onto the main road and headed for home.

The pain of Gran's death rose to the surface. My vision blurred, and I dashed the tears away. I couldn't drive and cry at the same time. Think about something else, I told myself. Focus! Where can we go? Is there a place Uncle Charlie won't think to look?

"God, I need your help!" I spoke aloud into the silence of my car. "What should I do? I have to get Jess and Liam away from the ranch! God, please show me where to go. I'm depending on you."

Montana. Ruby Hollow. Ben. Pictures flashed through my mind—a scene of thick green grass, high mountains, a rushing stream, a boy's smiling face. I hadn't been there in many years, but the names seemed to echo in the car. *Thank you, God!* I knew he had given me the answer.

Last winter, Gran's brother, George Marten, had passed away. Gran had gone north for the funeral. George's wife, Ruby Holloway Marten, had died a few years before, and they had not been blessed with children. Gran was his only sibling, so George had left her his ranch, Ruby Hollow, named for his wife. The ranch was five thousand acres, some of it along the wide creek running the length of the property, and some of it in the timberland covering the surrounding hills and mountains.

I had met Great Uncle George when Gran, Mama, and we kids went to Montana on a month-long vacation when I was almost twelve years old. Jesse was five, and Liam was just a baby. Papa couldn't come with us. He had our Texas ranch to run.

Uncle George had been a fun, smiley man. And then there was Ben, the teenager from the neighboring ranch who had taken time to show me all around Ruby Hollow ranch and teach me about the animals and plants there. His dad, a near neighbor, worked part-time for Uncle George. Ben. I didn't even know his last name. He had been amused at my interest in all things wild and had called me Nature Girl. We'd really hit it off, even though at fifteen, he was three years older than me. He had been a good friend.

So. Ruby Hollow. That's where we'd go. I doubt Ben would still be there. In any case, he'd probably forgotten all about me by now. Besides, I was no longer a child. I would manage on my own. At least I knew we would be safe at the Montana ranch. It's a long way from Texas—and Charlie. Gran never told Charlie about the ranch.

Shortly after Gran had returned from Uncle George's funeral, her lawyer, Mr. Miller, had come over. I was sitting with Gran and Mr. Miller in the living room when he told her, "You won't have to worry about keeping the ranch in order until you get there. George arranged for a man to help him when he was in his final illness, and if you want the same man to help you, he will keep the ranch up in exchange for your letting him graze his cattle in Ruby Hollow during the summer months."

"Sounds good to me," Gran said. "Who is the man?"

"It's George's neighbor from the next ranch. Eli Farley."

"Oh, yes. I remember Eli," Gran said, nodding. "He lives just over the ridge behind George's house. He's a fine man. If he would keep the place up for me, that's a good arrangement."

"I'll take care of it," the lawyer assured her.

After Mr. Miller left, Gran told me, "Sugar, I've left Ruby Hollow to you in my will. Since I had to sell your parent's ranch and horses, the Montana property will at least give you some options for restarting the horse business, if you wish. Montana can get cold, but it's a good land, and you'll get used to it after a year or so. With Sundance and Rosie, you can begin rebuilding the herd if you want. I know you will take care of Jess and Liam."

"Thank you, God!" I whispered, remembering the conversation. A steady peace settled on my heart. God was with me. A Bible verse popped into my mind. *"Be strong and courageous! Do not be afraid; do not be discouraged, for the LORD your God will be with you wherever you go."* God had given this promise to Joshua once. Now I felt he said it to me too.

CHAPTER 2

Time seemed to drag as I raced toward Doran, the closest town to our ranch in north Texas. I pulled into a parking space and went toward the red brick bank with its tall, ancient white columns rising gracefully in front. I would need money to get to Montana. My savings from rodeo competitions and ranch work were here.

Walking into the bank and up to the only teller at the window, I took out my phone, pulled up my account, and asked how much was in it.

Looking up at me kindly, she said, "Oh, Miss Tara. I was so sorry to hear about your grandmother's accident. How are you doing, my dear?"

"I'm okay, Mrs. Jacobs. Thank you for asking."

She shook her head. "It must be such a grief for you."

I nodded, not trusting myself to speak without crying.

"Well, it looks like you have about seven thousand dollars here," she said.

"Okay. I need to withdraw all but a hundred dollars, please."

Her eyebrows shot up. "What are you going to do with all that money, my dear?"

"I've got some horse expenses right now," I said calmly. "Until Gran's estate is settled, I'll have to take care of things myself."

Mrs. Jacobs was a nice enough lady, but she was also a terrible gossip.

"Sure, dear. I understand. It must be so hard for you. Do you want this in hundreds? Or would you prefer something smaller?"

"Hundreds will be fine, mostly. But could you, please, give me three hundred in fifties and twenties? Some tens would be good too."

"Okay." Mrs. Jacobs stood and walked back to the vault to get the money. On the way, she passed Mr. Mallory, the bank manager. I saw her stop and talk with him.

Mr. Mallory looked up and walked toward me. I felt nervous, but I straightened my shoulders and lifted my chin a bit.

"Miss Tara?" he said. "Why do you need so much money? I'm not comfortable giving a minor such a large amount of cash."

"Hello, Mr. Mallory," I said, smiling slightly. "Thank you for your concern, but I'm eighteen now. We have some expenses with the horses Gran had not yet paid. And this is my own money. I won it barrel racing at rodeos and branding calves."

"Oh, yes. I remember," he said, his frown clearing up. "Well, that's okay then."

I breathed a sigh of relief. "Thank you."

Mrs. Jacobs returned with the money. Counting it out for me, she placed it in a large manila envelope and handed it over. "Now you have a nice day, Miss Tara," she said. "I hope to see you at the funeral."

"Yes, ma'am," I said quietly, picking up the envelope and calmly heading for the door. I hoped Mr. Mallory wouldn't try to call the ranch and alert someone about my cash withdrawal.

The car had heated up in the warm Texas sunshine while I was in the bank. I climbed back into the sauna-like car, shaking a little from nervousness, and reached to turn on the air conditioner. As the cool air filled the car, my pulse slowed down. I took a deep breath, sent up a prayer of thanks, and headed for home.

The spring grass in the fields outside of Doran rustled in the soft breeze like waves on a silver-green sea, an ocean dotted occasionally with islands of live oak. Peace gradually settled into my heart.

Twenty minutes later, I turned off the main road onto the dirt track in the far back pasture. Though the road was deeply rutted in many places, it was smarter to enter this way. I drove slowly, avoiding the worst of the pits in the road.

I followed the dirt road below the level of the surrounding pastures, hiding my entry from anyone who might be watching from the house. The barn roof loomed ahead on my right, its gray shingles baking in the hot sun. I drove behind the weathered building, switched the engine off, and stepped out of the car into a silence broken only by the gentle breeze. Nobody was around. Good.

Hurrying to a corner of the barn where I could see the back of the house without being noticed, I could see the reflected light of the downstairs TV on the living room wall. From the barn, I slipped over to the bush foliage and followed it around the edge of the lawn over to the window to do some reconnaissance first.

I positioned myself where Jesse had stood behind the lilac bush. Sylvia, curled up in Grandpa's big leather chair with a bottle of liquor on the table next to her. She was probably drunk by now. The light of the television lit her face. Her eyes were closed, and I assumed she was asleep.

Carefully returning the way I had come, I retreated into the shadows behind the barn. I looked among the vehicles parked next to the barn. An old truck, a tractor, a flatbed trailer for hauling hay, and my old Corolla. Where was the big F-250 truck we used for hauling the horses to rodeos? Where was the horse trailer? They weren't in their usual places.

CHAPTER 3

My heart froze. Without the truck and trailer, I could do nothing to save the horses. I'd have to flee Texas with the children in my small car. Frantically, I opened the heavy back door of the barn and found the truck and trailer inside. Breathing a sigh of relief, I wondered why Charlie had moved them into the barn. Maybe he wanted it to be cooled off when he drove it.

The horse trailer, a Logan model with a small living compartment for the family in the front, was already hooked up to the back of the truck, ready to go, the combined bulk filling a good portion of the barn's interior. The trailer had slanted stalls for three horses, plus feed in the storage area. Just what we needed.

The panic in my heart melted into thankfulness. I wasn't sure Jesse would have known how to help me attach the trailer to the truck. Gran had always helped me before.

Following quickly on that thought, a wave of resentment washed over me. *This is my truck and trailer! Papa and Mama left it to me when they died. These are my horses! But Charlie's already making free with them, assuming his ownership. I know I'm small—only five foot two—and people say I look about fourteen. Mrs. Jacobs and Mr. Mallory sure thought I was underage. I wouldn't be surprised if Charlie thinks I'm still under eighteen, and he can do whatever he wants with my stuff, because now he's our only living relative. I'm sure he thinks he will be my guardian too.*

Glad for the unintended help of the hitched-up trailer, I could immediately leave with my family and my horses. *Thank you very much, Charlie!* I tossed my head and climbed into the truck. I hesitated to turn the engine on for fear Sylvia would hear it. Then I heard another motor arrive outside. Jumping out of the pickup, I ran to the small front door of the barn and peeked outside to see the UPS man pulling up to the house. He put his truck in park, jumped out with a package, and dashed onto the porch.

My heart pounding, I ran back to my truck and started the engine, knowing the noise of the other truck would drown out the sound of my own truck and hoped Sylvia wouldn't come outside. I drove the truck and trailer out behind the barn and parked there in the partial shade of some elm trees. Racing back to the small barn door facing the house, I watched the back of the house for a few minutes, leaving the truck idling behind me.

Sylvia didn't go to the door. Hopefully, she's still asleep. She'd have to be dead drunk not to hear that doorbell, I thought.

Once again, I followed the bushes and trees between the house and the barn. I dashed quietly from bush to bush, checking the back door and windows between each short sprint. I reached the big maple tree on the other side of the house, with its branches reaching high above the roof, almost touching the shingles.

Grabbing the lowest branch, I swung up into the leafy bower. I couldn't remember how many times Gran had scolded me for climbing up to my room this way. In only a moment, I was on the roof, tiptoeing across to Jesse's bedroom window. Jesse had left it open at the bottom. I heard the TV but no other sounds. Peeking through the windowsill open only a fraction of an inch, I tapped lightly on the glass.

Jesse jumped up from the beanbag planted in front of the TV and rushed over to me, followed closely by Liam. She helped me push the window up, then wrapped her arms around my neck.

"You're here!"

"Let me get inside, Jess, honey." I whispered.

Once I was inside the room, Jesse and Liam both threw themselves at me. Liam's shoulders shook as his tears soaked through my blouse. Tears filled Jesse's eyes, but she quickly dashed them away.

"I was so worried you wouldn't make it here before Uncle Charlie comes back!" Jesse whispered.

We clung to each other for a moment before I gently stepped back, keeping a hand on each of them. "Jess," I whispered, "did you pack your clothes?"

"Yes. They're in here." Jesse hurried toward the closet door and brought out two duffle bags, one for Liam and one for her, plus a pillowcase filled with shoes and boots. She'd also found two sleeping bags and added them to the pile.

"Good. Now, do you know where your winter coats are?" I asked, checking the bags carefully.

Jesse looked puzzled. "I've put in our spring coats. Isn't that enough?"

I shook my head. "No. We're going to need the winter ones too. And you'll want some heavy jeans, shirts, and socks. We're going to Montana."

"Oh!" Jesse blinked, her eyes opening wide.

"I don't think Charlie knows about the ranch up there. We should be safe."

Together, we looked at the top shelf of the closet and found Jesse's coat, with her jeans in a box next to it.

"I'll have to find Liam's and mine too," I whispered, heading toward the bedroom door. Opening it softly, I slipped over to the upstairs landing and looked downstairs.

I could see Sylvia, still sleeping in the big, leather chair downstairs, beyond the living room doorway. *Good. The TV's on. The noise will keep her from hearing us leave.*

I walked quickly down the hallway toward Liam's room. Grabbing his winter coat, boots, and blue jeans. I set them inside Jesse's room then turned and headed for my own bedroom further down the hall. Once inside, I threw a quick look around to see if there was anything else I'd need. There was a sleeping bag in my closet in addition to my winter clothes, so I grabbed it, stuffed my winter things into a duffle bag, and hauled them back to Jesse's room.

Jesse picked up the sleeping bags and headed for the window.

"Jess," I whispered, "can you take the sleeping bags over to the edge of the roof and drop them onto the lawn while I go to Gran's office and get the files on the horses? The duffle bags, too. Oh—and get your schoolbooks—and Liam's—when you're done with that."

Jesse headed for the window. "Sure." She climbed out the window and reached back for two of the sleeping bags.

Climbing out after her, I turned and looked at Liam, who was still sniffling from crying. "Wait here, Liam. I'll be right back. Can you find your schoolbooks?"

"My schoolbooks?" Liam whined a little, rubbing his arm across his face to dry the tears.

Jesse gave Liam a look, then nodded to me as she climbed out the window. "His books are over next to my desk."

"Okay, Liam, put them in your backpack." I turned away from the window, picked up my sleeping bag and coat, and followed Jesse toward the tree. We carefully dropped our gear off the edge of the roof.

The roof was in the shade, being on the north side of the house, which made it easier to cross the shingles in the warm March afternoon. The sun on the roof a month later would have been unbearable. The window to Gran's office was still open just a crack. I lifted the bottom rail and climbed inside.

Gran was old-fashioned and only used paper files. She didn't trust computers. She had kept the files in a small cabinet next to the desk. I pulled out the files marked "Horses" and checked to make sure all the papers were there. They were. All except for the big picture of Sundance. Charlie must have it, I thought. As I started to remove them, my eyes fell on other files with our names on them. Yes, we would need those too. Then I remembered the file on Ruby Hollow. I couldn't leave it for Charlie to discover. He would know at once where we were. I searched for the file and removed it as well.

This pile of papers wasn't big, but I needed something to put them in so they wouldn't blow away when I went down the maple tree. Let's see—where's Gran's go-bag? Going over to her closet, I looked around inside. There it was. It was full. I hated to disturb it, but Gran wouldn't need it anymore, I thought sadly, my heart aching. Dumping the contents onto the floor at the back of the closet, I refilled the bag with the files and turned to go back to the window.

We gathered at the foot of the tree—our bags scattered on the ground. Both the kids were wearing their backpacks with their books inside. Jesse picked up her duffel bag and one sleeping bag. Liam could only manage his duffel bag.

"Stay behind the bushes and head to the barn," I whispered, grabbing Liam's sleeping bag and the coats under my left arm, and slinging the bag with the files over my right shoulder. "I'll have to come back for the rest of it."

"Okay," Jesse whispered.

The three of us crept from bush to bush, glancing back at the house. But Sylvia didn't come to the back door. I breathed another sigh of relief when we slipped into the barn. One more trip back to the house, and we had everything ready to load into the trailer. I shut the barn's small door and turned toward the wide-open back exit.

"Let's get the horses," I said to Jesse.

Together, we went over to the corral, which was located partly behind the barn, with a gate where we could let the horses out. Standing in the shadow of the barn, I whistled softly for Sundance, who was drinking at the water trough. His head came up, dripping water from his mouth, and he turned to look at me.

"Come, Sundance," I said softly.

The big palomino stallion walked calmly over to me. Rosie, a sorrel with a light-red coat and strawberry-blonde mane, followed him. Rosie's latest colt, Dramatica Bueno, trotted along with her. His name reflected his father's descent from Doc Hollywood and his mother's Poco Bueno blood. We just called the colt "Bueno."

"Good boy!" I said, stroking Sundance's face as he nuzzled my neck. The halter slipped easily over his ears. Next to me, Jesse put a halter on her horse too. Bueno followed his mother wherever she went, so he didn't need a halter.

Jesse and I put the travel boots on the horses to protect their legs.

"Jess, that back road is badly rutted, but that's the way we'll need to leave. I want you to ride Rosie and lead the colt and Sundance. Follow me out to the road."

"Good idea," Jesse said, helping me carry our bags over to the trailer's living quarters. She opened the door and stopped. "Charlie's suitcase is in here," she said.

Moving forward, I grabbed his suitcase, his boots, and his jacket and carried them back into the barn where I threw them into a stall which hadn't been cleaned. Charlie's stuff landed in a pile of horse manure. I didn't care. Back at the trailer, I checked for more of Charlie's things. Refrigerator? Yes. He would have put something in the fridge if he had already loaded the rest of the trailer. I opened the fridge. Sure enough, there was a six-pack of beer. I grabbed the pack handle and carried it back to the same stall where I'd dumped Charlie's suitcase. *There. That should do it.*

Once more, I went over to the smaller barn door and peeked out at the house, standing quietly in the warm sun. No sign of Sylvia anywhere. Everything looks clear.

Jesse had helped Liam with his seatbelt and had mounted Rosie's bare back by the time I returned to the truck.

I put the truck in gear and slowly headed down the back road, careful not to raise any dust in case Sylvia looked outside. I didn't think she would hear the truck from the house though. The earthen bank above the road muffled the sound of the engine. Jesse followed with the horses.

I'd been driving this truck on the open road for a year now, taking Liam and Jess with me to rodeos, hauling the trailer with our horses. Jess was developing into a good barrel racer already, and Liam liked to participate in the Mutton Bustin' event where the children rode bucking sheep. Gran's health hadn't been great, and she had trusted me to look out for the children and myself.

My phone buzzed. I hesitated for a moment before answering, then, taking a deep breath, I said, "Hi, Jenna. What's up?"

"Where are you, Tara?" she demanded. "The party is already started, and you aren't here!"

"Oh. Right." *I wish I could be at that party instead of running away from Texas with Liam and Jess. The party would have been fun.* "I'm so sorry, Jenna," I said. "You know how I got a call from home at lunch. Well, Jess said there's been a problem here at the ranch and I had to leave school early to help with Jess and Liam."

"But I thought you were coming home with me this weekend!" she protested.

"I am sorry, Jenna. With all the problems here, I totally forgot. Can we get together another time?"

"Well, okay. But Mom's not going to be happy. She made your favorite cookies."

"Oh, how sweet of her. Tell her I'm so sorry, will you?"

"Sure."

"Listen, Jenna, I have to go now. I'm not going to be able to finish the school year. Could you pick up a few of my things from my room and take them home with you? I've left a note on the mirror in my dorm room for you. Sonia will make sure you get it. I need you to get some things for me. I hope that's okay with you. I'll get in touch with you when I can."

"Of course! Sure. I can do that. Wait. You're going to be away for the rest of the year? What's going on?"

CHAPTER 4

"Um, I'm sorry, Jenna. I can't talk anymore right now. Things are kind of crazy. I'll get in touch with you when I can. I'm not sure when. Thanks for helping. Gotta go. 'Bye!"

I stopped the truck and quickly turned the phone off.

Jesse rode up to my window leading Sundance, the colt sticking close to his mother. "Tara? What's wrong?"

"Jenna called me." I handed my phone out the window. "Jess, put this in the hollow of that old oak tree when you pass it. I think Charlie might be able to have us tracked through my phone. We need to leave it here. Yours too. Make sure it's all the way off before you put it in the tree."

"You didn't tell Jenna what happened or anything?" she asked fearfully, reaching out and taking my phone.

"No, honey." I shook my head. "We can't tell anyone. You know how people think Charlie is so great. I'm afraid someone will tell him where we are if they know. This has to be totally secret if we're going to get away."

"You're right," Jesse said. "It's just that—well, it makes me feel so alone not to have contact with anyone at all."

"I know. I feel that way too. But I think it's important, at least for now. But don't worry. I'll pick up another phone soon."

Jesse rode Rosie over to the old tree and dropped my phone into the dark hole in its side. Fishing in her jeans pocket, she found her phone, turned it off and slid it in after mine.

If we we're lucky, Charlie won't find out we were gone until tomorrow. By then, we should be out of Texas—out of his range. I'm sure he'll look for us locally at first and even call Jenna. It's best if she doesn't know where we are and what I'm planning. Charlie is sure to ask her what she knows, and he can charm anyone into telling him anything.

When we reached the paved road, I gently edged out onto the side of the road and got out of the truck. I opened the loading door to the horse trailer and pulled out the ramp. The road, a rural one, was free of all cars. Good. Nobody would see us leave. Except maybe Levi Carroll, our neighbor. We'd have to drive past his house on our way out. But Levi was one of the only people who didn't like Charlie, and I doubted he would say anything.

"Why are we going to Montana, Tara?" Jesse asked, dismounting and leading Sundance over to the trailer first.

"Charlie doesn't know about Gran's property up there. It's safe. Do you remember Ruby Hollow, the ranch Great Uncle George willed to Gran?" I asked. I led Rosie into the trailer, her colt following closely.

She scrunched up her eyes, trying to remember. "Sort of. Where is it?"

"It's near Elliston, a little town over the mountains from Helena." Jesse and I climbed into the truck. I put it in gear, looked both ways and pulled onto the road, heading away from Doran. I didn't want anyone from Doran telling Charlie they'd seen us driving the horse trailer through town. The drive would be a little longer this way but not much. "Ruby Hollow is the ranch Gran inherited from her brother, George. Don't you remember the time we visited there? You were five, honey, and Liam was a baby."

"Oh! Yes, I think I remember something about it. I remember Uncle George was always a smiley man telling funny stories. And he gave me Juicy Fruit gum. I don't remember much about the ranch, except it had a lot of thick, green grass. And wasn't there a pond where we had a picnic?"

I smiled. "Yes, there was! Do you remember Ben? He used to carry you on his shoulders."

"Um, Ben? Did he have dark curly hair?"

"That's him."

"I kind of remember him."

"Well, Ben lives in Montana next door to Great Uncle George's old ranch. Gran inherited it, and she left it to me so I can take care of you all there, honey. That's where we're going. Charlie won't be able to find us in Montana, I hope. Gran left the ranch to me so I could get the horse business back up and support our family. I've got all the ranch papers with me, and Gran never mentioned it to Charlie. In fact, I don't think anyone except Gran's lawyer knows about the place. And he won't tell anybody. He knows about Charlie. We'll be safe there."

"Good," Jesse said. "I'm really afraid of Charlie!"

"I don't blame you, Jess. I'm afraid of him too. But remember—we belong to Jesus, and he will keep us safe."

"Gran belonged to Jesus too," Jesse said. I could hear the doubt in her voice.

"She did ... and she still does. She's with him now," I said. "I don't know how to explain how I know we will be safe when Gran wasn't. Sometimes God lets bad things happen to people who love him—for reasons I don't understand. But I trust him, and I know in my heart *we* are going to be okay. It's just something I feel deeply. I prayed about it all the way home. God's got us, Jess."

Jesse thought about it. "I am not sure what to think right now. I'm still scared."

"Me too," I said. "So why don't we pray while we drive and ask God to keep us safe?"

"All right. Will you pray for us? But don't close your eyes!"

"Okay. Father in heaven, we are scared. But we know that you are with us. Please keep us safe and protect us. In Jesus's name, amen."

Charlie's face appeared in my brain, a sneer marring his leathery tan, his light-brown hair swept across his forehead, his green eyes blazing in anger. I remembered how he towered over me, filling me with fear the day he shot my dog. I could still hear him shouting, "Shut up, kid! Get in the house."

When I was young, nobody told me about domestic violence, but I had seen Charlie dish it out. This year in college, I learned more about it in one of my classes. Gran said it was family business, and we should keep it to ourselves. But I questioned the wisdom of keeping it quiet, knowing how dangerous Charlie could be. Personally, I avoided him whenever possible and tried to keep Jess and Liam away from him too.

A few hours later, after crossing the border into New Mexico, I pulled into a truck stop to pick up some snacks and a phone.

Back in the truck, I started the engine and said, "Jess, can you get out the list of horse motels? We need to find a place for tonight."

"Sure." Jesse reached into the glove compartment and got the list out. "Where should I look?"

"I'm aiming for Santa Fe. See what's available there."

"There's only two places, and one requires advanced reservations," she said.

I figured Charlie and the sheriff might try to track us through the horse motels, and I couldn't let them. But I had an idea.

"Here. Take the phone and dial the number of the place that doesn't need advance reservations, then hand it to me."

"King Horse Motel. How may I help you?" said the woman's voice at the other end of the line.

"Hi. This is Noralee Rodriguez. I'll be arriving late this evening in Santa Fe with my two horses and a young colt. Do you have a place for us?"

Jesse looked startled and mouthed, "Noralee Rodriguez?"

"Yes, we do," the woman said.

After making the reservation, I handed the phone back to Jess. "Uncle Charlie may check the horse motels to try to find us. But if I use Mama's maiden name, I think we'll be fine. I've got Mama's driver's license. I look enough like her it will work if they ask for identification. I don't think Charlie knows either name. Nobody ever called her Noralee. Just Nora. Even if he remembers Mama's last name, Rodriguez is so common he couldn't guess that was me. I plan to sign in as 'N. Rodriguez.' That should keep anyone from finding us. I don't like lying, but sometimes ..."

Jesse nodded. "I understand, Sis. It's okay."

I just hoped it would work. I wasn't used to lying about my identity. But with a murderer looking for us—well—it was necessary.

CHAPTER 5

Charlie Webster was sweating when he got off the flight in Houston on Friday. He was glad his stepmother was dead. His dad had no business leaving the ranch to her in the first place. Everything should have been his. Well, now it was. At least, the land, the few cattle, and the house were. But the horses belonged to the kids.

He brushed the thought aside. As their only living relative, he was sure to be appointed their guardian. Then he could do whatever he liked with the horses. And all the money in the bank too. As their guardian, he could use their inheritance for himself, and the kids couldn't do a thing about it.

Now all he had to do was convince Gino to hold off on collecting on his gambling debt until he could get control of the kids' horses and money.

All I need now is time. But will Gino listen? Charlie shrugged off his doubts.

Taking a taxi to Gino Vincenti's casino, he headed for the office door. Straightening his shoulders and pasting a grin on his face, he walked inside. "Hey, Gino, I've got some good news!"

Gino looked up from his newspaper and frowned. "I hope it's your payment."

"Better than that! I have a trained barrel racing quarter horse. He's a champion. He's worth more than my entire debt if you count what he can win in rodeos. Why, it would be even more than I owe in another couple of years."

Gino said nothing for a moment and stared at Charlie. "A trained barrel racer? How did you get a horse like that? Did you steal it?"

Charlie pretended to be offended. "Of course not. No! Well, okay, so it's not my horse yet. But see, my stepmother passed away this week, and her ranch and everything on it will be mine, including the horse, once I've been appointed guardian for my nieces and nephew."

"What's its name?" Gino demanded.

"He's called Hollywood Sundance. He's a grandson of Doc Hollywood on the top and descended from Sun Frost on the bottom. He's beautiful—a palomino. Here, I have his picture." Charlie fished the folded eight-by-ten print from his shirt pocket and handed it to Gino. "He's a big horse—seventeen hands high. And he's fast."

"Hm. How old is he?"

"He's seven. In his prime," Charlie said. "My brother and his wife didn't start entering him in barrel racing too early, and they never doped him. And did I mention that he's fast?"

"I'll have to take a look at him first," Gino said. He paused for a moment while Charlie sweated. "Okay. I'll give you a break until you get hold of the horse. But this better be legit. If I'm going to race him, there can't be any questions about his ownership."

"Great!" Charlie put on a wide smile. "I'll let you know as soon as I get possession of Sundance. The process might take a while. You see, the kids were wards of my stepmom. She just died, and since I'm the last living relative, I'm sure I'll be named their guardian. But as soon as I get his papers signed over to me—you know, all that legal stuff—then the horse is all yours."

"I want this 'legal stuff' to get settled fast, Charlie. Say, within two months. That should give you enough time."

"Sure, Gino. Two months ought to be long enough."

"I'm warning you. I'm not going to give you any more time."

Charlie flashed another smile at Gino before returning to the parking lot and hailing a taxi. He'd lost his Chevy Camaro to Gino in a poker game six months before. "I need a drink," he told the cab driver. "Take me to the Cantina."

Ten minutes later, Charlie was sitting on a bar stool drinking a cold beer, trying to relax. *Everything's under control*, he consoled himself. *Sylvia's watching the kids, with strict orders to keep Jesse away from the phone. I took Jesse's phone and locked it in the office—that way she can't use either her cell phone or the office phone to call Tara and tell her Evelyn's dead or about my plans for the stallion. Once I move the horse somewhere Tara can't find it, I can start the process of being appointed guardian for those miserable kids. The trailer's hitched up and ready to load Sundance and leave. It's a good thing I found the note Evelyn left on the counter saying Tara was supposed to spend the weekend with one of her friends from school. I'll call her tomorrow night after I've flown back and taken the horse away. She can wait that long to hear that her grandmother's dead.*

Charlie finished his beer and headed to his condo. He needed a shower and a good rest. The day had been exhausting. He hadn't planned to kill Evelyn. He pushed the remembrance of her dead face away. They'd never gotten along anyway. Forget her, his brain said. She doesn't matter.

After dinner at a restaurant, Charlie called Sylvia.

"Hello?" she mumbled.

"Hi, Babe," he said. "How's it going there? Are the kids under control?"

"Yeah. Haven't heard a peep outta them for a while," Sylvia slurred. "I think they're watchin' TV. I fed 'em lunch an' they went to their rooms. They were pretty upset, but they're quiet now. Their TV's goin'. I 'spect they're tired."

Charlie could tell she'd been drinking. "Sylvia, lay off the booze, okay?' I'll be back tomorrow after lunch. Think you can handle the kids 'til then?"

"Okay. No problem," Sylvia assured him.

"Good girl," Charlie said. "See you soon."

Sylvia stared at the silent phone for a moment then set it down. Somewhere in her foggy brain, she began thinking about the kids. How could it be eight o'clock already? Thinking they might be hungry, she struggled to get to her feet and stumbled into the kitchen. Opening the refrigerator, she looked to see what might be good for supper. Beef. Bread. Cheese. Yes, that will do. I'll make them some sandwiches and give them some milk. They won't mind if it's cold, she told herself, reaching for the meat.

Clumsily, Sylvia assembled the sandwiches and found some plates and cups. Setting them on the table, she called out, "Jesse! Liam! Dinner's ready. Come down here."

But there was no answer. All she could hear was the TV. *Well, maybe they've gone to sleep. Should I wake them? No. They've had a rough day. So have I.*

Evelyn had been a friend. Sylvia knew Charlie had hated his stepmom, but she didn't understand why. Evelyn had always been nice when she came into the beauty salon where Sylvia worked. The way Charlie was acting made her feel anxious. Something wasn't right.

She put the sandwiches on a single plate and sealed it with plastic wrap so it would be fresh later. If the kids got hungry, they'd find everything prepared.

Stumbling into the living room, Sylvia went back to the comfortable, big chair and poured herself another drink. *Tomorrow. I'll think about Charlie and this mess tomorrow.*

CHAPTER 6

The sun had set by the time we pulled into Santa Fe, New Mexico. We were all exhausted from the emotions of the day. Liam dozed fitfully. Jesse stared out into the darkening sky. When the truck stopped at a traffic light, Liam stirred and opened his eyes.

"There's a burger place up ahead," I said. "Anyone want to eat?"

"I do!" Liam said, yawning and perking up.

"Yeah, I guess I could eat something," Jesse said. She had been unusually quiet during the drive. Her tense, stiff attitude had me worried. I'd heard about posttraumatic stress from a friend at college whose brother had served in the war in Afghanistan. *Is Jesse suffering from something like that? Will I be able to help her get through it?*

"Okay. We'll stop for dinner." I stopped at the fast-food restaurant, parking in the shadows at the back of the parking lot. I pulled my hair back, twisted it into a low knot and fastened it by putting a pencil through it. Primitive but effective. I looked a little older, and different from any photos Uncle Charlie might give the police to use in finding us.

"Jess, you and Liam use the bathrooms, then get back out to the truck while I order dinner. I don't want anyone seeing the three of us together. Here," I said, pulling my baseball cap out of the glove compartment. "Wear this to hide your face a little."

I bought our dinner, praying the whole time nobody would notice Jesse and Liam entering or leaving the restrooms. A few minutes later, back in the truck, Jesse and Liam pulled out fries and burgers, eating hungrily while I drove to the horse motel. Once we reached our location for the night, I checked in and drove to a parking spot and unloaded the horses. I could eat later. I didn't have any trouble with identification during check-in since I paid cash, and they didn't ask for ID.

The horses were eager to get out of the trailer after such a long, exhausting day. Jesse climbed out of the truck to help me, brushing the crumbs from dinner off her clothes.

"Here, Jess. You lead Rosie and Bueno. I'll take Sundance. Liam, stay with me. We need to take off their travel boots and put the fly nets over the horses."

Sundance nuzzled my shoulder then lifted his head and whinnied. In the distance, another horse answered.

We led the horses over to the motel's stable for the night and led them in. The colt began nursing right away. With the fly netting over the horses, nobody would be likely to remember them later. Sundance was a beauty and very noticeable, not only for his coloring but also for his size. I needed to make sure he wasn't seen. The netting would help, and I'd try to wake up early so we could move the horses back into the trailer before daylight.

Once the horses were cared for, we walked toward the living quarters in the trailer. Liam yawned.

"Let's get some sleep," I said, lifting him up onto the first high step into the trailer.

Mama and Papa had bought the Logan trailer when Jesse was small. This trailer was large enough for our family to go to rodeos together back in the days when Mama was competing in the events, and we could haul three horses in it. Later, I took Jesse and Liam with me to the rodeos. I always said Gran needed the break from taking care of us, but the truth was, I also liked having my sister and brother with me.

Exhausted, we climbed up into the trailer's big bed together and each of us snuggled down in our own sleeping bag. Laying in the dark, I said, "We need to thank God for getting us out of Texas."

"Yes," Jesse agreed.

Liam squeezed his eyes closed. "Dear Jesus, thank you for helping us get away from Uncle Charlie," he prayed. "And please take good care of our Gran, now that she's up in heaven with you." He started to cry. Jesse and I both put our arms around him.

"Jesus, please be with us and keep us safe," Jesse said, tears evident in her voice. "We're sad. And we miss our Gran."

I couldn't speak for a moment. My throat constricted as I tried not to cry. Now that we had stopped for the night, and I didn't have to concentrate on driving or getting away from Charlie, I still couldn't let my own tears flow freely. I needed to be strong for their sakes. "Lord, we need you to show us what to do. Please protect us from Charlie. You are all we have now. Help us sleep well tonight and not have any bad dreams. Thank you. In Jesus's name, amen."

"Good night, Liam honey," I said, kissing his forehead. "Good night, Jess." I reached my hand over Liam and squeezed Jesse's hand. Gradually, my brother and sister fell asleep. Only then did I move my arm back under my own covers.

As I settled into the warm sleeping bag, my thoughts turned to Ben. *He's probably about twenty-two years old now. I wonder if he's married. No! He can't be! Or maybe he has a girlfriend.* My eyes blinked open. *Why do I care anyway?* I turned over restlessly, pulling my pillow with me. *I shouldn't expect him to remember me. He hasn't seen me in seven years.*

But in my heart of hearts, there was a secret place of daydreams where memories of Ben existed. Be honest, I told myself. He was a terrific guy. He's the reason I haven't been interested in any of the guys in Texas. They weren't Ben. The guys my age didn't even resemble him. Compared to him they are just children. All they can think about is having a fun time. Ben was thoughtful and responsible—he was my friend. And—to be honest—yes, I had loved him. This was the first time I had even tried to figure how I felt about Ben. Why had he spent so much time with me? Was it because his dad was working for Uncle George? Or was it because Ben genuinely liked me? Most teenage guys wouldn't have paid much attention to a kid who was almost twelve. He was extraordinarily kind. But what does it matter now after so many years?

I turned over in bed again. *I need to concentrate on the job ahead of me and not let my heart or imagination get in the way. We have such a long way to go before we reach Montana. Can I even get us there safely? What if ...* Somewhere along the corridor of my anxious thoughts, I fell asleep.

The first hint of dawn brushed the sky, awakening me Saturday morning. At first, I couldn't remember where I was. Then I saw Liam and Jesse curled up on the bed next to me, and the pain of losing Gran flooded over me again. But I didn't have time to cry right now. I breathed deeply and sent up a quick prayer asking God to help me be strong.

We needed to get back on the road and into Colorado before Charlie sent out the alarm.

I rolled out of bed and slipped outside to care for the horses. By the time I had fed and watered them and had put them back in the trailer, Jesse was up. She stuck her head out the door. "Tara, do we have any food for breakfast?"

"Look in that cupboard over the fridge. I think there's a box of Fruit Loops up there," I said. "Will that be enough for now?"

Rummaging around in the cupboard, Jesse called out a muffled, "Found it."

A few minutes later we were headed back toward the highway, munching cereal. "I'll get some real breakfast at a station somewhere," I said.

"Works for me," Jesse said.

"Me too," Liam echoed.

"Jess," I said, as I pulled into a station on the outskirts of Santa Fe, "while I pay for gas, could you shop around inside with Liam and get some milk and food for us? Here." I handed her a twenty-dollar bill.

"Okay. Come on, Liam." Jesse took the money, opened her door, and jumped down, Liam following right behind her. I waited a minute so we wouldn't be seen together, then went inside and paid cash for the fuel.

My legs welcomed the stretch while I filled the tank. Putting the nozzle back into its holder, I looked up to see a highway patrol car pull up to the other side of the pump. A young handsome officer got out and stretched. He looked over at me curiously.

I looked away, my heart pounding.

"You don't look old enough to be driving that rig," he commented.

I straightened my shoulders and looked him in the eyes. I forced myself to smile a little. What was it Mama always said when men told her she looked too young to have three kids? Oh, yeah. "Why, thank you, officer," I said calmly. "That is the nicest thing anyone has said to me all week."

He grinned and reached for the gas pump nozzle. I could tell he was going to start a conversation.

Please, Jess, stay in the store. He mustn't see us together in case the sheriff in Doran puts out an alert.

Just as the officer took the gas cap off his tank to insert the hose, his car radio crackled.

"All units. Accident on I-25, two miles east of town."

He swore, put the nozzle back, screwed on the gas cap and jumped back into his patrol car. Lights and sirens filled the air as he tore out of the gas station.

Liam and Jesse came out of the store looking startled. My heart was still in my throat. That was a close call.

"It's okay," I said. "He just stopped for gas, but he had to leave. You two get back in the truck."

Still shaking slightly from my close encounter with the highway patrolman, I pulled a roadmap from the glove compartment. Concerned the accident on the highway might keep us from driving to Denver on the freeway for an hour or more, I didn't want to risk any delays at this point.

Oh, good. There's another way. I can take the 285 North then switch to some smaller roads to take us west of Denver and eventually into Wyoming. This route would take longer than the interstate, but it would be less crowded, and I was sure we wouldn't see as many patrol cars. Bypassing Denver with all its crazy traffic sounded less stressful anyway.

I started the truck engine and carefully pulled out of the station. The sun was just coming up, and I doubted Sylvia would be awake yet. As soon as she awoke, she'd be calling Charlie—if she hadn't already discovered the kids were gone. Charlie might already be searching for us.

Once we were away from town and had left Texas behind, I felt I could breathe freely again.

CHAPTER 7

Sylvia yawned and stretched her arms out, like a kitten waking up. She sat up and looked around. Ugh. Her mouth tasted terrible, her eyes felt tight, and her head ached. She opened her purse and pulled out a small container of aspirin. Was there any tomato juice in the fridge? She stumbled into the kitchen and opened the fridge door. Yes, there was.

Sylvia sipped the juice and looked around the kitchen. Sunbeams danced on the countertops. The clock's face indicated it was nearly 9:00 a.m. Sylvia rubbed her eyes. Shouldn't the kids be up by now?

She walked across the dining area to the stairs, where she heard the TV still blaring up in Jesse's room. "Jess? Liam?" she called.

No answer.

Sylvia sighed. She pushed her long, blonde hair off her face and smoothed her stylish but rumpled clothes before dragging herself up the stairs and knocking on Jesse's bedroom door. Silence. She felt panic rising. Pounding on the door she commanded, "Jess! Liam! Open this door!"

But there was no answer.

Sylvia hurried into Gran's room and found a hairpin. Back at Jesse's door, she bent the hairpin open and inserted one end into the lock. Click. The door opened easily. But the room was empty. A puff of breeze hit her face. She stumbled toward the window and pulled it closed.

Uh-oh. Charlie won't like this. Facing Charlie did not appeal to her at all. He wasn't pleasant when he was angry. She slapped at a fly buzzing around her face and went back to the kitchen. *Charlie's flight should be landing at the airport in about two hours, I'll let him figure out what to do.*

Pulling out her phone, she called his number, but the call went straight to voice mail.

"Um, Charlie, this is Sylvia. The kids aren't in their rooms this morning. I don't know where they went. I found Jesse's bedroom window open. I think they climbed out and ran away. So, I'm going home. There's no point in staying here now." She ended the call. Let Charlie deal with it. There must be something very wrong if the kids ran away. Whatever Charlie was up to, she wanted no part of this.

Charlie raced out of the Amarillo airport into the parking area where he'd left Evelyn's car. With little regard to speed limits, he raced back to Doran and the ranch. Around two in the afternoon he drove through the gate and straight up to the barn. Jumping out of the car he ran over to the corral to find the gate open, swinging in the wind.

The horses! Where are they? He ran around to the next pasture behind the aging structure. Maybe the horses were out grazing with the cattle. His gaze swept over the field. Only five cattle were left. Evelyn had sold the rest of the herd. The cows were resting together in the shade of the trees along the irrigation ditch. But he could see no horses among them.

Hurrying back to the barn, Charlie swung open the big back door and looked inside. The horse trailer and the truck were gone. *How could Jesse have driven it? She's only eleven*

*or twelve. Tara! She must have come back to the ranch and ...
No! She couldn't know about Evelyn yet.*

Charlie pulled out his phone and dialed the sheriff.
"Dan, this is Charlie Webster. I just got back from Houston
and found that the kids are gone. I left them with Sylvia,
but they ran away sometime during the night. The horses
are gone too. Can you come out here?"

"Okay. I'll be there in a few minutes," Sheriff Dan
Bradshaw said. "Don't worry, Charlie. We'll find them."
Slamming the office phone back in its cradle, Sheriff
Bradshaw looked over at his deputy.

"Come on, Tyrel. The Webster kids are missing. We've
got to get out to their ranch." He headed toward the door,
clamping his tan cowboy hat over his thinning hair and
hitching his belt up higher beneath his middle-age paunch.

"Yes, sir." Deputy Sheriff Tyrel Morgan headed for the
patrol car. Young, in his mid-twenties, and lean, Tyrel was
a head taller than the sheriff. His dark-brown hair, short
on the sides but longer on top, was hidden by his hat. He
slid into the car next to Sheriff Bradshaw.

"Tyrel, tell me what you know about the Webster kids,"
Bradshaw said.

"Well, I only know Tara, the oldest. She used to hang
out with my little sister, Jean, every summer. They went
to grade school together. Jean sometimes goes to rodeos
with some of their friends to watch Tara perform. Tara
was a barrel-racing champ in the kids' division with a big
palomino stallion named Sundance, although I think she
may have graduated to the adult division by now. She's
taken a lot of prizes at rodeos, like her mama used to. Um,
let's see. I think she has a younger sister and brother. Their

folks died in a boating accident down on the Gulf a couple of years ago, and she and the younger ones moved in with their grandma, Evelyn Webster. I know Tara went to that fancy girls' school—Olivia Stokes High School. She may have graduated by now. That's about all I know."

Bradshaw nodded. "Okay. I just got a call from her uncle, Charlie Webster. He says the youngsters ran away. I don't know if Tara was with them or not. We need to check it out."

The spring sun was hot when they pulled into the ranch driveway twenty minutes later, where Charlie was anxiously awaiting them on the front porch. He stepped down and strode toward the patrol car.

"Hi, Dan. I really need your help." Charlie nervously tugged on his ear.

"Take me through what happened, Charlie," Bradshaw said, climbing out of the patrol car.

Shaking his head, hands on his hips, Charlie recited the events of the past forty-eight hours since Evelyn's death. "I left Friday afternoon to take care of some urgent business in Houston. Sylvia came over to watch the kids. She said they were watching TV in Jesse's room. She stayed here to watch them. When she got up this morning, the kids were gone. Jesse's bedroom window was open, so they climbed out that way. The horses are gone too. So's the horse trailer and the truck. I know Jesse drives the truck around the farm, but I didn't think she'd take it and the trailer out on the road!"

Sheriff Bradshaw looked up from his notes. "Where's the older girl—what's her name—Tara?"

"Supposedly, she went to some friend's house for the weekend. I don't know which friend. I couldn't get in touch with her." Charlie shrugged, a worried furrow between his eyes. "She doesn't know about Evelyn yet."

"I see," Sheriff Bradshaw said thoughtfully. "Then I doubt the kids have gotten very far. The odds are they've gone over to a friend's house too. But why take the horses?"

"I can't imagine." Charlie said, scratching the back of his head.

Tyrel stood back watching and listening.

"Charlie," said the sheriff, putting a hand on his friend's shoulder, "Tyrel and I will start hunting for those kids. Do you have any ideas about who their pals are?"

Charlie shook his head helplessly. "I don't spend much time here at the ranch with the family. I live in Houston. I wouldn't even know where to start looking."

"Those horses are going to be pretty hard to hide. I think if we put out a local alert about the kids and the horses, we'll hit pay dirt," Bradshaw said. "We need to get a description and license plate numbers out to the local highway patrol too."

"Okay," Charlie said. "The files should be in Evelyn's office. Come with me."

Sheriff Bradshaw turned to Tyrel before following Charlie into the house. "While I go with Charlie, you go search the barn and the pasture. See what you can find."

"Yes, sir." Tyrel pivoted and headed toward the barn, searching the ground for prints of any kind, but the dust in front of the barn was too thick to show anything definite. Once he was inside, he saw a profusion of prints. From the size of them, it looked like three different kids. The largest of the footprints led to one of the stalls. Inside, he found a suitcase with some boots and a jacket on the floor—in the manure—and a six-pack of beer. What were these things doing in a stall? He cocked his head in puzzlement.

He followed the footprints out the opened back door of the barn. They were centered on an area with wide tire tracks, then some truck tire tracks. Looked like a truck and horse trailer. Yes, and there were horse hoofprints leading out of the corral and down into a dirt road running along a gully over the tire tracks. Looked like a smaller car had traveled the road into the ranch sometime that same day. The truck and trailer tracks ran over those of the car. He followed the rutted road out to the highway. There in the dirt he noticed an indention where the trailer ramp had been let down. They must have loaded the horses here.

Tyrel returned to the barn. Parked beside it was an old truck with flat tires and a compact car. Was this Tara's car? He'd noticed her driving something similar a few times. He radioed the police station. "I've got a plate for you to run." Giving the number, he waited while the deputy at the desk ran it. Sure enough, the car belonged to Tara.

So, Tara's been here. That's her car. But did she take the other children, the truck, and horses? Or did she catch a ride from a friend before the weekend to go to some party or something? He pondered the evidence and concluded she must have taken the kids and horses with her.

Stepping inside the house, he followed the sound of voices up the stairs to what looked like an office, where Charlie was furiously going through Evelyn's files again. Bradshaw stood next to him waiting calmly.

"Where are they? I know the files were here!" he said, his voice rising in panic. "Evelyn must have moved them!" His face was red and angry.

"What files?"

"The ones on Sundance. The ones on the truck and horse trailer."

"Calm down, Charlie," Bradshaw said. "We can look the truck information up at the office."

But I need those papers!

"Don't worry, Charlie, we'll find the horses and the kids. The papers are probably somewhere else in the house or with Evelyn's lawyer." He patted Charlie's shoulder. "Trust me, Charlie. I've got this. Now what do the truck and trailer look like?"

"Huh?" Charlie jerked his attention back to the question.

"The truck and trailer. What do they look like?"

"Oh. Um, the truck is a Ford. An F-250. Some dark color, I think. The horse trailer is a Logan model. Brown stripe over tan."

"Okay. That's enough to start with. We'll go back into town and start the search. Why don't you have a beer and sit back and relax here at the house while we take care of things? You can look around for the papers after you've calmed down. Don't worry. Right now, you're upset. The papers will show up eventually." Bradshaw looked over at Ty. "Let's get back to the office. I'll send out an alert to our local highway patrol." He walked out into the hallway.

Charlie couldn't seem to unwind. "Get back to me as soon as you hear anything," he demanded, following them out.

"Sure thing, Charlie," Sheriff Bradshaw said, nodding. "Let's go, Ty."

Back in the patrol car, Tyrel said tentatively, "He's mighty upset, isn't he?"

Bradshaw shook his head sadly. "Death can mess with people. They often get real tense like that. They focus on little things because it takes their minds off the bigger tragedy. Charlie always gets that way when things go wrong. He's been that way since we were kids."

"Hm," Tyrel said noncommittally. *Obviously, Bradshaw is sympathetic toward his long-time buddy. But personally, I wonder why those kids would run away. Would they take their grandmother's papers with them? Would a twelve-year-old girl even think of taking papers? Not likely. And why would they take the horses? Looks to me like Tara must have been there. She's older. She might think of the papers, and she would certainly take the horses. They're her livelihood. Why didn't Charlie meet the sheriff's eyes when they were talking? Why did he seem so much more upset over the horses than over the kids? What was really upsetting him? Charlie's behavior and mannerisms seemed very suspicious. I'll have to talk this over with Dad after work. Maybe he will have some ideas.*

"Did you see anything out there in the barn?" Bradshaw asked.

"Yes. I saw the footprints of three different kids," Tyrel said. "They were fresh. Looks like someone rode the horses down the back road to the highway then loaded the horses into the trailer out there. I think Tara is with them. One of the sets of prints is about the right size for her. Either that, or someone else helped them load those horses."

"Who? A neighbor? A friend? Why would those kids leave?" Bradshaw wondered aloud. "You'd think they would be comforted to have Charlie there. He's a great guy. Everyone likes him. Let's talk to Sylvia after I send out the alert. She might know something." Grabbing his radio, he put out a report to be on the lookout for a dark colored F-250 towing a tan and brown horse trailer.

Tyrel kept his thoughts to himself. He knew better than to argue with his boss.

Sylvia was still hung over when they reached her house. She answered their knock with a bag of ice on her head.

"Sylvia," Bradshaw said, "can we ask you some questions about this past weekend?"

She frowned, nodded, then held the door open for them. Tyrel stood back to watch Sylvia while the sheriff interrogated her.

"Let me get this straight. The kids were upstairs in one of the bedrooms last night?"

Sylvia winced and nodded. "Yes. After Charlie left, Jesse took Liam upstairs to her bedroom. I figured they wanted to be alone, since their grandma had just died, and they didn't know me very well. As soon as they went inside, they locked the door and turned on the television. I made them dinner later, but they didn't answer me when I called them. I figured they were exhausted and had fallen asleep. This morning, the TV was still on. I knocked on the door, but nobody answered. I picked the lock to get in, but they weren't in the room. I saw the window was open and figured they went out that way. Flies were getting inside, so I closed it. Then I called Charlie and left a message."

"Did you hear them leave or see anything?"

Sylvia slowly shook her head and winced again. "No."

"Do you have any idea where they might have gone?"

"No. I told you, they don't know me very well. They were very polite when we met, but they never confided in me."

"I see." Sheriff Bradshaw nodded. "Well, thank you, Sylvia. If you think of anything, give me a call." He handed her a business card.

"Okay."

"Well, that's that." Bradshaw said with a shrug, heading back to the patrol car. "We'll have to find out who their friends are and canvas them. The kids are probably at some friend's place."

CHAPTER 8

Back at the ranch, Charlie called his friend and legal counsel, Jeff Blake. "Jeff, I need your help. The kids have run away and have taken the horses with them."

"I'm sorry to hear that, Charlie." Jeff paused. "Uh, you know, the wife and I have plans this evening. I don't really have time to drive all the way out there. Can you meet me at the park? Usual place?"

"Okay. Be there in twenty minutes."

Jeff was already waiting in his bright red Mustang when Charlie pulled up in Evelyn's battered car. "Come get in my car, Charlie," Jeff said, rolling down his window. "It's air conditioned." He smiled, brushing his longish brown hair off his forehead. He was dressed casually in a blue polo shirt and white slacks.

Charlie frowned, but the thought of air conditioning won. He got into the Mustang with Jeff.

"What's going on, Charlie?"

"You know Evelyn's dead, don't you?" Charlie asked.

"The news got around." Jeff nodded. "Sorry to hear that."

Charlie shrugged impatiently. "Yeah. Well, last night the kids ran away—and they took the horses with them." He shifted his shoulders impatiently and frowned.

"I see. I think." Jeff looked quizzically at Charlie. "It's the horses, not the kids. Right?"

"Oh, I'm worried about the kids too." Charlie tried to put on a show of concern. "After all, they might be in trouble somewhere."

Jeff wasn't fooled. He knew Charlie had little regard for those children. "Where do you think the kids went—with the horses?"

"They're probably holed up at some friend's place, but I don't know where to begin looking," Charlie said. "I thought Tara was with a classmate, but now I'm not so sure. Bradshaw's deputy thinks she came home and took the kids and horses away."

"She's the oldest?"

"Yeah. And she's feisty. Hard to manage."

"I see. But it's still about the horses, isn't it?"

Charlie shrugged. He couldn't fool Jeff. "I need to give her big palomino stallion to Gino to help pay off my gambling debts."

"Won't Tara fight you for him?"

"She won't have a say. I'm her only living relative. She's a minor, and I'll be appointed as her guardian," Charlie snapped. "But Tara can't possibly know about the deal with Gino. How could she? I just made that arrangement."

Jeff sat silently for a moment then looked across at Charlie. "Let me ask you this, Charlie. Where were you when Mrs. Webster fell down those stairs?"

Charlie evaded Jeff's look. "I was in the barn hooking up the horse trailer." He shrugged, looking away.

"I see," Jeff said. Falling silent, he thought for a moment then said, "I'll bet the kids called Tara about Mrs. Webster's death."

"They couldn't. I told Sylvia to keep the kids off the landline downstairs, and I took Jesse's phone away and put it in the office, then locked the office door so Jesse couldn't use either her cell or the office phone to reach Tara." He added lamely, "I felt the news would be easier for Tara if I told her in person."

Jeff looked at Charlie, weighing what he had heard. "I wouldn't let Bradshaw know that if I were you."

"Do you think I'm stupid or something?" Charlie demanded angrily. "Of course, I didn't tell him that. And I didn't do anything to Evelyn. She fell down the stairs all by herself."

"Okay! Okay. So, let's see what we have. You think Jesse took Liam and the horses and drove away?"

"Yeah. She could do that. She drives the truck around the ranch hauling things all the time. Going out on the road wouldn't be a problem for her. But I don't think she's driven it yet with the horse trailer attached. Tara does, though."

"Well, if Jess is driving the truck and horse trailer, she is going to get into big trouble if the highway patrol stops her. How old is she?"

"Twelve."

"Where do you think Tara is?"

"She's probably at a friend's house. Jess may know who Tara went home with, but she's gone. We just need to locate her friend somehow. Bradshaw says he's going to look for the younger kids."

"Good. Shouldn't take long to find them. Not with the police and highway patrol looking for them. A truck and horse trailer aren't easy to hide." Jeff looked at his watch. "Charlie, are you making arrangements for Evelyn's burial?"

"Uh—sure," Charlie said. "I'll head over to the funeral parlor tomorrow morning. Thanks for reminding me. With all the confusion over the kids and horses …"

"Hang in there, pal," Jeff said as Charlie climbed out of the Mustang. "Call me if anything comes up."

CHAPTER 9

After work Saturday evening, Tyrel headed over to his parents' house instead of his own apartment. Seeing the light in his dad's study, he cut across the grass and knocked on the French doors.

"Come on in," his dad called, looking up from his book.

Tyrel opened the door and stepped into the study. Leather-bound books lined one wall, law books and historical volumes his father loved. On the other walls hung desert paintings in pale, delicate colors, paintings his mother had done over the years. His dad, Judge Morgan, was sitting in his favorite chair of dark, worn leather.

"What's up, Ty?"

Tyrel sighed and dropped into in a matching chair nearby. He shook his head. "Dad, Charlie Webster called the office today and reported his niece and nephew were missing, along with their horses. Tara, the oldest niece, is supposed to be away at a friend's place for the weekend, but we don't know where. With this coming right after Evelyn's death, it seems suspicious to me. Bradshaw and I went over to the Webster ranch to check things out." Tyrel filled his dad in on the details and gave his own take on the situation. "I think Tara went home and took the kids and horses away with her somewhere. But I don't know why she'd do that.

There's something wrong about this whole situation." He scratched his head and shrugged.

"Hm. How does Tara get along with her uncle?" Judge Morgan asked.

"I don't know. Is Jean around? I thought she might be able to shed some light on this since she and Tara have been friends for years."

"Jean should be home within the hour. Why don't you stick around for dinner and tell me more about this situation in the meantime?"

Tyrel's stomach growled. "Yeah," he said with a grin. "That sounds like a good idea. I'll go tell Mom." He headed for the kitchen. "Be right back," he called over his shoulder.

A few minutes later, an iced tea in one hand, Tyrel rejoined his dad in the study.

"Dad, I just have a feeling about this case," he said, frowning. "Something isn't right."

"What do you mean?"

"Well, look at it. Their grandmother, who has taken care of them since their parents' accident, suddenly dies in another accident while Charlie is at the farm. Bradshaw asked him where he was when the accident happened, and he claimed he was in the barn at the time. But he looked away when he said it. I felt Charlie's responses to Bradshaw's questions were all wrong. Something doesn't smell right to me. But Bradshaw won't even consider questioning Charlie's answers. Says Charlie is just grief-stricken." Tyrel shook his head. "I never heard of Charlie feeling anything good about his stepmom. None of this adds up."

"You've got good instincts, Son. What else?"

"I have a gut feeling Charlie isn't telling everything he knows about the accident, the kids, Tara, or those horses. Something feels off, but I can't put my finger on it."

After dinner, Tyrel broached the subject with his sister while washing dishes. "Jean, do you know anything about Tara's relationship with her Uncle Charlie? How do they get along?"

Jean paused, trying to find the right words. "Tara is scared of Charlie," she said carefully. "He always acts so—so charming—in town. But Tara said he gets mean at home when he doesn't like something or doesn't get his way. She said he's violent. He's hard on the horses and they run away whenever he comes near them. When Sundance was about six months old, Charlie was visiting their ranch, and he got mad and took a swing at the colt with his fist. Ever since then, Sundance goes into a panic whenever Charlie comes near him. Sundance bucked him off once when he tried to mount him, and Charlie got really mad and hit the horse in the face—again. Charlie killed Tara's dog a year or so ago too."

"I see." Tyrel rubbed his face. "Did Tara say anything about how her grandmother reacted to that?"

"You've got soap on your face, Ty," Jean said, bursting into a fit of giggles.

Ty smiled and wiped it away. "About Tara—you were saying?"

"Yes. She said her grandma screamed at Charlie and told him to get off her property and not come back until he could control himself. Those two didn't get along at all."

"Thanks for telling me," Tyrel said, looking out the window, deep in thought.

"What's wrong, Ty?" Jean asked curiously. "Did something else happen?"

"Yes. The kids ran away and took their horses with them. We don't know if Tara took them or if they got someone else to help, but I saw three sets of footprints, all of them either kids' prints, or one set is a small woman's prints.

Tara isn't very big, so it might have been her footprints. At least, that's what I'm guessing."

Jean frowned thoughtfully. "That was probably a good thing, Ty. According to her, Charlie wants that ranch more than anything. She said Charlie has always resented his dad leaving the ranch to Evelyn for her lifetime, and that Charlie wouldn't get it until after she died."

Judge Morgan, who had been finishing his dessert in the dining room, came into the kitchen. "Do you have any idea where Tara would go, Jean?"

Jean shook her head. "I can't think of any place. But she will do everything she can to make sure her uncle doesn't find them. She said Charlie is pretty violent."

"I see," said the Judge. "Jean, Tyrel, I'd like you both to keep this information to yourselves. I have a feeling it could be dangerous to say anything."

"Dangerous?" Jean asked.

"Call it a hunch."

"Okay, Dad." Tyrel said. Jean nodded her head in agreement.

"I'd like to speak with Tyrel in private for a few minutes, honey. Ty, come back into the study."

"See you later, Ty," Jean said, punching him in the shoulder and heading for her room.

"Son, you be careful," Judge Morgan said, looking into his son's eyes.

"I will. I brought up Charlie's angry behavior today to Bradshaw, but he flared up in his friend's defense. He and Charlie go way back, and I realize I shouldn't say anything else to him about my suspicions. He wouldn't believe me, and he'd tell Charlie for sure."

"I agree. Keep it to yourself. Don't mention it to the other deputies either. But please, Ty, keep me informed. I can be a sounding board and provide some outside help.

You need to keep in mind how violent Charlie is. I know he'll inherit the ranch now. He had plenty of motive for wanting Evelyn dead. If he did murder her, then he's going to try to eliminate anyone he thinks is on to him. Murder becomes a habit. It makes people go a little bit insane too. So be careful, Son."

"Murder?"

"Yes. That's what I'm thinking," Judge Morgan said thoughtfully.

"Do you think he would murder the kids?" Tyrel was shocked.

"I don't know. Maybe. Maybe not. But Evelyn? Probably."

"Okay, Dad. I'll be careful."

Miles away to the north, Tara, Jess, and Liam crossed over into Colorado long before Charlie got the call warning him they were gone. The farther the truck and trailer got from Texas, the easier Tara breathed.

There were horse motels along the new route where they could stop. The horses were more stressed to be on winding, back roads, but Tara didn't have a choice. To travel on the main highways would mean the highway patrol might spot them if Sheriff Bradshaw had put out a regional alert. Tara had to drive slower and stop more frequently to let the horses rest along the way, checking them carefully at each stop.

They stopped for the night in Laramie, Wyoming. Tara's tension level gradually dropped. She began to realize they were going to make it—they were going to escape. The younger kids relaxed too.

CHAPTER 10

By mid-afternoon on Sunday, Charlie couldn't wait any longer for the sheriff to find the kids. He jumped into Evelyn's car and drove the couple of hours to Tara's high school. He hadn't been able to raise anyone on the school office phones, and Tara wasn't answering her phone either. He needed to know if she was at a friend's place or if she had really come back to the ranch and taken Jess, Liam, and the horses away.

He parked under a shade tree at the school. There weren't many cars in the parking lot. In the distance, he saw a janitor pushing a cart. Walking swiftly in that direction, he said, "Excuse me. Would you know where Tara Webster's room is?"

"Tara?" the janitor said, his eyebrows going up. "Didn't you know? She graduated last year."

Charlie stared at the janitor, his mouth hanging open for a moment, then pulled himself together. "Oh, yes. I forgot." he said. "Thanks for your help."

"No problem, sir," the janitor said, nodding his head politely then turning again to his cart. He stopped and looked back. "I heard she might have gone to West Texas A&M, but I'm not sure about that," he called back.

University? But isn't Tara still seventeen? Isn't that a little young for college? His brain resisted the thought. *If she's eighteen now, she's no longer a minor, which means ... no. There must be some mistake. She had to be a minor. Otherwise ... But Tara had always been a smart kid. She might have graduated early. That might explain it.* Charlie tried to reason with himself.

A shiver ran down his spine. He turned and raced back to the car and headed for the university. Tara could be a problem, but what if nobody ever finds her or the kids? What if she were to have an accident too?

The buildings and grounds of the university campus with its many trees and wide green lawns in Canyon, Texas, sat peacefully in the golden lights from the warm glow of the western sun. Charlie climbed out of Evelyn's car and headed for the administration building.

Closed. Of course. He had forgotten it was Sunday. He shook the door handle angrily and walked away.

There were groups of students hanging out on the lawns. He saw some young people loitering along the sidewalk. He had no idea where Tara's dorm room was, but one of these kids might know. He strode purposefully toward them.

"Hey, there," Charlie called out, looking anxious.

"Yes, sir?" A tall young man answered for the group.

"My niece, Tara Webster, attends here. Her grandmother just died, and I haven't been able to reach her. I know she was going to a friend's place for the weekend, but I don't know which friend. Can you help me?"

The young man shrugged. "I don't know all the students. What does she look like?"

"She's Hispanic. Pretty. Not very tall. Long black hair to her waist."

A second guy from the group spoke up. "She's in my Comp 1 class. I can take you over to her dorm, and you can look around. Someone there might know where she went."

"Thank you." Charlie said with a smile. "That would be so helpful."

The student ambled down the sidewalk toward the next dorm. "I think she lives in this one."

"Okay." Charlie hurried into the dorm and walked down the ground floor hallway, knocking on doors to see if anyone there knew where Tara's room was. Most of the students were out of the building or not responding to his knocking. Finally, he found someone who pointed out Tara's room.

Charlie nodded. "Thanks." He knocked on the door, but nobody answered. Walking quickly back outside, he found a student-aged janitor emptying trashcans.

"I need to find my niece. She isn't in her room. But I need to know where she is. Her grandma just died, and I need to contact her. Her name is Tara Webster. Could you let me into her room to see if there might be any clues there—like a phone number or something?" Charlie managed to look helpless.

"Sure. That's sad about her grandma." He walked up to Tara's room and unlocked the door, then stood and watched as Charlie searched it.

Inside the room, Charlie noticed there was more than one bed. Which was Tara's? Ah! There was a note on one of the desks.

Hey, Sonia, I have to leave school for a while. My grandmother just died. I need to go home and take care of my sister and brother. Jenna may come by to pick up some of my stuff.

So, she knows about her grandmother. How on earth did Jess contact her? Maybe someone from the ambulance service, the funeral home, or the hospital. Who called her? Well, it doesn't matter. What does matter is finding her as soon as possible. Her friends might know where she went. But who are her friends? The note says Jenna. Jenna who?

Charlie continued to look around. On the wall above her desk was a picture of Tara and another girl. He reached up and removed it. Stepping back to the student in the doorway, he held the photo up. "Who's this?" he asked.

"Um, I think that would be Jenna Johnson. Yeah, I've seen her and Tara together a lot."

"Ah. Jenna. Right. Do you know her address, by any chance?"

"No, but Mrs. Collier, who works in the office might. She's in charge of housing. She may be able to help."

Charlie chewed his lower lip. "It's just too bad the office is closed today. I really need to get hold of Tara as soon as possible."

The student nodded his understanding. "I have Mrs. Collier's number." The student pulled out his iPhone. "I'll send it to you. I'm sure, since it's an emergency, you could call her today. Normally, she doesn't like us to call her on weekends."

"Thanks." He smiled charmingly at the student. A moment later, Charlie had Mrs. Collier's cell number. "You've been a great help," he said as he turned away.

"Glad to be of service, sir," the student said with a smile, responding to Charlie's charm. "I hope you find Tara. She wouldn't want to be away from home at a time like this."

Charlie smiled, gave a brief nod, and walked away. Quickly punching the number into his phone, Charlie waited for an answer.

Mrs. Collier knew nothing about the family tragedy, but she did have Jenna's phone number. So sorry about her grandmother—she hoped Tara would be okay.

Walking toward his car, he punched in Jenna's home phone number.

Jenna said Tara had told her about having to go home to take care of her sister and brother, but that was all she had said. No, she didn't know about Tara's grandmother. Sorry she couldn't help him locate his niece.

Charlie started to panic. *Where's Tara? Where's that stallion?*

CHAPTER 11

Sunday morning, Liam was still too sleepy and grumpy to wake up when the sun rose over Laramie. I carried him to the truck cab where Jesse and I managed to buckle him in. Jesse, though, was wide-awake. She had been in kindergarten the last time we were here, but she could not remember much about that trip.

We were far enough away from Texas now that I felt more comfortable driving on the main highway, and I didn't think a Texas alert would reach the police here. As we pulled onto the road, the beams from the rising sun hit the thick clouds above the distant blue, snow-capped mountains, turning them bright pink. The view was startling against the deep blue of the sky and the mountains.

Jesse gasped. "Wow! Look at that, Tara! Have you ever seen such a sky before?"

Liam opened a sleepy eye to look then promptly closed it.

I smiled. "Yes. When we were here last time, I saw those sunrises. Aren't they awesome? The clouds here are some of the most unusual ones I've ever seen. You're going to love God's sky art in Montana!"

"I'm gonna *paint* it." Jesse said. "Can we get some paints and paper somewhere?"

This was the first time Jesse had opened up or shown any enthusiasm since I'd raced home to get them away from

Charlie. The whole time we'd been driving, she'd been too quiet. Not that she was ever a chatty sister, but she had never seemed this tense and silent before. Now she seemed to be pulling out of it a little. I breathed a cautious sigh of relief. I knew she wasn't through the stress yet, but she was making progress.

Jesse had been showing quite a bit of skill lately in art class. She was gifted. Maybe her artwork would help her get over the trauma of what she had seen. I sent up a quick prayer for her.

We crossed into Montana, making it as far as a motel with a horse pasture not far from Bozeman, where we stopped for the night. The drive wasn't much farther to Helena, but I wanted to reach it during the daytime, which would help me find the ranch turn-off more easily.

Charlie was frustrated. Instead of looking for the kids on Monday, he had to finish planning Evelyn's funeral, which would be on Tuesday. He found it hard to pretend he was sad and had nothing better to do than plan for the funeral. He allowed some of his anxiety to show when he explained to the funeral director and the pastor about the children's disappearance and the ongoing search.

The pastor was kind to him. He patted Charlie on the back and said he would pray for the kids' safety.

Pray? I don't think God's out there. Those prayers won't get beyond the ceiling, Charlie inwardly scoffed while outwardly putting on an act of thanking the pastor for his kindness. *I need to get busy hunting those kids. I hope this funeral is over quickly and doesn't take up too much time.*

"Are you planning to sell the ranch, Charlie?" a neighbor asked curiously.

"Sell the ranch?" Charlie was shocked at the idea. If he sold the ranch, he would no longer have capital to draw on for gambling. He shook his head slowly. "No, it's our family ranch. I couldn't do that. I may hire someone to live on it and keep the place up and watch after the kids though."

Relax, he told himself. *This will all be over by Tuesday. I can get started on the search again as soon as the funeral is over.*

CHAPTER 12

Monday morning dawned clear and fresh, the sun just beginning to color the clouds pink.

"Wow! Look at those mountains!" Liam exclaimed, pointing to the snow-capped peaks near Big Timber, Montana, where we had stopped the night before. Across the valley, mountains rose dramatically— white against the blue sky. The store clerk said they were called the Crazy Mountains. Later, when we went through the pass before Bozeman, Liam fell silent, overwhelmed by the great towering cliffs. After the plains and rolling hills of Texas, these mountains inspired awe. Liam had never been this close to them before, and Jesse was too young to remember much about our last trip to Montana.

Jesse still wasn't saying much. She mostly stared out at the scenery and followed any instructions I gave when we stopped for gas or for the night. Most new days seemed to start with silence. Sometimes she pulled out of it as we drove, like she did in Laramie, and other times she simply didn't talk much at all.

Early in the afternoon, we reached Helena. "Look!" Jesse said excitedly, breaking her silence and pointing at a group of stores. "There's a Hobby Lobby! Can we stop?"

"Yes," I said, pulling off at the next exit and backtracking. *This will take her mind off the shock and pain of seeing Gran killed. She's always happy when she paints. I should buy some art supplies for Liam too. He might like to paint when Jesse does.*

"We should pick up some groceries while we're in town too. The ranch is way up in the mountains," I said when we had bought art supplies and were all back in the truck. "I saw a Walmart on our way here."

Milk, eggs, meat, bread—the list of things we would need was long. We packed most of the groceries into the back seat of the truck, but Jess ended up having to fit a couple bags around her feet.

This should be enough to get us by for a week, maybe more. Not sure what the storage situation will be like at the ranch. Surely, the electricity will be off. We'll have to use the trailer's refrigerator until we figure out a place to store things, I guess. Great Uncle George told Gran the place was energy independent though. I don't remember much about our last trip. I wonder how it works. Did he use propane or what?

Once back in the truck, we headed across Helena toward the mountains beyond. Seeing the green grass and buds on some of the trees, winter looked to be nearly over. But it was awfully cold here compared to Texas. We'd kept the heater running since Colorado. Clearly, we were going to need to make some adjustments to live here.

We drove out of town on Highway 12 toward the west. Before us, a long, winding road headed up into some steep mountains. Switchbacks made it easier to drive up the slope, but we had to go extremely slow with the horse trailer. Back and forth across the mountainside we drove, rising higher, ever higher, into the sky. A deep canyon clad with evergreen trees dropped away on our left, while the road led us up, up, up into the clouds.

"Christmas trees!" Liam exclaimed. "They're everywhere!"

I laughed. "Yes, they are. Isn't it beautiful?"

Jesse smiled and drank in the scenery, her eyes moving from the slope on our right to the steep drop-off on our left. "It's sure a long way down," she said looking out over the valley.

I glanced briefly at the incredible view and rolled down my window. The sun shining down on the lower parts of the mountain released the sharp smell of pine into the air. "Can you smell the trees?" I asked.

Liam and Jesse both sniffed.

"It smells good," Jesse said. She took another deep breath. "Is Ruby Hollow up here?"

"It's just on the other side of this pass," I said. "We'll be there in a few minutes."

"Roll up the window," Liam demanded. "The air is freezing me!"

Laughing, I did as he asked. When we neared the top of the pass, we drove into a cloud so thick we could hardly see. Fine misty rain brushed the windshield. I turned on the wipers, creeping along slowly through the fog.

Suddenly, we were out of the cloud, looking down on the other side of the pass. There were many thick clouds above, but they were higher than the mountain peaks. A cloudy mist hugged the road around us but disappeared as we moved downward.

"We must be on top of the world!" Liam said, his eyes open wide.

On both sides of the road, alpine meadows stretched out, with evergreen trees towering into the sky around their edges. Ahead and far below, we caught glimpses of another valley.

"It's so big and—and wild," Jesse said in amazement. "Is the ranch nearby?"

"Yes. Not much farther now." I drove slowly down the mountain, fearful of the steep descent, searching for the turn-off to Ruby Hollow.

"There it is," I said with satisfaction. I pulled off the highway onto the wide entry of a dirt road. Set back from the road was a fence and a locked, metal gate. I pulled up to the gate and put the truck in park. A carved wooden sign greeted us with the words Ruby Hollow Ranch inscribed on it. The center of the drive beyond the gate was overgrown with grass. "We're here!" I said cheerfully.

Liam and Jessie craned their necks to get a good look at everything in sight.

"Where's the house?" Liam asked.

"It's down this road a ways," I said, jumping down from the driver's seat to get a closer look at the gate's simple padlock on a chain. Sorting through the ranch keys I'd discovered in the files, I found a key marked "front gate" and inserted it into the lock. Undoing the chain, I swung the gate back and drove the truck and horse trailer through, then went back to close and lock the gate behind us.

"I'm not sure what the road is like," I said, looking doubtfully at the ruts in the road at the entry area. "The horses are tired. The road's probably just fine, but I'd feel better if—Jess, let's saddle up Rosie. You can ride her and lead the other horses while I drive the truck in."

"Great!" Jess opened her door and jumped down. "I'm tired of sitting in this truck." A frigid burst of wind whipped our hair every which direction. "Burr! It's cold! Hand me my coat, Tara."

"Can I ride too?" Liam asked.

"Um—well, not while Jess is leading Sundance. He can be a handful. Later, when we get to the house, you can ride Rosie for a while," I said, brushing my hair out of my eyes.

"Okay," Liam sighed.

"Here. Put this on." I reached in the back seat and pulled our coats out. "Here, Jess," I said, climbing down from of the truck, passing her jacket before swiftly donning my own.

"Thanks. It sure wasn't this cold in Helena," she commented.

"Well, it was sunny there. We're up in the clouds now at a higher elevation. It's going to be colder here."

Jesse and I pulled the horse trailer doors open and lifted the ramp down. The horses were eager to get out too. This had been a long, grueling drive for them.

I saddled Rosie for Jesse, who mounted up, reached out and took Sundance's reins. Bueno, the colt, moved up next to his mother, ever eager to be close to her.

I put the ramp back up and closed the trailer door.

"See you at the house!" Jesse said, nudging Rosie toward the side of the road. "Wait." She drew Rosie to a stop. "How far is it?"

Sliding into the driver's seat, one hand on the open door, I paused. "I'm not sure. It seemed to take a long time to drive this road before. Maybe a mile. Maybe two. Wait for me to get ahead of you. I'll lead."

"Okay," Jesse said, a smile lighting up her face. She seemed more relaxed this afternoon.

A creek ran along the left side of the road, but golden willow branches with silvery pussy willow buds hid most of it from sight. There were hints of green in the pasture on the other side of the thick willows. Dark green forest covered the mountain, lining the road on the right. Tiny yellow buttercups sprinkled the roadside, nodding in the damp air, decorating the fresh green grass shoots pushing their way up through last year's dead and matted grass.

The road took a winding route alongside the steep slope, and the creek meandered through the willows below.

"Look! Snow!" Liam said excitedly. "Can we build a snowman?"

"Sure," I said. "There's probably some close to the house too." This was going to be a challenge. Texas was already warm, and the horses had lost their winter coats. We'd have to use their blankets until summer. Maybe longer.

Turning a corner, we saw the valley spread out before us, a huge red barn on the right-hand side. About a half-mile away on the left, we saw Uncle George's log cabin with a small log barn next to it on the far side of the creek.

The road ahead branched at the huge red barn. I turned left, crossed a small bridge, and followed the winding drive up the hill toward the cabin.

There were two horse paddocks on the hillside with tall pole fences. Green grass shoots pushing up through the dead grass from last year were thicker in the sunlight in the paddocks. But there still wasn't enough grass for the horses to graze. Not yet. Where would we get hay? I wondered. Will the neighbors have some? Did Uncle George store some in the big red barn we just passed?

Uncle George loved horses too. I remembered him telling me when he was young he competed in roping and bull riding at the rodeos. He was too humble to brag, but Gran said he often won the top prize. Chances were, we'll find some hay stored somewhere around the ranch. I remembered he had horses last time we were here. He would have stored hay for them, surely. We'd look around later.

Barbed wire fences bordered the outside of the property and divided large pastures within the valley. I knew the property opened into an expansive pasture somewhere up ahead. This stretch was mixed evergreens, willows, and pasture.

The cabin nestled among some bare, leafless fruit trees, with firs rising behind it. Tight little buds on the fruit tree branches held the promise that beauty would soon burst forth. In front of the log home, daffodils nodded in the garden around the house, cheerful and welcoming. Next to the front door was a wooden bench. A small barn stood next to the cabin with a corral on one side. I stopped the trailer near the barn door to unload the horse gear.

Jesse, bringing in the horses, cantered up the road below, crossing the bridge, her long black hair blowing in the wind. She pulled up next to me. "Do you want the horses in the corral or the barn?"

"Let's put them in the corral. It's cold, but they can run around in the sunshine for a while. Leave one of the barn doors open so they can go inside when they want. There's a water pump next to that trough. I'll water the horses, and you toss some hay in the feed box."

"It's awfully cold here, Tara," Jesse complained again, hugging her coat around her. "Isn't the grass too short? We're almost out of hay. I think we have enough for another two days, but after that, will we be able to put the horses out in the pasture?"

"No. You're right. The grass is too short. I don't know when it will start growing tall here in the mountains. There's a chance it will take another few weeks. In the meantime, we'll have to find hay for the horses. There might be some in one of the barns."

"In this barn?" Jesse said, looking at me with a question in her eyes.

"Maybe. We should go check out that big red barn across the field too. Chances are, Uncle George stored some there." I frowned, worried about the feed problem. "The pasture grass needs to thicken up and grow another six inches in height before I can turn the horses out into the fields, I think. But I don't know much about this mountain grass. Young grass would mess up their digestive systems at this point. Too much fiber in it. Until we're sure it's okay, we'll have to give hay to the horses. Since they've already been eating green grass in Texas, they won't be happy, but they can get along with it for now."

Working together, we settled the horses and the colt into the corral then turned toward the house. Liam was already exploring, chattering all the while, looking in windows, checking out the trees. Two big boulders towered behind the barn. His face brightened, and he headed for them at a gallop, scaling the first one quickly.

"I'm going to pull the truck up closer to the house to unload, Jess. Could you please get Liam down off those boulders? The last thing we need is for one of us to get hurt."

"Liam!" Jess called. "Get off the rocks. You'll fall."

"Aw-w-w-w," he complained. "I won't either."

"Well, Tara's in charge, and she said to stay off the rocks. We're gonna do what she says," Jess declared, reaching up to help him down.

I pulled the truck up behind the corral next to the boulders. This seemed like a good parking place, sheltered by the rocks and trees. As I walked toward the cabin, I sorted through the ranch keys looking for the one we'd need to get inside. At the cabin door, I inserted the key labeled "house."

As the door swung open, sunlight from the door and the front windows lit on the furniture covered with protective cloth. There was a faint smell of dust in the room. I pulled the cover off the couch while Jess did the same for a big, leather chair. Liam uncovered the kitchen table, calling out about each new discovery he made in our new home.

Jesse sneezed. "Oooo! This is dusty!"

"Let's take the covers outside and shake them," I said. "Come on, Liam. Bring some of the dust covers outside." A few shakes, and the sheets were ready to fold and put away.

"Let's stack these in a corner until we find a better place to put them," I said, dropping the furniture covers in a corner away from the kitchen.

There were light switches next to the door, but nothing happened when I flipped them on.

CHAPTER 13

"The electricity is off," I said. "Oh yeah. I remember Uncle George used to talk about the place being energy independent. Hm. I'll have to figure out what he meant by that. Jess, did you see any solar panels?"

Jess walked back outside and looked up at the roof. "Yes. There are two panels.

"I wonder where the switch is to turn them on?"

I walked back inside and went over to the sink where I turned the faucet on. "No water either." I looked under the sink. Turning the knob on the water line didn't produce anything. "There must be a shut-off valve somewhere." I looked in the bathroom. "No. Isn't there either."

Jesse and Liam looked at each other, then at me.

"Doesn't this place have water?" Liam wanted to know.

"I'm sure it does," I said. "I just have to find where it turns on."

"We'll help you," Jesse said. "Come on, Liam."

"What are we looking for?"

"See those pipes under the sink?"

"Yeah."

"We're looking for pipes like these with knobs on them."

"Okay."

We spread out, the children going outside while I checked the laundry room.

I finally found the main water valve near the back door that opened off the small laundry area near the kitchen. I turned the valve and heard the pipes filling, clanking loudly as the water pushed the air out. Water sputtered and splashed in spurts in the kitchen sink, then settled down to an even flow.

"I found it!" I shouted to the children.

Together we looked at the spitting, uneven flow.

"Why's it doing that?" Liam asked.

"Because it's been off for a while and there's air in the pipes," I said.

I put my hand into the icy water. How can the water flow so strongly without electricity? I wondered. Is there a water tank on the property somewhere? I would have to look into this.

A woodstove stood in the kitchen, a small pile of wood, kindling, and newspapers next to the stove. This was something I knew how to manage. In no time, I had a fire going in the stove and a big pan of water on top. We'd use it to wash up later.

"Let's unload the groceries from the truck," I said. "We need to get our things inside. Let's just bring them into the kitchen and we'll sort them afterward."

Together, we brought the food into the house, and I began putting things away. There were too many items needing refrigeration, so I set some of it aside until I could figure out where to store it.

Jesse was exploring the cabin when Liam burst through the front door all excited. "Tara! There's a door in the mountain!"

I laughed. "A door in the mountain? Show me!"

He grabbed my hand and dragged me outside. Jesse followed us. "Look," Liam said.

Sure enough, there was a door built into a stone wall on the side of the mountain near the back corner of the house, which looked like it might have been a cave at one point. I lifted the bar across the front of the door and opened it. The sound of splashing water met our ears. Reflected light showed a small room with a cement trough on one side, water coming from a pipe lowdown on the wall. The water spilled out into the trough then disappeared through a drain at the other end. Against the wall were shelves.

"Oh, look! A little creek!" Liam said, dashing over and putting his hands in the water. "Yikes!" He pulled them out and shook off the drops of water. "That's freezing!

"I think this is what the pioneers called a springhouse," I said as I stepped inside. "I remember Uncle George carrying a can of fresh milk into this room and setting it in the little creek. This is like a big refrigerator. You can put things down in the water to keep them cold, and you can put other things that need to be kept cool on these shelves." I ran my hand over the smooth wood, remembering smells of jerked beef, fruit, and cheese. *This is where I'll store the perishables.*

"Wow," Liam said in awe. "It's cold in here, but not cold enough for ice cream. Where are we gonna put that?"

"Maybe in the refrigerator in the house," I said, smiling at him. "But I don't think there's any ice cream yet. We have to figure out how to turn on the electricity, so we can turn on the refrigerator and freezer. Uncle George used this room to stock up on things they needed to keep cold, so he didn't have to drive into town a lot. We can do that too."

"Smart," Liam said, nodding his head.

I noticed another pipe coming out of the mountainside near the bottom of the back wall. *Interesting,* I thought. *The pipe crosses the floor next to the stream then goes out under the front wall of the room where the small stream exits the springhouse. Hm. I see. The stream trickles down the hill, but it looks like the pipe goes underground, toward* the cabin. This room is a little higher than the cabin. The water tank must be buried in the earth behind the wall. If the pipe comes out of the bottom of the tank, that would explain the good water pressure in the kitchen. I wondered if the tank could be spring fed, or if it had to be pumped?

Jesse walked around the dark, cave-like springhouse. "Hey, I remember this place. Didn't Mama bake cookies and store them here?"

"I think so," I said, smiling at her. "I'm glad you remember."

Shutting the springhouse door firmly behind us, we walked back to the cabin.

"There are two bedrooms," Jesse said. Both bedroom doors were opened showing one room with blue curtains and twin beds and another room with yellow curtains and a queen size bed. But there were no blankets on them. Maybe there were some in the closets.

"Can I sleep in the blue room?" Liam asked.

"Sure. Do you want to have it all to yourself?"

Liam hesitated. "Um, can Jesse sleep in here too?"

Jesse hugged him. "You're sweet, Liam." Jesse investigated the other room with its queen-size bed. "I guess I'd rather have my own bed. Tara has cold toes."

"I'll take the big bed then," I said, laughing as I stepped into the cheerful room with yellow curtains and looked around. The window faced east, with the bed against the north wall and a closet along the wall facing the window. The log walls gave the room a faint aroma of evergreen trees.

Between the two rooms was a bathroom with a tub and shower. "Maybe if we can figure out how to turn on the electricity, we can get some hot water and have baths tomorrow." The trip had been long. There was a shower in the trailer, but showers weren't as good for getting warm as baths were.

But no matter how much we searched we could not find the solar panel switches in the cabin's dim light.

"I guess we'll be like pioneers tonight and heat water for baths on the stovetop. We can look for the turn-on switches tomorrow."

"I like being a pioneer," Liam said, nodding his head in approval.

"Let's get the extra blankets out of the trailer," Jesse said. "It's gonna get really cold here tonight, I think."

We quickly gathered our clothes, sleeping bags, blankets and other miscellaneous gear from the trailer and got settled into our new home. I found more blankets and sheets in the closet in my bedroom and added them to our supply. By then the water on the stove was boiling. I filled our mugs with a hot chocolate mix then started warming hotdogs in another kettle. The smell of the woodstove reminded me of pleasant times back in Texas when Mama, Papa, and we kids had gone camping together.

The meal was simple and satisfying. We dined by candlelight as the sun dropped steadily downward.

"Tomorrow, when the light's better, we can all look for the switches for the solar panels, okay?"

"Yeah," Jesse said, "it's kinda dark in here now."

"If we can't turn on the 'lectricity, will we have to live like pioneers still?" Liam wanted to know.

Jesse smiled.

"Probably," I said. "But we're gonna find those switches. I don't like the idea of having to heat up our water for baths on the stove! It's a lot of work, buster!"

Liam sighed. "I wanna live like a pioneer, like Davy Crocket."

"I imagine you'll get plenty of chances to do that outside," Jesse said. "There'll be tons of work to do here, just like in the pioneer days."

"Work!" Liam scoffed. "I wanna go hunting and fishing!"

Jesse and I both laughed.

"The horses aren't used to this cold weather," I said, looking at Jesse. "We need to put their blankets over them and stable them in the barn for the night."

"Okay." Jesse swallowed the last of her hot chocolate and stood up. "Let's go."

Sundance, Rosie, and the colt were happy to see us, and even happier when we covered them and led them into stalls in the barn. Jesse and I brought in hay from our diminishing supply in the trailer, enough to satisfy the horses until morning. Together, we closed the barn doors when we left, locking in the warmth the horses' bodies would make. They should be fine.

Jesse and I looked out over the darkening valley together. "It's a good place," she said. "It's so beautiful! I think we're gonna be safe here."

"I think so too. This will be a challenge—getting used to the way Uncle George set things up—learning how to run a ranch this big—but we can do it, Jess. Have you noticed the fruit trees have little buds on them?"

"Yeah." She nodded solemnly. "It should be beautiful in a few weeks."

Back inside, Jesse and I washed the dishes then we all used the remaining hot water to wash our hands and faces before bed. Liam was yawning by the time the sun finally dipped below the mountains across the pasture. We slipped thankfully into our beds. Liam fell asleep as soon as his head hit the pillow.

"Tara," Jesse said as she crawled into her sleeping bag and pulled a thick blanket over it, "God is watching over us. I can feel him now."

I sighed in relief. "Good. I can too. I'm sure we will be safe here."

Lying in bed watching the moonrise, I whispered, "Father in heaven, thank you for this safe place to live. I don't know much about this ranch, so would you please show me what to do? I'm afraid to ask anyone around here, because I don't want word to get back to Texas we're here. I give this problem to you and thank you for protecting us. Please give me wisdom! In Jesus's name, amen."

Peace filled my heart as sleep claimed my body.

CHAPTER 14

Tuesday morning dawned bright with a cloudless sky overhead. Charlie had planned a quiet, private ceremony for Evelyn Webster's funeral, but a surprising number of her friends from church and town showed up to honor her, and to offer Charlie their condolences. All Evelyn's neighbors showed up too.

Charlie arrived at the church with his cowboy hat in hand, wearing all black. He looked deceptively sad and alone. Others patted him on the back, offered words of encouragement, and said nice things about Evelyn. Charlie soaked up the attention, nodded and pretended to wipe a tear from his eye.

"Yes, it has been a hard week," he said with a sigh. "First, losing Evelyn then, having the kids run off like they did." He shook his head. "I hope we find them soon."

Tyrel moved quietly among the guests, listening to comments. All the ranchers near the Webster's place were there as well as many people from town. Since most of the ranchers or their wives worked in town to make ends meet, this was a good time to listen and ask a question here or there to get people talking about the Webster ranch. He noticed Levi Carroll, Evelyn Webster's nearest neighbor, hadn't joined the commiserating crowd around Charlie. He wandered slowly to the back of the room where Levi stood.

"Levi," Tyrel said with a nod.

Levi nodded back and sent a brooding glance toward Charlie.

"You've heard about the Webster kids missing, haven't you?"

"I have," Levi said solemnly.

"I was wondering if you might have any ideas about where they might have gone. I saw three fresh sets of footprints behind the barn. Looked to me like Tara was there to help her sister and brother take the horses and leave."

Levi hesitated and glanced again toward Charlie. "Ty, I figure if Tara took her brother an' sister an' them horses away, she had good reason. I don't really know nothin', though." He paused. "I may have some ideas. But I'm not tellin'. I'd trust Tara if I were you. She's levelheaded. Since her parents died, she's been watchin' out for the youngsters and doin' an excellent job of it. Evelyn's health hadn't been good, so Tara took on most of the work durin' the summer months an' most weekends. If she took them kids away, she had good reason for doin' it. Leave her be, Ty." He looked steadily at the deputy for a moment, underscoring his words with a stern glance.

"What do you know, Levi?" Tyrel asked.

"Nothin'." Levi's voice grew harsh.

Tyrel tried another tactic. "Do you know anything about Charlie's relationship with Mrs. Webster?"

"Well—I can tell you that there wasn't no love lost between Evelyn an' Charlie, an' he ain't nearly as likable as folks seem to think."

"Was he ever rough with Evelyn or the kids?"

Levi said dryly, "I never saw him be anything but nice— when he knew others was around. But I've come to the front door a time or two with vegetables from my garden to give to Evelyn, an' the way he talked to her wasn't pretty. Evelyn had a black eye a time or two. I don't think she got it fallin' down no stairs, nor runnin' into any doors neither. An' that's all I'm gonna say." He turned and walked away.

The information wasn't much to go on as far as evidence, but it confirmed his suspicions. Tyrel remembered a rumor from their high school years about Levi and Charlie. Charlie had stolen Levi's high school girlfriend, Mary. Levi had liked her tremendously, but she only had eyes for Charlie. After dating Charlie, Mary soon found herself in a family way and had to leave town to go live with her aunt until the baby was born. She kept the baby and got a job in another town. Levi had helped her relocate. He'd tried to convince Mary he loved her, but she was done with men. After that, he'd wanted nothing to do with Charlie.

After the service, Tyrel headed to his parents' home to talk with his dad. *I'll drop by Levi's shop soon and see if Levi is willing to part with any more information. Seems like he knows more than he's letting on.*

CHAPTER 15

I awakened to the sun rising outside my window. For a moment, I was disoriented. Then I remembered we were at Ruby Hollow. The house was silent, which meant the kids were still asleep. The room was cold, and I wasn't eager to leave the warmth of my blankets. I reached out for my clothes lying on the chair next to the bed and pulled them back under the blankets with me to warm them up a little before putting them on.

My heart ached as my thoughts turned to Gran. She'd done all she could to help us after Papa and Mama died. This ranch was the best gift she could have given me. A place of safety where I could bring the children. A place where we could raise horses and build a new life.

Outside, the early sun shone down on the log barn, raising steam from the roof as the day warmed up. I thought of days gone by and Sundance. I'd raised him from the day he was born. I remembered Papa coming into the house one frosty morning in the spring of the year I turned twelve, smiling and saying, "Well, Tara, it looks like you've got your very own colt!"

I'd rushed out to the barn to see the wobbly gold and white colt. Papa said, "He looks like a good one. His sire and dame are both good performers, and I'd say he will be too."

From that day on, I'd spent every spare minute working with Sundance, currying him, training him, and talking to him. We became pals. He was a quarter horse with an impressive pedigree. I was the first person he allowed on his back. Papa taught me how to gently train him to accept a saddle and rider.

Later, Sundance let Mama ride him too. She was an expert horsewoman. But Mama was the only other person he would allow on his back. Papa didn't even try to mount him. Mama entered Sundance into a local barrel race when he was three years old, and he won easily. Over the next few years, I rode him in barrel racing myself, and he continued to win at almost everything he did.

After Mama and Papa died, and we moved to Gran's ranch, Charlie tried to ride Sundance. But the big blonde horse would have none of it. He was frightened of Charlie. He bucked him right off. Charlie got up, furious at the horse. He hit Sundance in the head and tried to mount again. But Sundance reared and broke away, galloping toward the high fence, taking it in an impossible leap.

"I think Charlie must be a little crazy," Gran had said. "He knows better than to hit horses in the face. At least, he was raised to know better."

From then on, Charlie couldn't even get near the horse. Sundance screamed with fear, reared up, and raced off every time Charlie approached him. Gran told Charlie to leave the horses alone. Her demand enraged him so much he punched Gran in the face, giving her a black eye.

"Don't you try to tell me what to do, old woman!" he shouted.

We were all afraid of Charlie, especially after Papa and Mama died. But Gran tried to shield us from him by taking the brunt of his anger herself.

Because our parents were gone, I started saving the prize money I won in barrel racing and roping and branding calves for nearby ranches to help pay for my own schooling, putting aside some of my earnings for Jesse's future education. I raced in the summer to continue earning money. Now it seemed like another lifetime. A time for me to lead our family and keep the younger ones safe. The money I had withdrawn from the bank should keep us through my July birthday, I figured, maybe longer if I was careful and if the horses didn't need a vet.

Looking back at my days at West Texas A&M, I sighed. *College looks like it's out of the question now, at least for me. Mama and Papa wanted me to go to college, but I'll have to put that off, at least for a few years. I need to take care of Jess and Liam and get the horse business going. Maybe I can finish college later.*

Jess can get a scholarship and some grant money for college when the time comes. Her grades are excellent, and our Native American heritage will be another avenue toward grants and scholarships. The Social Security survivor benefits she gets will help too. By the time Liam's ready for college, I should have the business going well. I hope.

Under the warmth of the blanket, I pulled on my blue jeans and knit top. With a rush, I got up and grabbed my coat and socks. Montana was cold!

The fire had burned out in the woodstove. Picking up some kindling and small chunks of wood next to the stove, I lit a new fire. After a few minutes, it was going fairly well. I closed the lid and stood there in my coat, hoping it would get warm quickly. The cabin had a fireplace stove insert to help heat the cabin, but I'd have to round up more wood first.

The clanking noises from building the fire had awakened Jesse and Liam. I could hear them stirring in the other room. I walked over to their bedroom. "Hey, sleepyheads. Good morning!"

"Umph," Jesse said, pulling the covers up over her head.

Liam blinked and looked around, but stayed under his warm blankets too.

"I've got the fire going. You just stay where you are until it gets a little warmer while I fix breakfast."

"Whatcha making?" Liam wanted to know.

"How about pancakes?"

"Um. Good choice," Jesse mumbled.

"Will you make me a Micky Mouse pancake?" Liam asked.

"Sure," I said. "I'll call you when it's ready."

The kitchen was cold, but it warmed up quickly around the stove. I laid bacon slices in one of Uncle George's big frying pans. While it sizzled, I whipped up batter for pancakes, and beat some eggs to scramble. Twenty minutes later, breakfast was ready.

"Jess, Liam, it's on the table," I called.

Jesse came out of the bedroom, hair rumpled, a blanket wrapped around her shoulders over her pajamas, wearing tennis shoes on her feet with the laces dragging on the floor. Liam was fully dressed with his coat on, ready for the cold. They pulled out chairs and sat at the table while I put hot plates in front of them.

"Pray quick!" Liam said hungrily.

I smiled. We bowed our heads. "Father God, thank you for bringing us safely here, and thank you for this food. Amen."

After breakfast I asked, "Jesse, after you are dressed, would you wash the dishes? And Liam, could you dry them?"

"Okay," they said in concert.

"I'm going out to feed and water the horses." I stepped outside, alone in the cold, Montana morning. Or so I thought.

CHAPTER 16

Ben Farley walked from the weathered ranch porch on the other side of the hill from Ruby Hollow. He clamped his cowboy hat down over dark brown curls, its shadow hiding his eyes from the early morning sunshine. His lambskin lined denim jacket hung open over his blue plaid shirt. *Maybe I'll have time to stop by the Country & Ranch store and see if they want an ad—after I'm finished with class.* He zipped his jacket up, the air still a little chilly.

He stopped suddenly and sniffed the air. *Wood smoke? Now where would that be coming from?* The Farley ranch had propane heat. He stepped off the porch and felt a faint breeze blowing from the north. *The only place to the north is Ruby Hollow.*

Pulling out his cell phone, he touched a number on his speed dial.

"Ben?" a sleepy male voice sounded at the other end of the call.

"Yeah, it's me, Dad. Um, did Evelyn Webster say anything about coming up to the ranch this week?"

"No, she didn't. Why?"

"Well, someone must be at the cabin, because I smelled wood smoke coming from that direction just now."

"Hm. I hope it's not someone else trying to use the cabin. Are you going to check it out?"

"Yes. I'm going over there now."

"Take Jingle, Son, not the truck. The engine makes too much noise."

"I will, Dad. I'm going to saddle up and ride over. That way I can come in quietly and see if it's Evelyn or a trespasser."

"Okay. Good plan. But take your rifle along—just in case."

"Will do," Ben said. "I'll call you when I know the scoop."

"Be careful."

"Of course, Dad. You know me. I can sneak up on anything or anyone. 'Bye."

Ben put his phone back in his pocket and headed for the barn where his mare, Jingle, was stabled. "Hi there, Jingle," he said, rubbing the white blaze down her nose. "Ready to go?"

Jingle snorted.

Ben threw a blanket over the mare's back, pulled his saddle off a rail, and swung it onto the horse, cinching it tight. He grabbed a bridle and held the bit in his hands for a minute, warming it up before slipping it over Jingle's head and buckling the leather strap. He led the horse out of the barn, ground hitched her, and stepped back into the house to grab his rifle. He shoved it into the scabbard, scooped up the reins and climbed into the saddle.

Maybe Evelyn is at the ranch. But wouldn't she have called if she were coming? If that's her over at Ruby Hollow. I wonder if she brought her grandkids along. Didn't the kids' parents die a couple of years ago, and doesn't Evelyn have custody of them now? Ben nudged his horse and headed toward the narrow pass through the mountains between the two ranches. *But surely Evelyn would have called first. I'll just have to wait and see who's there.*

Dark evergreens covered the narrow gap between the hills separating the Farley ranch from Ruby Hollow. Pine needles muffled the sound of his horse as he rode swiftly through the forest. Ben slowed the horse to a walk when he was within sight of the ranch buildings, stopping in the shadow of the boulders behind the corral.

A door slammed, and a girl in a red coat came from the house, long black hair falling to her waist as she walked swiftly toward the barn. She looked Native. He saw her reach up and pull her hair back, looping it in a big knot. He waited a few minutes, looking the place over carefully. A good-quality horse trailer stood by the boulders next to the barn along with a dark blue, almost new F-250 truck. The vehicle spoke of money, so this was not a squatter. But who was the girl? Could she be related to George Marten?

Ben waited. She came out of the barn again leading a beautiful palomino with a blanket over its back. Ben decided the situation wasn't dangerous and nudged his horse with his knees. Jingle snorted and took a step forward on the pine needles.

The girl whirled around, her eyes wide.

Ben heard her gasp. He rode forward, stopping about fifteen feet away to avoid frightening her. "Hello," he said, touching the front of his cowboy hat politely. "Ma'am, this is private property," he said gently, continuing forward at a slow, steady pace.

The palomino stallion pulled toward the approaching mare, but the girl held him back.

"Yes, I know it's private property," she said with a soft, Texas drawl. "It belonged to my grandmother. Now it's mine. Who are you?"

Ben's eyes widened. "You must be Tara, then."

The girl nodded.

"I'm Ben Farley. My dad, Eli, manages this ranch for your grandma."

"B-Ben?"

He smiled and nodded. "Yes, ma'am."

"Oh!"

CHAPTER 17

Ben dismounted and stepped toward me, leading his horse. "You said your grandma owned this ranch but now it's yours? What happened?"

"Gran died," I said, searching his face.

"She died?" Ben asked. "I knew she was ill, but I didn't know it was that bad yet."

"It wasn't. She—she fell down the stairs." I couldn't bring myself to tell him about the murder. Not yet. I felt tears coming to my eyes and dashed them away with the back of my hand.

"I'm so sorry, Tara," he said gently. He looked sympathetic. "I know this must be hard, after losing your parents—and now your grandma." He shook his head slowly.

I took a quick breath and lifted my head. "Wait. You knew my parents died?"

"George told Dad. He kept us informed about your family. I was terribly sorry to hear about their deaths."

"Then you can understand why I brought Jess and Liam up here—to get away from Texas for a while. We need some time to heal."

"I understand. If there's anything I can do to help you, I will."

"Thank you." I hesitated a moment, wondering how much to tell him. "Um ... could you please not tell *anyone* we're here? I just can't cope with others dropping in right now. You're fine because I know you. But I just don't want neighbors or anyone else dropping in until we're ready."

"Sure," Ben said with a nod.

Just then the cabin door opened, and Jesse stepped out hesitantly. "Tara?"

"It's okay, Jess," I said. "It's Ben Farley. I don't know if you remember him or not."

"Oh!" Jesse's eyes flashed as she looked back at me then at Ben again.

Ben smiled. "Are you the girl who used to love Juicy Fruit gum?"

Jesse hesitated a moment. "I still do."

Ben fished in his shirt pocket and pulled out a packet of gum, separated a piece for Jesse and handed it over.

Jesse's face lit up in pleasure as she took the gum. "Thank you, Ben," she said shyly.

Liam came out to join us. Ben went down on one knee in front of Liam and studied him. "You must be the baby I saw last time you were here."

"Well, I grew up!" Liam said, standing tall, his arms akimbo.

"You sure did. What's your name, cowboy?"

"Liam"

"Glad to meet you, Liam," Ben said, standing and shaking Liam's hand. "Are you too old for Juicy Fruit gum?"

"Nope!" Liam said, his eyes gleaming.

Ben pulled out another piece and offered it to Liam, then turned to me. "How about you, Tara?"

I quickly shook my head. "No, thanks." I suddenly wondered if Ben still thought of me as the child of seven years ago.

Ben turned back to Jesse and Liam. "I'm sorry to hear about your Gran," he said. "Tara told me she passed. It's a hard thing you all are going through." He looked over at me. "I'll help you get settled. I'm sure there are a number of things about the ranch you could use help with. And you definitely need to know about the wildlife around here."

I nodded. "Yes. Thanks." I suddenly remembered the solar panels. "Would you know where the switches are for the solar panels?"

"I sure do, Nature Girl," Ben said, grinning at me. "They're in the laundry room. I'll show you."

Nature Girl. He still remembers the nickname he gave me the summer we spent together. I felt funny inside and a little light-headed for a second. *He remembers!*

Ben and I walked back into the house together, Liam and Jesse trailing behind us. He led me to a cupboard located behind the dryer in a corner of the laundry room. "Here they are," he said, opening the cupboard, pushing aside a box of laundry detergent, and flipping some switches hidden on the wall behind them. "That will turn on the solar panels and get things going."

"No wonder I wasn't able to find them."

"Tara," Ben said apologetically, "I need to head for class now. I'll stop by this evening to see if you need anything and tell you more about the place."

"Thanks, Ben. We'll be fine now that we've got everything turned on. But I do need to know more about this ranch."

I followed him out onto the front porch as he walked over to his horse and mounted. He waved as he rode off, and I waved back. Then, breathing in the cold, fresh air, I turned and took in the view stretching out before me. Pastures with a faint hint of green stretched across the valley. The hills were clothed with pine and fir trees, with a few aspen groves near the meadow. The sky was so blue and so wide, I could lose myself in its beauty. All this was now mine. I felt overwhelmed by the thought of managing this ranch.

I took a deep breath. "God, you're gonna have to help me. This is a big ranch, and I hardly know how to begin running it, this being Montana not Texas."

"Jess, Liam," I called, walking back into the house. "Get your coats and riding boots on so we can take the horses out to explore the ranch."

"How big is it?" Jesse asked as she and Liam came out, buttoning their coats.

"There are five thousand acres, partly pasture, partly trees. The creek runs the length of the property."

"Five thousand acres?" Jesse said wide-eyed.

"Yes. Enough to raise not only horses but cattle as well if we want. Are you ready to go look?"

"Yeah," she said, heading for the barn with Liam right behind her.

I saddled Sundance while Jesse saddled Rosie. She and Liam mounted the mare while I mounted Sundance. Together, we headed down the road into the valley. We left Bueno in the barn where he would be safe and warm. "Let's check out the other barn first," I called back over my shoulder. "We need to see if there's any hay in there."

Steam rose from our lips and from the horses' nostrils in the chilly morning air. An eagle swooped across the sky above us as we headed across the field.

"Look, Liam. An eagle!" I pointed.

"Whoa!" Liam shouted.

Both Rosie and Sundance stopped.

Jesse and I both laughed.

"Ignore him, Rosie," Jesse said, clicking her tongue and pressuring the horse with her knees.

I nudged Sundance. The big stallion twitched his ears and moved forward.

Soon the big barn loomed over us, steam rising from its shingles in the morning sunshine. Dismounting Sundance, I tied his reins to a fence rail while Jess and Liam did the same with Rosie. Together, Jesse and I pulled the big barn doors open, amazed at how neat and clean it was inside. Back in the shadows I could see a tractor and various attachments—a hay mower and a plow, and several other pieces of farm equipment. We spread out to explore the barn.

"Hey, Tara," Jesse called a few minutes later. "Come see this."

I followed the sound of her voice. She had discovered a milking room on one side of the barn. "It's big enough for five cows! We could start a little dairy if we wanted."

"Are you willing to get up at four in the morning every single day and come back again at four in the afternoon to milk the cows?

She thought about it for a moment, then regretfully shook her head. "No. I guess not."

"Beef cattle will be enough work. We have plenty of room here to raise them if we want," I said.

"Well, it was a nice thought," Jesse sighed.

"Yes, it was." I smiled. Jesse was starting to open up again.

"I'm gonna check behind the barn to see if there's anything more out there," she said, moving away from the milking room.

Back in the main barn, I saw a ladder rising toward a loft. I was about halfway up the ladder when I heard an engine roar. Liam shrieked. He was standing behind the tractor's steering wheel, gripping it tightly as the tractor lurched through the barn's open door.

"Liam!" Hurrying down the ladder and racing after him, I jumped up onto the short running board right as the tractor stalled and the engine went silent. I reached across

Liam, turned the key off, and dragged it and its chain away from the tractor's ignition switch.

"It tried to buck me off!" Liam yelled, his eyes wide.

"Oh, Liam!" I gasped, hugging him close, sinking onto the tractor's seat. "Don't ever do that again!"

"But the keys were in it."

"Yes, I see. But that does not mean you should turn it on. You could have been killed!"

"But I wasn't," he said with a shrug, quickly recovering from his momentary fright.

Whatever am I going to do with this fearless little brother of mine? I shook my head. "Climb down now while I put the tractor away."

"What happened?" Jesse said, racing into the barn breathlessly.

I explained and added, "I'm going to put the tractor back into the barn." I held up the keys. "It looks like this was Uncle George's key set."

There are more keys on this ring than were in Gran's file for the ranch. I wonder what they all go to? I led Liam over to Jesse. "Here. Hold onto him while I put the tractor back."

A few minutes later, having replaced the tractor, I put the keys in my pocket and continued my exploration of the barn. I climbed back up into the loft. "Jess!" I called. "There's enough hay here to get the horses through the summer if we need it!"

Jesse joined me in the loft. "How are we gonna get it down?" she asked, always practical.

"There's a rope and pulley set-up by the window. I can put the bales on the platform there and lower them into the truck, then drive the hay up to the other barn and push it out onto the barn floor. They aren't very heavy. They're thirty-five-pound bales, like we had for the horses back in Texas. But it's still too much for you to lift, Jess. I'll do it."

"We'll do it together," Jesse said. "If it's too much for me, it's probably too much for you too. You aren't that much taller than me."

"Okay." I laughed.

Climbing back down the ladder, I went outside and looked at the green fields. We'll have to mow some of that hay this summer. How will we manage all the heavy work? Who will help me hitch up the equipment?

Well, Lord, I prayed silently, *you brought us here safely. You know how we are going to manage this. I'm leaving it in your hands.*

"Let's mount up and ride back to the house and get the truck," I called to Jesse and Liam. "I think we can get at least one load of hay up to the smaller barn before lunch. We can explore the rest of the ranch later."

As Jesse and I loaded the haybales onto the pallet and lowered them down to the truck, I thought about this new ranch. *Will I be able to make a go of it here? We're far from town. Will I be able to find clients to buy the horses I will raise and train? What will I do during the long winters?*

My heart was anxious. I took my concerns to God. "Father, I have a lot to learn about this new place. There are new challenges to meet. Help me day by day to do what must be done. I don't know if I'll want to stay here forever, or if I'll want to go back to Texas someday. I trust you to tell me what to do. Be with us and bless us. Help me keep the children safe from Charlie. Help me know what is best for Liam and Jesse. Father, I place everything in your hands. Thank you for loving me."

Before leaving for Helena to shop for warmer jackets and have some lunch, I fished the set of keys from the tractor out of my jacket and tossed them onto the top of the tall dresser in my room and promptly forgot about them.

Little did I know how important those keys would prove to be someday.

By the time we returned, the solar panels had produced enough energy to provide hot water in the house. We would be able to have hot baths before bed.

One never realizes how important such things are until they aren't there anymore, I thought as I washed my hair later in the evening.

CHAPTER 18

Wednesday morning, Tyrel Morgan was driving his patrol car through town checking for anything out of the ordinary. But all was quiet. He was mentally cataloging the information about the missing Webster kids. Where could they have gone? Tara was just a little older than his sister, Jean, who was a senior in the local high school. The two girls had usually spent a lot to time together during their summer vacations, and he'd seen her often around the house. He would ask Jean more about what she knew. She might have some ideas.

Mark and Nora Webster had lived in another town about ten miles away before they died. They'd had friends and neighbors he could ask. Yes. He'd start with those neighbors.

Tyrel considered his dad's choice of profession and pondered whether or not he would like to be a judge too. Maybe someday he would follow in his dad's footsteps, but for now, he wanted to find out about law enforcement from the inside, working cases. Which would be a great asset when he applied to grad school later. Besides, he liked the challenge of keeping the peace.

This case was proving to be difficult, mainly because the sheriff was such good friends with Tyrel's chief suspect. He sighed. Concentrating on finding the kids first, then solving the suspected murder sounded like a better option.

Their friends might have some ideas. He'd be off duty this weekend. He could drive over to the next town and look up Mark and Nora Webster's friends then.

Charlie backed his car into a parking space outside a new brick building on Doran's main street. Walking through the doorway, he searched the directory for John Miller, Attorney at Law. There it was. Room 212. He turned and took the stairs two at a time.

Opening the office door, Charlie walked up to the secretary at the reception desk and gave her a charming smile. "Hi. I'm Charlie Webster. I believe I have an appointment with Mr. Miller?"

"Oh, yes," she said returning his smile. Reaching for the phone, she spoke into the receiver. "Mr. Webster is here, sir. Shall I show him in? Okay."

"Come this way, Mr. Webster."

"Charlie," Mr. Miller smiled gently and rose from his desk. He came around to extend a hand. "I'm sorry to hear about your loss."

Charlie nodded solemnly. "Thank you. Lots of folks came to Evelyn's funeral yesterday. They were most kind."

"I'm glad to hear that, Charlie. Have a seat. Now, what can I do for you today?"

"Well, I can't find my stepmother's will, and I don't know how things stand regarding the ranch. I was hoping you could tell me." Charlie leaned back in the comfortable chair and crossed his legs nonchalantly.

John Miller picked up a file on his desk, opened it and looked through the papers. "Um. Yes. By your father's will, you inherit the ranch upon Evelyn's death. Which means, it becomes yours outright."

Charlie nodded. "That's what I thought." He paused. "But what about Mark and Nora's children? What has been done about appointing a guardian for them, in the event of Evelyn's death?"

Mr. Miller paused. "Evelyn Webster's will is privileged information involving only the people to whom she gave instructions."

"The children are missing, John!" Charlie protested. "Isn't there anything that can help me find them?"

The lawyer's eyebrow rose ever so slightly. Evelyn had warned him about Charlie's aggression. Apparently, Charlie did not respect legal privilege. And he was altogether too familiar in the way he addressed him, calling him by his first name when they weren't even acquainted. He absolutely would not tell Charlie Webster about the Montana ranch. He knew his client would not have wished it.

"I have seen nothing in the will giving any indication about where the children would be." He wasn't lying. There was no mention of the Montana ranch in the will, only that everything belonging to Evelyn Webster was to go to Tara. "Also, it is my understanding Tara, being eighteen, is going to be appointed guardian for her younger brother and sister. Mrs. Webster specifically named her to be their guardian."

"Oh, no. She's still seventeen," Charlie said confidently.

"No. According to the dates here, she is eighteen now."

"She is? I thought she was still seventeen!" Charlie felt his life slipping away, sliding down, down, down into danger, toward death. He marshaled his thoughts and tried to stay calm. He frowned cautiously at Mr. Miller. "Is that wise? I don't see how she could continue college and still care for the younger children. They'd all be better off with me. Could you talk to someone about this for me?"

"I'm sorry, Mr. Webster, but I represent Evelyn Webster and, of course, Tara, since she's mentioned in Mrs.

Webster's will. I cannot represent you in this conflict. I can tell you this—most likely the court would not take guardianship away from her." Mr. Miller shook his head. "Tara has proven herself to be a very responsible girl these past two years. She's been working, performing in rodeos, and helping her grandmother manage the ranch and take care of her siblings. She's earned her own money during summer vacations and manages it well. Her grades are good. Fantastic, in fact. She earned a 4.0 GPA in high school. And she will have her inheritance to help support the younger children as well as some Social Security survivor benefits because of their parents' deaths. All of which should be enough to provide for them."

Charlie frowned. "Well, just think about it."

"Hm," Mr. Miller murmured noncommittally. He was not going to reveal anything more about what he knew.

"Are you *sure* there isn't anything in Evelyn's will to give me a clue about where those kids are?" Charlie looked grim. "I'm worried about them. In light of Tara's disappearance, I want to be appointed as the children's guardian when they are found. I find it totally irresponsible for Tara to take them and run. Surely the law would agree."

Mr. Miller brought his fingertips together in front of his face and considered. "Child Protective Services usually oversees situations like this."

"Who do I need to speak with there?" Charlie asked. "How long does it usually take to appoint a family member as guardian?"

"My secretary can give you a name and number to call at CPS. In this case, it will take a few months to settle on guardianship. The children aren't here to speak for themselves."

"Months!" Charlie was aghast.

John Miller's eyebrows rose. "Is that a problem?"

Charlie forced himself to calm down. "No. No. Of course not." Charlie sighed in frustration. "Sheriff Bradshaw has put out a local alert for the kids, and the police are looking all over this part of the state for them. I think they're probably running scared because their grandmother died, and their parents are dead too."

"I see," Mr. Miller said, standing up, indicating the interview was over. "Thank you for coming in, Mr. Webster. I'm sorry I could not be of more help."

Charlie stood. "Thank you, John." He smiled with practiced warmth, held out his hand and gave Mr. Miller a hearty handshake. "So, um, please let me know if you find anything else in Evelyn's papers you think could give us a lead to finding the kids."

John Miller gave a noncommittal, "Um."

When Charlie had left, John sat at his desk and stared thoughtfully at the Webster file. Why indeed had those children run away? He got the feeling they were afraid of Charlie, which went along with what Evelyn had told him.

He remembered the day Evelyn Webster had come to his office to make a will. When they reached the subject of the children, Evelyn had said if something should happen to her, then Tara should be their guardian if she were eighteen or older. He had protested. Surely their Uncle Charlie should be the children's guardian since he was their only living relative.

But Evelyn had been firm. "I wouldn't leave a *dog* to Charlie!"

He had been shocked, but after she left, little snatches of conversation came back to him. Like the time years ago when his nephew, Karl, had come over after school all bruised up. He'd been in a fight with Charlie on the playground. He'd said Charlie was picking on him because he was shorter than the other boys. Karl had told Charlie to leave him alone, but Charlie had only become more infuriated and had followed the teasing up with a beating.

He remembered Levi Carroll, Evelyn's neighbor, openly disliked Charlie too. Strange. Charlie had always seemed like such a nice young man. Being a lawyer, however, Mr. Miller felt cautious and preferred to reserve his judgment.

There was one thing he could do to help Tara. He picked up the phone and called the sheriff's office.

Tyrel answered. "Sheriff's office. This is Deputy Morgan. May I help you?"

"Deputy Morgan, this is John Miller, Evelyn Webster's lawyer. I want to speak to the sheriff about the search being made for the Webster children. Is he there?"

"I'm sorry. The sheriff is out. May I take a message?"

"Yes. I understand the sheriff has issued a local alert for the Webster children. I feel you should know Evelyn's will names Tara as guardian for her brother and sister. She is almost nineteen, she is in college, and she is highly responsible. More than likely the courts will confirm this appointment to guardianship. Although nothing has been settled at this time, I would advise the sheriff of Tara Webster's position. Mr. Webster just came to my office trying to find clues about the children's possible location. I had nothing to tell him, nor would I if I did. I feel it would not be wise to inform Charlie Webster of their location if you happen to find the children. This matter should be taken up only with the court. I have no proof of any wrongdoing on Charlie Webster's part, but that is my professional opinion as Evelyn Webster's attorney. That is all. If the sheriff wishes to call me, here's my number."

Tyrel wrote quickly, then read the message back. "Thank you, Mr. Miller. I will tell the sheriff."

Well. That certainly confirms my impressions, Tyrel thought. *I wonder what Sheriff Bradshaw will say?*

CHAPTER 19

Charlie drove back to the ranch in fury laced with fear. *Who would have thought Tara was eighteen? She looks younger, with that wide, innocent gaze of hers. I'll just have to find her. And when I do—well, there's one good way to stop her. But it will have to look like an accident.*

After he cooled down, Charlie contacted Jenna, Tara's best friend. Arriving at her house, he heard some noise coming from the back yard and walked toward it. "Hello. Anybody here?"

"Hello," a pleasant woman stood up from a group of ladies and came toward him. "May I help you?"

"Yes. I'm Charlie Webster, Tara Webster's uncle. I'm looking for Jenna. Is she here?"

The woman nodded. "Yes, Mr. Webster. She is."

"Call me Charlie," he said, giving her a charming smile.

"Okay. Charlie. Come over to the shade and have a glass of lemonade while I find Jenna," his hostess smiled.

When Mrs. Johnson and her daughter returned to the group, Charlie said, "May I have a word in private with Jenna?"

"Sure," the girl said. "Come into the house." She led him into the living room with its long stretch of windows overlooking the back yard.

"How can I help you, Mr. Webster?" Jenna asked.

"I'm trying to locate my niece, Tara," Charlie said. "I know you two are good friends, and I wondered if you knew of any place she might have gone with her sister and brother? Her grandmother passed away last week, and Tara and the younger children have disappeared."

Jenna looked away. She was very aware of Tara's feelings about Charlie. She remembered the phone call Tara had received from Jesse, and the short conversation she'd had with Tara later that same day. "I wish I could help you," she said politely, "but I haven't seen Tara lately, and I have no idea where she might be." She fixed wide, innocent blue eyes on Charlie.

"Did she ever talk about any place she liked a lot?"

Jenna smiled. "Other than rodeos? No."

"Is there a special young man in her life?" Charlie grinned charmingly and tipped his head to the side.

Jenna shook her head. "No. Tara hasn't shown interest in anyone that I know of. She's friendly, but she's not dating anyone."

Charlie bowed his head and sighed. "Well, if you hear from her or have any ideas about where she might be, would you give me a call?" He fished a business card out of his pocket. "Take my card."

"Thank you," Jenna said politely, showing him to the door. "I hope everything will turn out okay."

"Me too," Charlie said, walking with Jenna to the front door. "Thank you for your time."

Jenna nodded and opened the door. Watching him drive away, she shook her head. If Tara had disappeared, she must have had a good reason. This was beginning to sound serious.

"What did Mr. Webster want?" her mother asked quietly, coming into the house.

"He wanted to know if I had any idea where Tara might be," Jenna said. "She disappeared with her brother and sister. I don't know where she went, but if I did, I wouldn't tell him. Tara says he's a monster. She wouldn't like me to tell him a thing, even if I knew."

"Well, you know Tara better than I do," her mother said thoughtfully. "Do what you think is best."

Jenna stared out the window. Where was Tara? Was she okay?

Ben thought about Tara and her family as he headed down the mountain to attend classes. Tara has turned into a real beauty. She was a cute little girl last time I saw her. But now—wow! *She's got to be the prettiest girl I've ever seen.*

He slowed his truck going around the curves. The Helena Valley lay just beyond the green ranchland far below the mountain highway. *I don't like the idea of Tara being up there all alone with the kids. The property isn't posted, and people sometimes try to camp there. What if the wrong kind of people show up at the ranch? Dad and I have chased off a few. I'll pick up some more No Trespassing signs at the hardware store after class and post them. I should take Goliath over to the ranch, too, and leave him there to guard them.*

Looking out over the smaller hills and valley on his way down the mountain, Ben gave this problem to God. "Father in heaven, please watch over Tara and her brother and sister. Keep them safe. Show me how I can help. I sense Tara is nervous, maybe even afraid of something. Be with her thoughts today, and put your peace in her heart. In Jesus's name I ask this, amen."

He parked in the college campus parking lot and headed for class.

"Ben!"

He turned. "Hi, Nikki."

She's a pretty girl, too. Great personality. Nice figure. Rich parents. But there's something hard about her eyes. She's not a Christian. She isn't interested in the same things as I am. She's not interested in church or the young adult meetings we have there. I don't mind being her friend, but it's best if I were to keep some distance between us. I don't ever want to become involved with someone who doesn't share my faith. I don't want her to think I'm interested in more than friendship.

"Some of us are getting together over at Montana City Bar and Grill tonight. Want to come?"

Ben knew all about those parties. Everyone usually ended up drunk. "Thanks for the invitation, Nikki, but I have some work to do this evening."

"Aw, Ben," she pouted. "Can't you put it off ... for me?" She looked up into his face, invitation in her eyes.

"Thanks, but I really can't."

"Oh!" she tapped him on the arm playfully. "I'm beginning to think you don't like me!"

"I like you fine. You are a nice girl," Ben said, smiling. "But I'm a working man with a long way to go to establish myself. I can't take time out right now."

Nikki sighed and took his arm. "Well, if you can't come, you can't. Maybe we can do lunch together. Lorene and I are planning on heading for Hardee's at noon. How about it?"

"Sure," Ben nodded. "Hardee's it is. See you there."

"It's a date, then." she said.

A date? I don't think so.

CHAPTER 20

Jesse and I were moving hay into the log barn next to the house when we heard a truck coming up the road. It must be Ben. Glancing at the driveway, I saw Liam race out to meet him as he pulled into the ranch yard.

"Hi, Liam," Ben called, stepping down from the truck.

"Hi, Ben," the boy said enthusiastically. "I was hoping you'd come back."

Jesse and I came out to greet him too.

"Tara? Is it okay that Ben knows we're here?" Jesse whispered anxiously. "What if he calls the ranch in Texas and talks with Charlie?"

"I think we're safe," I said softly. But what did I know about this older Ben? I felt a trembling inside warring with the joy. I sent a silent plea from my heart to God's. *Let us be safe.*

"Hey, Tara," Ben called. "I was thinking about how isolated this ranch is for you. I just put up some more No Trespassing signs near the ranch entry, but I think you may need a little more protection from unwelcome visitors than that. I have an idea." Ben smiled and headed toward Jesse and me.

"Oh?"

"Yes. Would you be comfortable having a dog around?"

"I love dogs."

"Me too!" said Liam enthusiastically.

"Okay. I was wondering if you might feel safer if I brought my dog over here. I'm away most of the time at class, and he'd be happier with people around, if you're okay with it."

"Sure. We'd love to have him."

"Good. I'll bring Goliath over. He's a terrific watchdog. I'd feel better if he were here."

"Goliath?"

"Yes. But I call him Golly most of the time."

"How big is he?" I asked suspiciously.

"Oh, smaller than a horse." Ben grinned. "He'll keep the big game and any strangers away."

"I'd like that," I said. "Bring him over."

"Sure thing. I'll bring him over tomorrow."

"Thank you, Ben." I smiled.

Ben smiled back, holding my gaze for a long moment.

I remembered that moment later with a warm glow when my head touched my pillow.

But before I went to bed, I called Jenna. She answered right away. "Jenna, it's me. Don't say my name."

"Okay."

"My grandmother died. We are in danger from my uncle, Charlie. I've had to take Jesse and Liam away for a while until it is safe to come back."

"Charlie came here today asking for you," Jenna said softly.

"Did you tell him anything?"

"No. There was nothing to tell. Besides, I wouldn't ever tell anyone anything you don't want me to."

Relief washed through me. "Thank you, Jenna."

"Where are you?"

"I can't tell you. You are safer not knowing."

"Okay. But if you need help, just call me."

"I will. But I wanted you to know I'm okay, and we have someone to help us where we are now."

"Who?"

"A good friend. I need to go, Jenna. I don't have a lot of time on this phone. Could you put any news about us or Charlie or Doran on your Facebook page if you hear anything unusual? I'll check your page every day, but I won't communicate on it. I'll call you when I can."

"Okay. I can do that. Be careful."

"I will. Pray for us, Jenna."

"Yes. I will."

"'Bye for now."

"'Bye."

The sun peeked through misty clouds rising above the creek and meadows in Ruby Hollow. Looking out the kitchen window as I fixed breakfast, it was as though I was overlooking a soft, white shifting sea filling the space between the house and the big barn across the pasture.

"Oh, how beautiful!" Jesse breathed standing next to me and surveying the cloud layer. "This looks just like the land of Jack and the beanstalk!"

I laughed. "It does, doesn't it?"

Jesse shivered and pulled her sweater around her more tightly. "Burr ... it looks cold out there.

"Yes, but it will get warmer. Look on the bright side. By July, you'll be complaining about the heat." I reached into the cupboard and pulled out some dishes. "Jess, could you set the table while I make pancakes?"

"Sure."

We had eaten breakfast and cleaned the kitchen when we heard a truck making its way through the fog toward the cabin. Like a sea creature emerging from the tule fog, it rose and purred to a halt in the driveway.

"There's Ben!" Liam grabbed his coat off the hook by the door and ran outside.

Ben opened his truck door and stepped down, then looked back and said, "Come on, Golly." A dog jumped out of the truck and stood wagging his tail.

"Wow!" Liam said, staring at the huge black and white dog.

"He looks like a bear." Jesse said.

Ben smiled and held Golly's collar so he wouldn't be too rowdy with the children. "Hold out your hands so he can smell you."

Cautiously, they held out their hands for a sniff and a lick. After completing the greeting, Golly sat in front of Liam and barked twice.

Liam, who loved dogs, wrapped his arms around Goliath's neck. "Hi, Golly!"

The big dog wagged his tail ecstatically.

"Golly is huge, Ben! What kind of dog is he?" Jesse asked, ruffling Golly's fur while Liam hugged the gentle giant.

"He's a Saint-Dane—half Saint Bernard and half Great Dane."

"I like him!"

"He seems to like you, too, Liam" Ben said. "He is very protective, and I think he will make you feel safe. He's a good watch dog."

Golly isn't the only one that makes me feel safe. Having Ben here has made all the difference. I smiled, watching the interaction between Liam and the big dog.

The fog started to lift off the meadow, gradually floating up and fading in the sunlight. What a lovely day this would be.

CHAPTER 21

The next week passed quickly on the Montana ranch. Near the house, we found Uncle George's greenhouse, complete with peat pots and many containers for water. Gran and Mama had used similar things in their gardens back in Texas, planting seed in the peat pots and letting them sprout on sunny windowsills, then transplanting them into the garden with plastic cartons full of water by each plant. During the day, the water would heat up and by night, the tender plants would stay warm and not freeze.

"Do you want to start a garden like Gran and Mama used to have?" I asked.

"Yes," Liam said firmly.

"Sure," Jesse said with a casual shrug. Her face looked sad, as though the mention of Gran and Mama drew her back into isolation.

I could see she wasn't okay yet. "Would you like to do some painting later today, Jess?"

She looked out over the fields and mountains. "Yes, that would be nice."

"Okay. Let's buy some seeds when we're in town and start them in the greenhouse. We can use the plastic cartons filled with water inside the greenhouse because it's still so cold at night. After we've got the greenhouse ready for planting, you and Liam can paint."

Liam's enthusiasm for the greenhouse was beautiful to see in the following weeks. Soon little green sprouts began to grow, promising a harvest of vegetables and fruit.

Golly followed Liam everywhere, though Jesse drew the line at letting him into the greenhouse. "You know he'll wag that big tail of his, Liam. He'll sweep all our little plants off the shelves. Make him stay outside."

"Aw," Liam sighed. "Okay, I guess."

Jesse's collection of delicate paintings grew day by day as she painted pictures of the wildflowers around the property. As new wildflowers popped up around the creek and in the meadow, she painted every new bloom faithfully, quizzing Ben about each flower's name. What Ben didn't know, we looked up online at the library. Jesse wrote down the dates each type of flower bloomed and faded away, methodically cataloging them.

Life began to fall into a new pattern. Ben usually stopped by the house briefly to check on us each day after class. I looked forward to seeing him, but he was so busy with studies and his own family's ranch, he couldn't stay long. I learned his dad, Eli, had undergone surgery and was staying in Bozeman with Ben's older sister and her family while he recovered. Ben's mom had died when the children were young, and Ben didn't remember much about her. Carolyn, his sister, was four years older. Ben said they were close.

As we gradually settled in, the days grew slightly warmer. I checked Jenna's news from Texas on the computer at the library each week to see what was happening in Doran. Other than the initial news about us missing, nothing new was reported. My tension level began to drop, and I cautiously let my guard down. But Jesse wasn't feeling secure yet. She was still haunted by memories of seeing Charlie kill Gran.

"Jess? What's wrong?" I sat up in bed and held my arms out to her late one night.

"I dreamed about Charlie throwing Gran down the stairs," she sobbed. "Then he grabbed me and threw me down the stairs too!"

"Oh, honey!" I pulled her into my bed, tucked the covers around her, and let her cry on my shoulder for a while.

"I dream about it sometimes, and I don't know how to make the dreams go away!" she wailed.

"Jess, when I was scared once, Mama told me that Jesus has power over bad dreams. She prayed a special prayer over me." I stroked her hair. "Do you want me to pray the same thing for you? What Mama prayed for me?"

Jesse sobbed as she nodded her head.

"Father in heaven, we know this dream is not from you but from our enemy, the devil. Tonight, in the name of your son, Jesus, our Savior, we ask you to take this dream away forever. We ask you to fill Jess with your peace and joy. In Jesus's name, we break the power of Satan over Jesse's dreams. In Jesus's name, we ask that this dream will never return. Amen."

Jesse's shoulders relaxed as she nestled against me.

"Mama also gave me a verse to say before I went to bed at night. It's found in Psalm 4:8. It says, 'In peace I will lie down and sleep, for you alone, O Lord, will keep me safe.'"

"I like that," Jesse murmured, repeating it softly. Soon she fell asleep on my shoulder.

I sighed and pulled the blankets up over Jesse's shoulder. "Lord, show me how to help Jesse. I know you are with us. Please give me wisdom."

CHAPTER 22

Texas was growing hotter by the day. Charlie pulled into the ranch driveway in Evelyn's old car. Inside the house the air was stuffy and unbearably warm with the afternoon sunshine coming through the windows. While he waited for the cool air from the air conditioner to flood the house, he opened the refrigerator to grab a beer.

"What? No beer?" Remembering he'd put it in the horse trailer refrigerator, he cussed. Did those kids take the beer? He stomped outside and crossed to the barn. One of the stalls was open. Looking in, he saw the beer scattered in the hay and manure and swore again. Picking up two cans that didn't look too filthy, he stalked back into the house and put the cans in the fridge.

"Now where will I find a clue to where those kids went?" he muttered, looking around. "Upstairs? Yeah. The office. Evelyn might have something in her files." He took the stairs two at a time. In the office, he opened the top drawer of the file cabinet, and pulled out a handful of files.

Two hours later, Charlie still hadn't found a clue about where the kids could have gone. Their other grandparents were in Mexico and spoke only Spanish. Would they have gone there? No. Probably not. They've only seen those grandparents once or twice. They had to be at some friend's place. But where?

The house was cooler now. Charlie sighed and rubbed his neck. He walked downstairs and stared out the living room window overlooking the ranch. If only Dad had left the ranch to me, I wouldn't have sold off the cattle. I would have kept this place running and would have plenty of resources to pay off those blasted gambling debts. He looked at the empty pasture except for five cows left out of a herd of forty. I'll have to sell them to come up with a payment for Gino.

He thought back to those early days growing up on the ranch. He'd been the only child, loved and pampered by both his dad and mom. But when he was six, they had split up. His mom had taken him with her to Houston, away from his dad, away from the ranch. From that time on, he'd only spent the summers with his dad.

Then his dad met Evelyn. A few months later, they were married. By his eighth birthday, Charlie had a baby brother, Mark. He'd hated the baby from the moment he saw him. Mark would get to stay with their dad. Mark would step into his shoes as the son of the house, while he had to go back to Houston for the school year.

Many years later, when Mark and Nora died in a boating accident, Charlie rejoiced. His hated enemy was gone. The ranch would be all his someday—after Evelyn died. He heard she had cancer. When the opportunity to remove Evelyn from his path came, Charlie took it with pleasure. Now everything would be his. He could rebuild. Life was starting to look promising. But where were those kids? Everything depended on finding them.

Reading a Bible verse about God's protection to Jesse and Liam every night at bedtime, and praying with them, stopped Jesse's nightmares. Memories of Mama singing me to sleep prompted me to sing the same songs to my sister and brother as they lay in bed at night, gentle songs of praise and worship. Songs about Jesus.

Jesse continued to communicate a little more, but overall, she was still too quiet, and I could feel a tension in her.

Each morning I helped the children with their lessons, checking the children's work to make sure they understood the assignments, and working closely with Liam, whose reading skills were not great yet. Sometimes, I would read to them from books we checked out at the library.

The grass grew quickly. By the last week in April, it had grown enough for me to put the horses out in the upper paddock to graze. Horse blankets were still needed when we weren't riding the horses, as the weather continued to be too cold for them, considering they had come from Texas. I figured adapting fully to Montana weather would take several months for them, just like us.

"Are we going to keep Bueno or are we going to sell him?" Liam asked, leaning over the fence beside me while Jess practiced on Rosie.

"Do you want to keep him?"

"Yes. I *love* Bueno."

"Okay. We'll keep him. Do you want him to be your horse?"

"Yes! Yes!" he shouted.

Jesse and I laughed. "Then he's yours."

Liam ran down to the pasture calling the horse's name. "Bueno! Bueno!" Golly trotted behind, his tail wagging.

The colt, hearing Liam's voice, lifted his head and trotted to meet Liam.

"You're *my* horse now, Bueno," he said, gently putting his arms around the colt's neck.

Jesse and I exchanged looks and smiled. We both remembered the day we had met our very own horses.

CHAPTER 23

Saturday morning, I arose early to get a head start on work before the children were out of bed. The spring sunshine lit up the pasture below. A bumblebee flew from flower to flower in front of the house, drinking the nectar. In the distance, a meadowlark's song trilled an enchanting melody.

I breathed deeply, loving the delicate scents left after last night's rain, the earthy smell of damp soil drying, wildflowers nodding in the wind, and the new spring grass. I heard the muffled clip-clop of hooves on pine needles coming from behind the barn and turned to see Ben riding toward me through the dark trees. How tall and strong he looked. I strolled over to join him, hands in my pockets, as he dismounted and tied his horse to the corral.

"Hi, Ben."

"Hi Tara. I need to ask you something."

"What is it?"

"Your Gran had an agreement with Dad. We'd watch out for her ranch in exchange for pasture and hay for our cattle and horses. It's about time for me to bring the cows over. Is our agreement with your Gran still good with you?"

"Yes, of course. When did you want to bring them here?"

"In about a week. Will that work for you?"

"Yes. That's fine. Where are you putting them?"

"In the south pasture," he said, motioning with his hand. "We'll start them there, then move them into the next pasture a couple of weeks later. I move them around a lot, which will keep them from over-grazing the meadows. Dad and I have ten cow-calf pairs, plus ten pairs that belong to you now. Your grandmother had us sell her calves for taxes and expenses last fall, and the plan was to do that every year."

"Oh, good," I said with relief. "I don't see any reason to change plans. Is there anything I can do to help?"

Ben shook his head. "No. I'm going to ride out and check the fences in the first two pastures today. I want to be sure the cows aren't tempted to escape."

"Okay. When you're finished, drop by the house. You can tell me more of what I need to know about the ranch and how things work then."

"I'll do that," Ben said, touching the brim of his hat and turning toward his horse. He reined in and turned back for a moment. "By the way, we also have your grandma's two mares at our place. I'll bring them over with the cattle."

"Two mares? Good. Do you know how old they are?"

"One's nine years old, the other is five."

"Ah. Good breeding stock?"

"Yes, I'd say so. Though they don't have fancy pedigrees, they're both quarter horses. Your Uncle George rode the older horse in the rodeo and won some good prizes. But it's been a while since the horses have been worked like that." Ben turned and waved. "See you later this morning, Nature Girl." Ben smiled, his voice warm and lazy. Turning away, he nudged his horse forward, down the long drive toward the meadow.

Nature Girl. I felt as though the years since I'd followed him around had melted away. Yet now he seemed so much more interesting. From the look in his eyes, I knew he was seeing me differently too. My hand crept over my stomach to calm the butterflies.

I forced myself to think about the reality we faced. With two children dependent upon me, I couldn't let myself be distracted by my growing attraction to Ben. I'd think about the horses. How nice it would be to have two more mares to breed and train. This will be a good start for building my own horse business. Thank you, God, for these extra mares.

After he had checked the fences, Ben stopped by. "Hey, I have some hamburger makings over at our place. I thought you might like to do a barbecue for lunch."

"Great!" Liam exclaimed. "I'm starved."

"Thank you, Ben. Hamburgers would be nice. You don't need to do that, but I'm grateful."

Jesse watched silently.

"No problem. I'm glad to help. I'll be back shortly with the food." He grinned and headed back over the mountain path between our two ranches. Twenty minutes later, he returned in his truck. Bringing an armload of grocery bags into the kitchen, he dug out the meat. "You want to make some hamburger patties while I get things started at the firepit?"

"Sure." We hadn't used the firepit yet. I put the hamburger, buns, ketchup, mustard, and pickles on the kitchen island while Ben went into the barn and fetched barbecue coals and lighter fluid he had stored there.

Uncle George had built a small, outdoor barbecue pit into the center of the open patio in front of the house. Paved with flagstones with wooly thyme growing between them, the patio area gave off a pleasant, earthy smell. The fruit trees had also bloomed into a cloud of delicate white blossoms tinted with pink.

"Ben, what kind of trees are these?" Jesse asked.

"Apple trees. This fall, you'll have more apples than you know what to do with."

"Can we make applesauce?" Jesse turned to me.

"I think so," I said. "I helped Gran make some applesauce last year. It's not hard."

"There are some Nanking cherry bushes further down the hill too. They make great jam and syrup," Ben volunteered.

"Ben, the last time we were here, Uncle George had a picnic table set up out here. What happened to it?" I asked.

"It kinda fell apart. Your uncle chopped it up and used it for firewood. But there's a folding table and some lawn chairs in the barn."

"Can I carry something?" Liam said, tagging along as Ben headed that direction.

"Sure, cowboy!" Ben grinned down at Liam.

A few minutes later, Ben and Liam had set up the lawn chairs and a table in front of the house.

The meal Ben prepared was delicious. As we feasted in the fresh mountain air, I felt the tensions of the morning melt away. Liam climbed every tree around the barbecue pit, and I asked Ben about his life now, while Jesse listened in silence.

"Since I saw you last, I graduated from high school and began classes at the college in town. I'm just about done now. I studied business and advertising and have a few clients already. Not many, but it's a start," he said. "Dad's been sick and had to have an operation, but he's better now. He's enjoying his stay with my sister, Carolyn, and her family in Bozeman while he recovers. I'm taking care of our ranch and yours while Dad's away." He looked over at me. "What have you been up to, Tara?"

"Well, after Mama and Papa died, Gran took us in, and we've been helping around her ranch. She sold off most of her cattle because she couldn't handle the work. She only had a handful of cows left. She was battling cancer. She had to sell our ranch and most of the horses. She let us keep Rosie and Sundance so I could use them to restart our horse ranch later. Rosie had a colt this spring, which we were planning to sell. But I think we'll keep this one. It's Liam's horse now. And, of course, I've been doing barrel racing. Someday I want to raise and train horses for that event. There's college too. I had to leave when Gran died. Do you still go to the same church in Helena? The one we visited when we were here before?"

"Yes. I'm involved with the young people's group, and I play guitar in the worship band at church."

"Do you sing?"

Ben nodded. "Yeah. I enjoy it. Do you want to come to church with me Sunday?"

I hesitated. "Well—not yet, Ben. We need some time to heal and adjust. But maybe in a few weeks, we will be ready to go. Just not now." I looked up at Jesse, who had wandered over to the horses. Was she ready to be around others yet? Or was she still too shocked at what she'd seen? I wasn't sure. She was doing better. Maybe it was time for her to get involved with others her age again. But I didn't want to rush her.

"Hm." Ben's gaze turned toward Jesse and Liam. "Okay, Tara. But remember, you are always welcome to come to church with me if you want."

"Thanks." I felt flustered. I wanted to tell him more, but I changed the subject. "You mentioned telling us about the animals here?"

Ben smiled. "Yes. You all need to know about the wildlife." He turned to Jesse and Liam, who came over and sat next to us, eager to learn about Montana wildlife. "The main animals you'll have to watch out for are moose, elk, deer, bear, and mountain lions. The moose come down to the creek to eat willows. They will attack you if you get too close. So, stay away from them. The deer and elk graze in the meadows and on the hillsides. You won't want to get too close to them either. They are sometimes feisty, and you might get hurt. The bears come around if they smell fruit or meat in the garbage. You need to keep the garbage pail shut and locked up in the shed next to the barn until you take it to the dump." He paused and looked at me. "Did you find out where the dump in town is?"

"Yes, I bought a dump pass last week."

"Good. The mountain lions stay mainly in the hills, but sometimes they stalk the horses and cattle. Not often though. Just remember, they are sneaky and will come up behind you. If you stay together, you should be fine. They don't like groups. I'll bring some bear spray over and show you how to use it in case you need to."

Liam's eyes were big, bursting with excitement. "I've never seen a bear or a mountain lion or a moose in the wild. I can hardly wait!"

Ben laughed. "You'll probably see the moose and deer first. They come down frequently. Remember, keep your distance. There are other little creatures you'll meet, too, but none of them are particularly dangerous."

"What kind of animals?" Liam wanted to know.

"Oh, there are rabbits and squirrels. Raccoons and skunks, too, but they come out mostly at night."

"Skunks? Eeeeew!" Liam wrinkled his nose.

Ben laughed.

I stood to clean up our picnic. Ben followed me inside and parked his hat on a wooden peg on the wall near the door, grabbed a dishtowel, and helped me dry dishes. My hair now swung freely around my face and down my back. I pulled it into a loose knot to keep it out of the water.

Ben grinned. "You sure don't look like the skinny little kid in braids I met seven years ago."

I laughed. "Did you expect me to?"

He shrugged. "Kind of. I keep forgetting you've grown up."

"I could say the same for you, Ben Farley. At first, I didn't recognize you at all. Not with that big black mustache."

Ben fingered the luxuriant growth above his lip and smiled.

"It is a very nice mustache," I said, grinning at him.

Liam and Jesse played together under the trees while Ben and I talked. I put the kettle on the woodstove for hot tea later and sat down at the kitchen table with Ben.

"Tara, I get the feeling you aren't telling me everything about what happened in Texas," Ben said softly. "If you don't want to tell me, that's fine. But if you do want to talk, I'm here."

Ben had a quiet authority about him. I felt safe in his presence. Should I tell him? With all my heart, I wished I could pour everything out to Ben. But would he understand? Maybe I could tell him just a little.

I hesitated, then carefully chose my words. "Gran was murdered, Ben. With Gran's death, there are a lot of problems I need to work out to keep this family together and—and safe. Having you here is a blessing from God."

Ben blinked. "Murdered? Wow. That *is* heavy."

I covered my face with both hands for a moment then took a deep breath and looked up at him. I suddenly knew I could trust him completely. "Uncle Charlie pushed Gran down the stairs. Jesse saw him do it, but Charlie doesn't know. That's why I had to get the kids away from Texas. I'm sure Charlie is going to insist on being their guardian. He'll get the sheriff to hunt us down. I-I don't know where I stand legally in this. But if Charlie finds us, he's going to find out Jess knows about the murder, and he will kill her. He'll probably kill us all. He wants to sell Sundance to pay off his gambling debts. He owes a lot of money. I'm really afraid of him."

Ben reached out and put his hand on my shoulder. "Whatever happens, I will be here for you, Tara." He paused. "I think it would be a good idea if you would talk to the sheriff. He goes to our church."

"No!" I said, panic rising in my throat. "Ben, please! Please don't tell anyone at all! The sheriff would have to report to Texas he had found us, and the sheriff in Doran is a good friend of Uncle Charlie. We can't risk it, Ben."

He looked at me steadily for a moment. "Okay. You've got my word, Tara." He paused, looked away briefly then turned back to give me a quick hug. "I need to finish a paper for class this afternoon, Tara. But I'll be back after church tomorrow to show you around the ranch. Look for me around one o'clock."

"Okay. We'll be ready."

Ben stepped out into the sunny afternoon. "See you later, Tara," he said, looking over his shoulder at me and clamping his cowboy hat onto his head. "And don't worry. I'm on your side."

"Thank, you, Ben. See you tomorrow." I watched him climb into his truck and head down the drive before joining the children under the trees.

I watched his truck disappear down the road. *I'm glad I told him. With Ben's help, I don't feel quite so alone.*

CHAPTER 24

Tyrel Morgan pulled into the small parking lot in front of Levi Carroll's hardware store. He had waited until late afternoon when things were slow. The clerk pointed to the back of the store when he asked for the owner. The aisles were crowded with a multiplicity of gadgets. Hoses, sprinklers, fertilizer, mousetraps, small metal parts. A wonderful kaleidoscope of sights and smells, and a handy collection of useful items. At the back, Levi was arranging spring flowers in the small garden section.

"Mr. Carroll?" Tyrel said, closing the distance in long strides.

Levi Carroll looked up and frowned. "I told you all I wanted to say."

"And I thank you for that. I just need to know a few more things and was hoping you would help me."

Levi sighed. "What do you need to know?"

"I wanted to ask you a little more about the Webster kids. At the funeral, I sensed you had more information about them. Did you see them leave the ranch?"

Levi rubbed his chin. He looked around nervously. "Yeah. I did. Tara drove in through the back. She parked her car behind the barn an' climbed up that tree by the house an' went in through a bedroom window. Few minutes later, I saw her an' Jess an' Liam climb down an' carry their bags through the barn. Then I saw them take the horses." He paused and looked around to make sure nobody was listening. "Listen, Ty, Evelyn an' those kids got good reason for being scared of Charlie. He's a mean one. I seen him beat their dog, the one they had before he shot it, and I seen bruises on Evelyn's cheeks a time or two. They didn't get there by her runnin' into no doors, neither. It's a cinch that Charlie put 'em there."

Tyrel stood silently, nodding his head.

Levi spoke again. "You know, not everyone's the same at home as they are in public. Charlie had a dark side to him. Most people never saw anything but that pretty smile of his. But bein' neighbors, I heard things once in a while. He could be violent. If those kids didn't do what he wanted, he'd yell and lash out at 'em. Evelyn too."

"Why didn't she report it to the sheriff?" Tyrel asked.

"Guess she had some feelings about family bein' private," Levi said. "Some folks are like that. Keep ever'thing inside the family. It's not smart and makes the abuser feel like he can do it again and again. There's nobody to stop him, neither."

"Do you think he might have done anything serious to hurt those kids or Evelyn?"

Levi nodded his head and looked up to meet Tyrel's eyes. "You bet I do."

"Do you have any idea where those kids might have gone?"

"Mebbe. But I'm not sayin'." Levi looked determined. "Tara can take care of herself an' those kids just fine. Leave 'em be, Tyrel."

The deputy studied Levi's face. Should he persist in his questions? No. Not yet. "Okay, Levi. Thanks for your help. If you think of anything more, call me, okay?" He fished in his shirt pocket, pulled out a business card and handed it to Levi.

"See you 'round," Levi said. "An' you be careful, boy. If Charlie hears that you're nosin' about, he'll make trouble for you. An' don't worry. I won't say a thing. Less he knows, the better."

"Thanks again, Levi. Be seeing you." Tyrel turned and left. *Well, Levi just confirmed Charlie is trouble. Levi's right. This fits with what some folks are saying about Charlie. I'll need to be careful in this investigation. This is a small town and people's main entertainment is talking about their neighbors. I wouldn't want it to get back to Charlie. He shouldn't know he's under investigation. Better keep it under wraps.*

His next stop was the church. Pastor Bill Watts welcomed Tyrel into his office. "Hi, Tyrel. Sit down. How's work going for you?"

"Pretty good," Tyrel said. "Pastor, the reason I came by was to ask if you remember any friends of Tara Webster's parents."

"Hm. Why do you want to know?"

"Well, they might be able to give me some pointers about where those kids went."

"I see." Pastor Watts shot a sharp look at the deputy. "I remember her dad and mom used to hang out with Lem and Marge Smith. Marge would know who was in their group."

"Thanks, Pastor. That will help." Tyrel smiled and stood. "Would you mind not telling anyone I asked about this? I have a feeling it's dangerous."

Pastor Watts looked surprised. "Really? Well, I won't say anything since you asked."

"Thanks. I appreciate that." Tyrel smiled and turned. "See you next Sunday."

"Take care," the minister said, frowning slightly. "Dangerous?" he said to himself as the door closed behind Tyrel. "Hm. I don't see how."

Across town, Charlie was thinking about Jenna. He had hoped she might know something helpful. So far, he'd hit a brick wall in his search. He was in a foul mood. Once in his car, he swore viciously and sped back to the ranch. When he arrived, he walked over to the pasture fence. There weren't enough cattle to pay very much of his debt to Gino. He swore again. But only the cattle heard him cussing, and they ambled off toward quieter pastures just as his phone rang.

"Charlie, I just learned Deputy Morgan has been asking questions about you around town," Jeff Blake warned him.

"What kind of questions?"

"Well, the clerk at the hardware store heard Morgan asking Levi Carroll what he knew about you, and the clerk overheard Levi say something about you hitting Evelyn."

The world spun for a moment as the news sank in. He focused intently on the problem.

"Charlie? Are you there?"

"Yes. Sorry. I was just surprised."

"*Did* you hit Evelyn?"

"No! Of course not! It's a lie."

Silence. Then Jeff said, "I hope you are telling me the truth, Charlie. I can't defend you adequately if you aren't honest with me."

But Charlie had chosen his course. "What do you think I am, Jeff? I wouldn't hurt a woman!"

"Okay. I believe you. Just thought you'd like to know about Deputy Morgan questioning Levi."

"Thanks, Jeff."

For the rest of the afternoon, Charlie anxiously wondered what to do about Levi Carroll.

CHAPTER 25

"Jean, may I ask you some more questions about Tara Webster?" Tyrel asked as he took a bite of a chocolate chip cookie.

"Sure. What can I tell you?"

"I'm trying to find Tara and her sister and brother. Tell me about her. What's she like?"

"She's quiet, but she's not shy. She's confident and logical but not stuck up. I think she had to grow up fast after her parents died. She feels responsible for Jess and Liam, as their big sister. She acts way older than her age, she's not the party type, and she isn't easily excitable."

Tyrel gulped down some milk. "Good. Now, I'm trying to figure out why she took her family and ran away. What do you think, Sis?"

Jean stared at him, thinking it over. "Well," she said at last, "I think she ran away from her Uncle Charlie."

"I think so too," Tyrel said. "Can you tell me why you think that?"

"Sure. Tara said Charlie was sometimes violent at home. She said he hit her and the younger kids many times, and he often called her grandmother names. She saw him hit her grandma a few times. Tara was afraid of him. If something happened to her grandma, Tara wouldn't want to wait around for Charlie to come home and take charge.

She once told me most people think he's a terrific guy, but he's a completely different person at home. He's dangerous. He has a violent temper."

Tyrel nodded thoughtfully. "Okay. Then let's assume she and the kids took off in order to get away from Charlie. Where would she go?"

Jean hesitated for a minute, wondering whether she should tell what she knew. Finally, she said, "I think she would go to a ranch her grandma inherited somewhere up north."

"Did she mention any towns?"

"No. She told me a little about the ranch last year. Before her parents died, their family went up there. I think the ranch belonged to her great uncle. Tara really liked it there. After she moved in with her grandmother, Tara kinda clammed up and didn't say much. If she wanted to get away, I think she might have gone to that ranch," Jean said. "Don't tell anyone, Ty. If Charlie finds out—well—I'm afraid of what might happen." She shot a nervous glance at her brother; not sure she'd done right by telling him about the ranch.

Tyrel returned her look. "Don't worry, Sis. I'm keeping everything under my hat. The only person I might discuss it with is Dad, and you know him. Wild horses couldn't get him to talk about an ongoing case."

"That works for me," Jean said, looking relieved.

The young deputy stood up. "See ya' later, Jean. And thanks for the help."

"Ty," his mom said, stopping him on his way out of the house, "take this with you." She smiled and handed him a paper bag. "It's cookies."

"Thanks, Mom. You're the best!" Tyrel took the bag, sniffed the scent of warm chocolate chip cookies, kissed his mom's cheek, and headed out the door. His apartment was only a few blocks away, just enough space for him to have a private life, but still close enough to drop in for dinner regularly.

Back at his apartment, Tyrel added Jean's information to his growing list. Nibbling cookies as he wrote, he gradually became aware of sirens in the distance. Getting up from his table, Tyrel walked over to the window for a look. There seemed to be a fire downtown. Something was lighting up the buildings in the distance. He reached for his uniform shirt and badge. He might be needed.

As he drove closer, he noticed the fire appeared to be coming from the same block as Levi's store. Tyrel parked his car on a side street and raced toward the flames.

Sheriff Bradshaw came running up behind him huffing and puffing. Together, they pushed through the crowd, their badges flashing in the light of the flames. Deputies Malone and Delgado, the night shift, were already there. Fire hoses sprayed powerful jets of water at the fire inside Levi's store, trying to keep the doorway clear as two firemen came out carrying a stretcher to the ambulance.

Tyrel caught a glimpse of the victim. Levi's face was covered with soot, his hands looked black with burns, and his eyes were closed. They could see his chest rising and falling with jagged gasps as he struggled to breathe.

One of the firefighters clamped an oxygen mask over Levi's mouth and the paramedics loaded him into the ambulance, slammed the doors shut and headed for the hospital in the next town, the closest one in the area.

"Was anyone else in the building?" Sheriff Bradshaw shouted above the noise to a firefighter.

"Not that we know of," the man shouted back, shaking his head. "The building's going to go any minute. We can't save it. Step back, please!"

Reluctantly, Bradshaw and Tyrel moved away from the building. Minutes later, its roof crashed in, sending sparks and flames high into the sky as the firemen sprayed the nearby buildings to keep them from catching fire.

"Should I head over to the hospital in case Mr. Carroll wakes up or says anything? Or do you want me to stay here and investigate?" Tyrel asked his boss.

Sheriff Bradshaw waved toward the disappearing ambulance. "You go with them. I'll stay and ask questions here. This was probably an accident, but we need to be sure."

Tyrel returned to his car and headed down the road, his thoughts churning. Was this fire really an accident or just a coincidence?

Tyrel didn't believe in coincidences.

CHAPTER 26

Far away in Montana, I lay in bed looking out the window at the moonbeams dancing through the clouds. A sweetness filled my heart as I thought of how God had sent Ben to help us. Ben, my childhood hero—the one no other boy in my life could ever equal—the secret reason I had not wanted to date when the other girls were giggling with excitement over the boys in town.

But now, with so much depending on our remaining hidden, I couldn't afford to follow my heart. I had to keep my guard up to protect Jesse and Liam. Besides, I didn't know if we'd stay here in Montana or return to Texas ... if Charlie were caught.

A shiver of fear clutched my heart for a moment. Then I remembered the words I had read to Liam and Jess from my Bible before putting out the light. The Israelites were frightened when they reached the Red Sea and saw Pharaoh's army chasing them. But Moses told the people, "Don't be afraid. Just stand still and watch the Lord rescue you today. The Lord himself will fight for you. Just stay calm." The words from Exodus 14:13-14 stood guard at my heart's door, banishing the fear.

"I trust you, Lord." I whispered as I closed my eyes and pulled the blanket closer around me. "Thank you for sending Ben to help us."

God's presence comforted me as I fell asleep.

Sunbeams dancing across my face woke me the next Saturday morning. For a few minutes, I lay snuggled in my bed, reminiscing over everything we'd been through. "Thank you, God, for bringing us here to safety—and for sending Ben to help us," I whispered. "Lord, I'm looking to you for help. This is all new to me—running my own ranch, being responsible for my family—I'm counting on you."

I slid out of bed. *Ooooo! Cold!* I glanced at my watch. *It's almost eight o'clock. Ben will be coming over soon!* I grabbed my clothes and tugged them on, cold though they were. My fleece jacket had never felt so good before. *Will I ever get used to these chilly mornings?*

In the bathroom, I splashed my face with warm water, then held my hands under the faucet to warm my fingers.

A few minutes later, with a fire going in the woodstove in the big, open room, I reached for the oatmeal box and raisins, and pulled the eggs out of the refrigerator. By the time I had everything cooking, I could hear the kids moving around in the bedroom. I glanced out the window and saw Ben climb out of his truck, chin buried in his denim jacket, headed toward the house. My heart began to beat more rapidly.

Jesse stumbled into the room, her shoestrings trailing on the floor, hugging her blanket over her clothes. "What's for breakfast?"

"Oatmeal with raisins and scrambled eggs."

"Yum!"

Liam, also wrapped in a blanket, came into the room yawning widely.

A knock sounded perfunctorily at the front door and Ben stepped inside. "Good morning."

"Hi, Ben," Liam said, yawning again.

"Would you like some coffee or anything?" Jesse asked, looking around for a coffee maker.

"Sure. But you don't have to make it. Just point me at it and I'll put it together myself. I've already had breakfast."

I smiled over my shoulder and nodded toward the kitchen cupboard. "Coffee beans are in there. And good morning, Ben. I didn't see a coffee maker anywhere."

"Hi, Tara," he said smiling while reaching for the coffee makings. "There's an old-fashioned coffee pot in the cupboard to the right of the sink," he said, leaning behind me and opening the cupboard.

I felt a tremor at his nearness and caught my breath.

We sat down together at the table a few minutes later to bowls of steaming oatmeal, a serving bowl full of scrambled eggs waiting to be devoured, and fresh, hot coffee. Ben reached out his hands and said, "Why don't we hold hands while we thank God for this food."

As the kids and I ate breakfast, Ben sipped his coffee and said, "Tomorrow morning is church. Sure you don't want to go along?"

I hesitated, wanting the fellowship, but afraid to let people know we were here alone. And I was worried about Jesse's withdrawal. "Um, I wish we could go, but I don't think it's safe yet." I looked up at him hesitantly.

"Okay. I understand. Let me know when you feel safe. For now, why don't we go fishing down at the creek after breakfast?"

"Yeah!" Liam said.

"Where will we get the poles and bait?" Jesse asked.

"Everything's in the back of my truck," Ben said with a grin.

"Don't we need fishing licenses?" I asked.

Ben nodded. "Yes. You and Jess do, but not Liam. I brought those too. Everything's in my truck."

I stared at him in amazement. "Thank you, Ben."

He shrugged and grinned. "It's good to learn how to live off the land. Besides, Liam needs a hobby."

The younger children hurried to finish eating and ran to get the gear while Ben and I walked to his truck more slowly.

"Are you planning on going back to Texas later on?" Ben asked curiously.

"I'm not sure, Ben. Charlie inherits the ranch down there now that Gran is gone. Gran willed this ranch to me so I'd have some property of my own, because she knew she couldn't give me the Texas ranch. But I don't know a thing about ranching up here in the north."

"I could teach you," he said tentatively.

"Hm." I needed time to think about it. Would I like Montana? Would this ranch be a good place to raise and train horses? Gran thought so. I looked at Ben's profile. "Let's see how it goes. If the law catches Charlie, and it's safe to return—I don't know. I need to get the feel of things before making any decisions."

"How big is a moose?" Liam asked, running back to Ben, waving his new fishing pole.

"At their shoulders, they can be as tall—or taller—than I am," Ben said. "I'm six feet tall, so they are not small animals."

"Wow!" Liam's eyes grew big.

"You need to stay with Tara when you are out here in the meadows or in the forest. I'll teach her how to protect you. Don't play out here alone, Liam," Ben warned.

"Okay," Liam nodded.

"What about the bears?" Jesse asked. "Do they come down to the house?"

"Well, not usually. We have mostly black bears in this area. If you see a bear cub, stay away from it. Never come between a cub and its mama. Mostly, the bears here avoid humans. There's a lot to learn about the wildlife, but I don't want to tell you too much at once," Ben said. "The thing is, you are living in wild animal habitat. So, you have to stay alert. But for now, let me show you where you can fish."

"Here's your pole," Ben said reaching into the back of his truck and handing one to me. Jesse and Liam were already racing toward the creek.

"There are brown and cutthroat trout in the stream, kids," Ben said when we caught up with the children. They were sitting on the ground putting bait on their hooks. "You have to sneak up on them quietly and drop the line in the water near a pool, then let the bait drift into it. Make sure the sun is not behind you or the fish will see you. Think you can do that?"

"Sure." they said in unison, jumping up and running toward the water.

"Be very quiet or the fish will hear you coming."

They slowed down and crept in silence toward the creek. Jesse found a place she thought would work and drifted her line into a pool. Upstream, Ben showed Liam how to do it, whispering into his ear. Jesse was the family fishing pro, and she needed no instruction.

I smiled and walked to a shadowy place a little farther upstream and dropped my own line in the water. I wasn't particularly good at this, but I'd go along with it for the sake of the younger children. Jesse was into fishing, and she had a knack for it. Occasional squeals came from the children as they hauled in fish.

I felt a rush of excitement when a fish nibbled on my bait and took the hook. A short battle, and I had a good-sized brown trout on the bank, flopping around wildly. But now what did I do with it? Grab it? Eew!

Suddenly, Ben was there, laughing at me. "What? You don't want to touch your own fish?" He grabbed the fish expertly, removed the hook, and strung the trout on the fish line the kids had started

I laughed. "Thank you! I couldn't bear to touch the thing. Jess doesn't have a problem with the fish. She's great at this. But not me."

An hour later, with five fish on our line, we were ready to stop.

We headed toward the cabin. Halfway up the hill, Ben paused and motioned to a level area. "Your Uncle George used to practice with his horses here. The place grew over with sagebrush when he was sick, but I think there's rodeo dirt under the brush."

We all walked out to examine the field. The place was level, as Ben had said, but a lot of small bushes and weeds had grown in the sandy earth. I went to the middle of the field and knelt at a bare spot to check the soil. Lifting a handful of dirt, I let it sift through my fingers.

"What do you think?" Ben asked.

"Yes, it is rodeo sand." I looked up to study the area. "There's a lot of work we'll need to do before we can use it, but we have the time."

"I'll help," Jesse said.

"Me too!" chimed in Liam.

I laughed. "We'll have it cleared in no time, Ben."

"You might want me to bring the tractor down here to help pull out some of the larger bushes," Ben suggested.

"Yes, that would help," I said. "It will give us a good project to work on." I looked over the area, pleased at finding the practice field. We'd have to get some work gloves for this. "Ben, is there a shovel anywhere?"

"Sure. There's one in the small barn by the house. George kept it in a cabinet. I'll show you where it is. We can get started Monday after my classes are over. Sound okay?"

I nodded. "We'll be ready."

Later in the afternoon, Ben and I rode our horses out to check the second pasture's fences. The field was directly below the house.

"We have to keep an eye on the barbed wire fences here," Ben said. "Animals crawl through the wires and get them out of shape. See over there?" Ben pointed to a gaping hole in the fence. He swung down, and I joined him.

"This one will just take a minute." He pulled on his leather gloves and put the wires back into their correct notches on the posts. "There. Nothing to it." He straightened up. "Sometimes it gets pretty loose. Then I have to tighten the strands."

"I saw my dad tighten fences a few times. Gran hired someone to help with the chore."

We mounted up again and continued down the fence line, straightening where it was needed.

Later, Jesse and I put dinner together while Ben read a storybook to Liam.

By the time we finished eating, the kids were too exhausted to do more than fall into their beds. I walked with Ben out to his truck to say goodnight. He reached out and touched my cheek lightly. "Good night, Tara. You're doing a real good job. Everything will be fine. You'll see."

"Thank you, Ben. I'm so glad you're here. I don't think I could manage very well without you." I smiled, moved back toward the house, and waved.

Ben just stood by his truck for a moment, hesitating to leave. I felt the attraction vibrating in the air between us, but I kept walking. I needed to stay focused on protecting my family and not let myself be distracted by emotions, even though my heart pulled me toward Ben. Too much was at stake. "God," I whispered, "thank you for Ben's help. But please keep me from letting my heart rule my actions."

Some things are a lot easier said than done, I thought as I lay looking out my bedroom window at the stars, remembering my last moment with Ben.

CHAPTER 27

Ben drove into town on Monday and headed for campus. Parking, he climbed out of his truck and trekked across the parking lot toward the buildings.

"Hello, Ben."

"Oh, hi there, Nikki. How was the party?"

"It was fun. You should have been there." Nikki looked up at him, her lips curling into a flirty smile, a hint of invitation glinting in her green eyes. Lorene stood behind her, watching avidly.

Ben shrugged. "Parties aren't my thing. I'm not a fan of alcohol. But I do have some great friends at church. Would you like to come to one of our get-togethers? Everyone is friendly and we have a good time."

"No thanks," Nikki said. "Church isn't *my* thing. Want to go to coffee with us?"

Ben hesitated and looked at his watch. Smiling to take the sting out of it, he said, "Not today, Nikki. I've got to pick up some things for my business after class, then I need to head home."

Disappointed, Nikki pouted. "Oh, Ben. What's another twenty minutes?"

"Sorry. I really do have something I need to do."

"Oh, okay. Let's do lunch again tomorrow. You do eat, don't you?"

Ben laughed. "Of course. Hardee's? At noon?"

"Sure. See you there." Nikki smiled and walked away, her head moving close to Lorene's in muted chatter.

Ben watched them thoughtfully for a moment then pulled out his phone. "Hey, Max, would you like to meet me and a couple of girls from campus at Hardee's for lunch tomorrow?"

"Well, sure. Who are the girls?"

"It's Nikki and Lorene."

"Oh. I see. Isn't Nikki the freshman you've been inviting to our Bible study group?"

"Yeah, she's the one. She isn't a believer, but I thought she might be interested in coming. She isn't. Now she wants me to have lunch with her, and Lorene is supposed to come too. But last week when they invited me to meet them for lunch, Lorene didn't show. Turned out to be just the two of us. I felt it sent the wrong message."

"Sounds like she's got you in her sights."

"I think so. But I'm not interested that way. I need a wingman. Join us for lunch?"

"Sure. I've got your back," Max said. "Want me to bring Kate along?"

"That would be great, if you can get her to come."

"Okay. We'll meet you in Hardee's parking lot at noon. We can go in together."

"See you." Ben put his phone back in his pocket and smiled.

The following day, Ben met Max and Kate in the Hardee's parking lot. Nikki's car was already there. "Thanks for coming," he said, relieved at their presence.

"Anytime," Max grinned as they fist bumped.

"Sometimes a girl has to help rescue her cousins," Kate grinned, slipping her arm though his. "Last week, it was Jordan."

Ben laughed. "Who'd you rescue him from?"

"Some girl who's acting in the same play he's in down at Grand Street Theater."

"I see. Well, let's do this," Ben said, moving toward the restaurant door, taking Kate's hand. He grinned over at Max. "Thanks for loaning me your girl for a few minutes."

Max laughed as the three walked into Hardee's together.

Nikki was already there, but Lorene was not, just as Ben had predicted.

"Oh, there she is," Ben said casually, leading Kate over to the table. "Hi, Nikki. I'd like you to meet Kate." He released Kate's hand and ushered her into the vacant seat across from Nikki. "This is my friend, Max. I met them on my way over here and thought they'd like to have lunch too."

Nikki's smile was frozen. "Oh. Well, it's good to meet you both," she said stiffly.

"I'll go order," Ben said. "What does everyone want? My treat today." After a taking their orders, Ben headed for the counter.

"Tell me about yourself, Nikki," Max invited, sliding into the seat next to her.

By the time Ben returned, Nikki had started to thaw a little. When Ben sat next to Kate and put his arm over her shoulder, Nikki ignored him and deliberately turned her beautiful smile on Max.

After lunch, Ben stood up to leave along with the others. Nikki took his arm and looked up at him sweetly.

"I'll see you tomorrow," she said softly.

"Sure. See you later." Ben freed his arm, smiled politely, and walked away, leaving Nikki staring at his back.

CHAPTER 28

Tyrel's watch showed one o'clock in the morning when he returned home from the hospital. The doctor said Levi would probably live, but his recovery would take a long time. He had not yet regained consciousness and could not be questioned about the fire.

Exhausted, Tyrel sat down on the edge of his bed and pulled his boots off. He tossed his hat across the room to the big chair and lay back on the bed, too tired to undress. Sleep captured him the moment his head hit the pillow.

Sunlight filtering through the maple leaves outside his bedroom window woke Tyrel from a deep sleep. Lying in bed, he wondered where this case was leading. Did Charlie have anything to do with the fire at Levi's store? The idea seemed possible, even probable.

He rolled out of bed, grabbed his tablet, and added the fire incident to his list of unusual events. Doran hadn't had this much excitement in years. Was it all connected? He wanted to talk it over with his dad, who had a sort of sixth sense about these things.

Coffee. He needed coffee. And a shower to wake him up.

Twenty minutes later, wide awake and toweling his hair dry, Tyrel grabbed his jeans and a shirt. Nearly ten o'clock, Dad should be up by now.

Letting himself into his parents' house, Tyrel walked into the living room. Dad was sitting in his big chair, coffee in one hand, a newspaper in the other.

"Hello, Son," he said. "What brings you here on a Saturday morning?"

Tyrel grinned. "Well, I wanted to pick your brain again, if you don't mind, Judge."

"Go ahead. I take it you are working the Levi Carroll case?"

"Yeah, but I think it's more than that. I think it might be connected with the Webster case. I'd like to tell you what I've got and see what you think."

Bit by bit, Tyrel laid the facts before Judge Morgan, along with his theory. When he finished, he sat silently, waiting as his dad mulled it over.

Judge Morgan rubbed his chin. "Yes, I see what you mean, Tyrel. Problem is, you've got no evidence. Only suspicion."

"That's about what I figured," Tyrel said. "I'm not sure how to proceed from here. I'm afraid in a small town like this, more people could get hurt if Charlie Webster finds out they've talked to me. And I figure some of them are already thinking along those lines. The clerk at the hardware store for one."

"Could be," said his dad. "But you've still got to pursue the questions."

The two men sat silently for a few minutes, each lost in his own thoughts.

"Have you investigated why Charlie has been going back and forth to Houston? You'd think he would have plenty to keep him here in town at a time like this."

Tyrel shook his head. "No, I can't figure that out either. Surely, his employer would give him time off to manage family business. But maybe not. So how can you tell if a suspect is lying?"

"Hm." Judge Morgan cocked his head to one side. "He probably has a tell. Look for any gestures or eye movements indicating he's uneasy, which should tell you whether or not he's being straight with you. Then there's the looking to the left and down when a suspect is talking. There's the expressionless voice, covering his mouth or eyes, pausing a lot as he talks, sitting very still, changing his voice level. Those are some of the clues to watch out for. But sometimes shy people can seem evasive, too, making it difficult to figure out why people are responding as they do."

"Okay," Tyrel said. "I'm planning to talk to Levi Carroll as soon as he's conscious to see if he remembers anything about the fire. Then I'll talk to Charlie again."

"Levi might not say anything if he thinks Charlie is behind that fire. He might be too frightened. He might still be in danger. Have you thought of putting a guard on his room?"

"Yes," Tyrel said, "but Bradshaw doesn't think I've got a case yet, and he won't put a guard on Levi. He thinks this was an accident. He's been poker buddies with Charlie for years. They're good friends. Should I tell him about my evidence?"

Judge Morgan pursed his lips and shook his head "Ty, I don't think it's time to bring Bradshaw in yet. He's likely to tell Charlie, and that might put *you* in danger too."

Tyrel nodded. "I need to come up with some solid evidence fast. Bradshaw isn't going to believe me unless I have something solid."

"Yes, that's a problem." Judge Morgan paused, searching for words. "Son, you be careful. Don't let Charlie know what you're thinking or doing if you can. If he has murdered once, he has started down a bad path, and he'll murder again to keep himself safe. He's probably running scared, and that's an extremely dangerous kind of criminal, because they lash out whenever they feel threatened."

"Yes, Dad. I hear you. I'll be careful," Tyrel promised.

An hour later, Tyrel was searching for someone who might be a possible witness—Willie Peterson.

Willie had checked the alley carefully before entering it. When he was sure nobody was there, he crept out from behind the steakhouse standing next to Levi's hardware store and slipped over to the big dumpster at the back. Lifting the lid, he carefully leaned it against the building. Inside the dumpster he saw a foil-wrapped potato only half-eaten, and a fully wrapped corncob. With a satisfied grunt, he leaned over and pulled the food out, examined it, and slid it into his voluminous coat pocket. Using a stick, he moved other garbage around, but he didn't see anything else worthwhile so he closed the lid and faded back toward the shadows behind the brick building where he would eat his findings.

He had just finished unwrapping the corn when he noticed a pair of sneakers coming toward him and looked up.

"Hi, Willie," Tyrel said settling down next to the homeless man. "I brought you some of Mom's cookies." He held out a plastic bag containing a dozen freshly baked chocolate chip cookies.

Willie's caked teeth showed through a big smile. He reached out his hand for the cookies. "Thanks, Ty," he said. "I don't get dessert much. This'll go good with what I just found."

Tyrel waited for Willie to resume his meal before speaking. "Say, Willie, did you happen to see anyone besides Levi outside his shop last night?"

Willie glanced quickly at Tyrel then looked at the alley as he chewed his corn, savoring the flavor. He took another bite.

"I think someone tried to hurt Levi," Tyrel said.

Looking both ways to make sure nobody was coming, Willie leaned toward Tyrel and said in a low voice, "Yeah, I think so too. That weren't nice, Ty. Levi is my friend. He gives me food lots of times. I saw Charlie Webster go in the back door after closing time." Willie looked scared. "But don't you tell nobody I said so! That guy's pure poison!"

Tyrel's pulse leaped, but he remained calm. "What time did you see him?"

"Aw, I'm not sure," Willie said with a shrug.

"Was it dark? Or was it still light outside?"

Willie looked up at the sky. "Well, I saw stars up there. It was pretty dark."

"Anything else?"

"Hm. Let's see. Oh yeah. I saw Mr. Todd walkin' his dog. He lives a couple blocks away, an' he walks that dog ever' night."

"Good. I can check on that. Thank you, Willie." Tyrel stood up.

Willie smiled up at Tyrel, his eyes crinkled at the edges. "Yer welcome, Ty. Yer a good boy."

Tyrel laughed, "So are you, Willie. So are you." He patted Willie's shoulder and went back to the street, checking both ways before coming out of the alley to make sure nobody saw him. He did not want to endanger his one witness. Gossip was the main hobby of too many people in town. If someone saw him talking with Willie, word would get out. Charlie might hear about it. If he hadn't hesitated to kill his stepmother or burn Levi's shop, he surely wouldn't hesitate to kill Willie.

Tyrel headed back to his parent's home. His mom was in the kitchen, still baking cookies, when he arrived. "Mom, thanks for the cookies! They worked great!"

"What? You ate them already?" his mom looked surprised.

"No, I gave some to a friend who really appreciated them. Is Dad still in the study?"

"I think he's out watering the garden. Here. Take him a couple of cookies." His mom handed him a small plateful then reached for the lemons and pulled out the cutting board.

Tyrel headed out the back door and spotted his dad over by the rose bushes. "Mom sent some cookies, and I think she's making lemonade. Can you come back inside? I've got something."

Judge Morgan looked up and noted Tyrel's suppressed excitement. "Sure." He turned off the hose and headed back to the house with Tyrel. "Did you learn something more?"

"Yeah, Dad. But I don't think it's enough to make an arrest." He told his dad about Willie.

Judge Morgan nodded. "You're right. Willie's testimony won't be enough. A good defense lawyer would tear it to pieces. You'll need something more substantial. But this is a good piece of solid evidence upon which you can build."

Tyrel nodded. "Gotta go. I've got a ballgame to play." He grinned. "We're playing the First Baptists today. I think we'll win."

CHAPTER 29

Leaves on the trees rustled in the wind around the Lewis & Clark Library in Helena when I pulled the truck into the parking lot. The early May breeze was still cool, but I noticed most people at the library weren't wearing jackets. I pulled my coat closed and shivered. Why did Montana have to be so cold?

I didn't like leaving the ranch. But staying there all the time was lonely. Besides, the police probably wouldn't be looking for us in Montana. Jesse, Liam, and I went inside, pleased by the welcome breath of warm air greeting us.

"Jess, why don't you take Liam over to the children's books while I use a computer?" I suggested. I needed some uninterrupted time to search the internet.

"Sure. Want me to read you a book?" Jess asked, reaching out her hand to Liam.

I watched Jesse lead Liam away, then turned to the computers. I went to Jenna's Facebook page. Levi Carroll's store had burned down, she reported, and he had been severely injured. *Oh, no! He's a good friend. And he knows how brutal Charlie is.* A chill rushed up my spine. *I hope Charlie wasn't involved in burning down his store. Wouldn't that be just like him if he thought Levi was a threat.*

Bowing my head, I prayed silently for Levi then added a plea for our family. "Lord, help us find justice for Gran.

Help the law to catch Charlie. We cannot go home or even do rodeo unless Charlie is caught. We cannot do this ourselves. We are depending on you. Amen."

I wanted to keep an eye on what was happening in Doran, and it would be better if I could check Jenna's Facebook page daily on my own computer; but reception was intermittent where we lived, and I couldn't afford internet service.

We picked up groceries while we were in town and stopped for warm rolls from the bakery before heading home. Ben and Golly greeted us when we pulled into the ranch yard.

"Hi, Ben," I said, stepping out of the truck. "We went to the store and the library today."

"See any news from Texas?" Ben walked up to help me carry groceries into the house.

"Yes. I'll tell you later," I said quietly so the children wouldn't hear.

"I'm hungry," Liam said. "What are we having for dinner?"

Jesse laughed. "You're always hungry. I'll bet you grow a whole foot taller with all the food you've been eating lately." I hadn't seen her so relaxed since leaving Texas. "Let's help get the groceries into the house so we can think about it."

When we had unloaded and unpacked the groceries, Ben said, "You know, it looks like you have all the ingredients for campfire stew."

"What's that?" Liam asked, intrigued.

"It's a stew we guys make when we're camping." He shot a questioning look at me.

I smiled. "Go for it, Ben. I want to see what you can do."

"Okay. Liam, you find the potato peeler. Jess, I'll need a big knife to cut up this big chunk of beef, and another knife for the veggies."

"What about me?" I asked.

Ben smiled. "Do you have a large kettle?"

"Yes." I pulled my stew kettle from the cupboard. "Will this work?"

"Perfect," Ben said. "I'll use the electric stove for this since the woodstove isn't hot."

In no time, we were happily working together around the kitchen island, Ben and the children peeling, chopping, and cutting things for dinner, while I built a fire in the woodstove.

"Okay," Ben said. "The first thing we do is put a couple of tablespoons of oil into the kettle, heat it up, and brown the meat. After that, we'll add the carrots, potatoes, onions, and green beans." He deftly poured some oil into the kettle and heated it. Once the oil was hot, he picked up the bowl of beef chopped into bite-sized pieces, and dumped it in, too, the meat sizzling as he stirred it. A few minutes later, the meat was browned. "Hand me the veggies," Ben said.

Liam grabbed the bowl of vegetables and carried it over. Ben dumped it into the big kettle along with some boiling water from the tea kettle.

"Now we'll need garlic, salt, and pepper." Ben looked in the cupboard where the spices were stored, spices grown and gathered by Great Uncle George. "Ah. I see there's some dill weed in here. Let's use this too." Ben minced the garlic, added it and the spices to the water, gave it a stir, and put the lid on the kettle.

While Ben was working at the stove, Jesse leaned over to me and whispered, "Tara, I think God sent Ben to watch out for us."

"Me too." I put my arms around Jesse's shoulders. "God is taking good care of us, honey."

"This will be done in about a half hour," he said, turning the heat down to simmer.

I smiled. "I didn't know you were such a good cook, Ben. How did that happen?"

"Well, when my mom first became sick, I was about ten years old. She wanted my sister Carolyn and me to learn how to take care of ourselves. She had us take turns helping her cook. She sat on a stool in the kitchen and taught us step-by-step how to make dinner each evening."

"How nice." I hesitated then asked, "How old were you when she passed away?"

"I was twelve. Those times we spent in the kitchen together are good memories." Ben smiled reminiscently.

After we had eaten every drop of Ben's campfire stew, Ben and I did dishes together. When he had put the last dish away, Ben hung the dishtowel on a peg. "I've left something in the truck. Be right back," he said heading out the door. He returned carrying a guitar.

"I was wondering if I could keep my guitar here so we can all sing together once in a while. It would be fun."

"I'd love it, Ben."

"I wish you could be at my graduation this week," Ben said. "Dad is coming. So are Carolyn, my sister, and her husband, Joe. But we only received a few tickets earlier in the spring."

"Oh! I didn't know you were graduating."

Ben shrugged and smiled. "Yeah. The reason I brought it up is that we're having a graduation party over at our place later, and I want you and the kids to come. That is, if you want to."

"I'd love it. Thank you for inviting us. I'm looking forward to meeting your family and friends."

"Good. I'll count on you."

Ben and I went into the living area to join the others. Reaching over to the coatrack, he pulled a Bible out of his coat pocket and sat down in the big chair. "Would you like me to read you a story?" he asked.

"You aren't going to sing us a song?" I asked. He'd propped his guitar against the wall in the corner by the couch earlier, and I was curious.

"I will later." Ben smiled.

Liam crowded up to Ben's side expectantly while I joined Jesse on the couch. "What story are you gonna tell us?"

"I was thinking about a teenager named David." He flipped through the pages until he found the story. "This is the story about what happened with David after he killed Goliath."

Golly, who had been sleeping near the stove, lifted his head from his paws and barked.

"Not you, Golly," Jesse said while we all laughed.

Golly put his head back down on his paws and whined, his tail thumping slowly on the hardwood floor.

I settled back on the couch while Liam sat close to Ben and listened as he read about David, the shepherd-warrior whom the prophet Samuel had anointed to be the next king. He had played his harp for King Saul to try to help him relax. But the king, goaded by jealousy, threw his spear at David, trying to kill him.

David ran from King Saul. He fled across the desert wilderness to the springs of En Gedi, where King Saul could not find him. There, many other men came to help David. Together, they became an army, with David at the head. God trained him in leadership during those years in hiding and blessed him.

"David wrote these words about God in Psalm 91," Ben said. "Those who live in the shelter of the Most High will find rest in the shadow of the Almighty. This I declare about the Lord: He alone is my refuge, my place of safety; he is my God, and I trust him—If you make the Lord your refuge, if you make the Most High your shelter, no evil will conquer you; no plague will come near your home. For he will order his angels to protect you wherever you go—The Lord says, 'I will rescue those who love me. I will protect those who trust in my name. When they call on me, I will answer; I will be with them in trouble. I will rescue and honor them. I will reward them with a long life and give them my salvation.'"

Jesse put her head on my shoulder. I put my arm around her and looked over at Ben. Our eyes met and held.

"I believe those words," Ben said softly. "You are not alone. God is with you like he was with David. He will keep you safe." Ben bowed his head and prayed, "Father in heaven, thank you for these words telling us how you guard and protect all who trust in you. I ask for your protection over Liam, Jess, and Tara. Keep them safe and show me how to help them. In Jesus's name, amen."

Ben reached for his guitar and began playing Matt Redman's song, *You Never Let Go*. Sung in Ben's rich baritone voice, the song warmed my heart, as the words spoke of how God holds onto us, and we can depend on him no matter what.

We sat quietly together, thinking about the song, the crackle of the fire in the stove providing the only sound. Peace filled our hearts, washing away the fear that had followed us from Texas, quieting our questions, comforting our souls, and drawing us together.

CHAPTER 30

A car pulled up under the trees on the street outside the hospital in Doran, Texas, beneath a night sky twinkling with a profusion of stars giving little light, for the moon had not yet risen. A man wearing black slacks and a black pullover, reached over to the passenger seat, donned a black cap to cover his hair and black gloves to prevent leaving fingerprints. Emerging from his car, he followed the tree line to the darkest part of the hospital parking lot and cut across to a side door. Removing a small metal instrument from his pocket, he unlocked the door and slipped inside.

The nurses sat at their desks writing notes about their patients and talking among themselves. Nobody walking the hallways. Nobody watching the shadows.

One of the off-duty nurses had mentioned Levi's room number to a friend during lunch at the restaurant next door. The man in black had overheard the conversation. Slowly, hugging the wall, he slipped along the dim hallway until he reached Levi's room. Leaving the hospital room door open a crack, he walked over to the bed. In the dim light, the sleeping man's face was still recognizable, but his body was covered with severe burns. The intruder pulled a syringe out of his jacket pocket, removed the cap, and injected it into the patient's IV tube. Returning the syringe to his pocket, he carefully opened the door, and slipped back out into the night, undetected by a single soul.

Problem eliminated, he thought with satisfaction. Levi Carroll would never wake up, would never be able to tell anyone anything he might know. Learning Tyrel had been nosing around and talking to Levi was quite the lucky break for him. He was safe for now, with this witness eliminated.

Back at the hospital, hearing the alarm from Levi's monitors, the nurses rushed to his room, but they were too late. He was gone. They were not terribly surprised. The burns had covered too much of his body.

"Are you sure he died of natural causes?" Tyrel asked Doctor Benson.

The doctor was silent for a moment. "I thought he was doing well, Ty. I did not expect him to die. But the burns were bad."

"Are you going to do an autopsy?" Tyrel asked.

"Well, that's an expensive procedure," the doctor said, hesitating. "But I can do some blood tests at least. That should tell us something."

"I guess that will have to do," Tyrel said, shrugging.

The doctor looked at Tyrel curiously. "Have you spoken with Sheriff Bradshaw about this?"

"No, Doc. I haven't. It's just a hunch, not evidence."

"Okay," said the doctor. "I'll see what I can do. If everything's okay, I'll let you know. But if something is off, I'll need to tell Sheriff Bradshaw."

"Sounds good to me," Tyrel said with relief. "Thanks, Doc." Going behind the sheriff's back was a huge risk, but sometimes taking risks is part of doing a good job.

BURN VICTIM MURDERED! Morphine Overdose! Victim's Shop Torched! Arson Suspected at Store!

The Doran newspaper headlined the news.

At the breakfast table in Texas, Judge Morgan read the article. Tyrel had told him about his move to have some tests done. And Ty had been right.

At the same time in the library in Montana, I read the news on Jenna's Facebook page. Levi was dead? Murdered? And Levi knew how Charlie had treated us. Charlie—had he done this? Who else would have murdered Levi?

My hands were shaking when I finally turned the computer off. A feeling of helplessness and frustration filled my heart. Grabbing my coat, I found Jesse and Liam. "Come on. We need to go home."

Jesse looked up from the book she was reading to Liam. "Why such a short visit?"

I forced myself to remain calm. "I have some things I need to do at the ranch."

Jesse and Liam checked out their books, donned their coats, and followed me out to the truck. They chattered nonstop about the books they'd borrowed from the library as we drove home, oblivious to my silence, for once.

"I need some fresh air, so I'm going for a walk," I said when we reached the ranch. "Be back soon." I couldn't show weakness or fear in front of them. They needed me to be strong.

Just as I was leaving the house, Ben drove up in his truck. "I need to work in town this afternoon, but I wanted to make sure you have enough food for Golly first." He hauled a large bag of dog food from the back of the truck and set it down inside the cabin.

"What's up, Tara?" he asked, noticing my silence when he returned.

I took a deep breath. "Levi Carroll, our neighbor, was murdered in the hospital." I said, my heart aching for his family. My voice shook with fear. I started off toward the valley. "I'm going for a walk."

"Would you like some company?"

"Okay." I headed down the driveway, past the practice area where we'd been working, and on toward the big meadow at a brisk pace. Ben fell in beside me, his hands in his coat pockets, his cowboy hat shading his eyes, keeping pace silently.

On the other side of the creek, I left the road and walked through the tall grass. Ben followed quietly. There was a small pool on the other side of the meadow, shaded by aspen and maple trees in the summer, but they were just starting to bud with leaves now. I had often played at this small pool on our last trip to Montana. As I walked through the sweet-scented meadow, the tension slowly left my body.

Nearing the cascading stream, I saw some small, yellow wildflowers. Picking one, I stared into its golden center, so perfectly created. Moving toward the pool and the small waterfall, my hair brushed aspen tree branches, showering me with dew. Water trickled down my neck under my thin coat, sending a shiver up my back.

"You're cold," Ben said. He pulled off his jacket and wrapped it around my shoulders.

"Thank you, but aren't you cold too?"

Ben shrugged and smiled. "Not really." He paused, glancing over at me. "What's up, Tara?"

"I think Levi's murder is connected to Gran's. I think Charlie may have killed him too."

"Why would he do that?"

I shrugged. "Levi knows how Charlie really is. He might tell the sheriff."

"Would the sheriff believe him? You said he's friends with your uncle."

"I don't know. Maybe he would. But probably not." I fingered the flowers by the path.

"Isn't there anyone who could help you in Texas?"

I shrugged. "There's a judge in our town—Judge Morgan—who might help me. At least I think he would. Or I might be able to get in touch with Gran's lawyer. I'm not sure about that, though. I'm afraid to let anyone know where we are, for fear they'd tell Charlie, and I sure don't want him knowing Jesse saw him kill Gran. Jesse's life wouldn't be worth anything if Charlie found out. Neither would Liam's life or mine."

"If you told this judge what Jesse saw, would he help you to put Charlie away?" Ben asked, studying my face.

"I think he would believe me, but I don't know what he could do. Charlie is awfully popular around town. Nobody knows how he acts when he's alone with the family. And Jess is so young, a lawyer could confuse her in court. It would be a huge gamble, Ben."

"But Tara, with this possible second murder—the murder of your neighbor—even the sheriff would have to see that things are piling up."

"You think so?"

"Yes. The sheriff can't ignore the facts right in front of his face, and unless he's crooked, he's got to investigate for motive. Which will lead him right back out to Levi's place—next door to your Gran's ranch. I think this is just the beginning."

I sighed. "I hope you are right, Ben. But the sheriff may well be biased. He's a nice man, but he's Charlie's friend. And Charlie has sort of a magical charm about him with people outside our family. There's no way of knowing if the sheriff would even believe Charlie was guilty." I picked a few white and pink flowers absently.

"Isn't there anyone in law enforcement in Texas you could trust with the information about your grandma's murder?"

"Well, maybe. I've been thinking about it. My friend, Jean, has a brother who is a deputy sheriff in Doran. Tyrel Morgan. He's Judge Morgan's son. I think if I told Ty—" I shook my head. "But I'm still not sure it would be safe for us. Doran's a small town, and the walls have ears." My hand shook, and I dropped the flowers.

Ben saw my fear. "Tara," he said quietly, "if you could get a sworn statement from Jesse and send it to the deputy sheriff in Texas without giving away your location, would that help?"

"Maybe," I said. "That might work. Let me think about it. I'm scared, Ben."

Ben glanced at me. "Don't be afraid, Tara," he said, putting his arms around me, drawing me close to his heart. "For now, let's just work on keeping quiet about where you are. Pray about it. When you're ready, I'll help you. I have a friend who drives trucks. He could help send the letter from a different location—say, Kansas or Tennessee."

"I'll pray about it. I'll let you know if I feel it's safe after I've talked it over with Jesus."

"Okay." Ben stroked my hair gently. "Thanks for telling me what you and the kids are facing. I'll help you however I can."

Ben released me. "Let's get back to the house. I need to drive into town to meet with a client today."

We walked back across the meadows together. Delicate green leaves crowned the deciduous trees and soft green shoots tipped each evergreen branch. The fruit trees were blooming now, and the ash trees had sprouted bouquets of delicate white blooms. Snow no longer lingered in the shadows on the north side of the mountain. The scents of late April filled the air. The weather was warming up, but nothing like Texas.

"You all right now?" Ben asked when we reached his truck, studying my face closely.

I nodded. "Yes. Thank you."

"Okay. I'll see you after I get some work done."

CHAPTER 31

Ben headed for town, and I walked back into the cabin. Looking through Gran's files, I found the number for Gran's lawyer. I picked up my phone, went outside where the kids couldn't listen in, and punched in the number.

"John Miller's office, attorney at law," a feminine voice answered.

"Yes, may I please speak with Mr. Miller?"

"May I ask who's calling?"

"Um, could you please tell Mr. Miller this call is about a deceased client?" I hedged.

"Yes, ma'am."

Mr. Miller's voice came on the line. "This is John Miller. To whom am I speaking?"

"This is Tara Webster," I said.

"Tara! Everyone has been looking for you. Where are you and the children?"

"If I tell you, and you are my lawyer, do you have to tell others?"

"No, I do not," Mr. Miller declared firmly. "How may I help you, Tara?"

"I've taken Jesse and Liam away to keep them safe. You have Gran's papers. You will know where we are if you look through them. It's the ranch Gran inherited from Great Uncle George."

"Yes. I understand. Your grandmother told me a little about your Uncle Charlie. I assume you are hiding from him?"

"Yes. He is trying to take over our horses. He wants to sell them to pay off his gambling debts. I'm sure if he is named guardian for my brother and sister, he would use their inheritance to pay his debts. He said someone named Gino would kill him if he doesn't pay up."

"I see. Well, Tara, he cannot sell the horses without your permission. Their titles are in your name. You own them. Your grandmother told me that much."

"Good. But that's not the only reason I took the children away, Mr. Miller. Jesse saw Charlie push Gran down the stairs and kill her."

"What?" I could hear the shock in his voice.

"If Charlie finds out Jess witnessed him murdering Gran, he will hunt us down and kill her. He'd kill all of us. So, if you don't mind, I'd like to keep our location secret. Can you do that for me?"

"I certainly will," John Miller said. "Do you want me to tell the sheriff about the murder?"

"No! Please!" I felt panic rising in my throat. "Even if Jess tells what she saw, she's so young I'm afraid a lawyer might scare her while she's on the stand in court. Then Charlie would get away, and he'd find a way to kill her. Unless the sheriff can find more proof, I can't let anyone know about it. Besides, Sheriff Bradshaw is good friends with Charlie. He wouldn't believe Jesse."

"Okay, Tara. I'll keep this to myself." John Miller paused. "You should know that your grandmother named you guardian for those children. I've informed the sheriff. This will protect you from kidnapping charges, which Charlie might try to file. A local bulletin was put out on you a few days after your grandmother was killed. But nothing statewide so far. And I don't think there's anything in other states either. I don't think the law will look for you in the place you are currently living. But I can't guarantee that."

"Could you manage to transfer our Social Security survivor benefits to an account where I can get to them? We're going to run short on money otherwise. But don't open it in Doran. The people at the bank would tell Charlie about it. Could you open it in New Mexico, just to be on the safe side?"

"Sure. I'll see what I can do. Can I call you at this number?"

"Yes," I said. "But please do not share it with anyone."

"I won't. And I'll keep your secret, Tara. You can rely on me for that."

"Thank you, sir," I said. Relief filled my heart.

"Jess! Liam! Grab your sketch pads and pens. Let's go draw some pictures. I saw some new flowers over by the creek, and some baby birds in a nest."

Happily, we tromped across the meadow and plopped down near the flowers.

"Where's the birds' nest?" Liam asked.

"It's over in that bush," I said, pointing to a lone willow. "But go slowly so you won't scare the mama and papa birds. If they see you, they might attack."

"Okay," Liam said, standing and creeping toward the nest.

The warm sun and the pungent aroma of grass and flowers filled the air. I closed my eyes and breathed in the sweet, wild scents.

Lord, thank you for helping me today. Show me what you want me to do. I need your wisdom.

Later that day, I walked out to the barn while Jesse and Liam went down to the creek to fish. Fishing had quickly become one of their new favorite pastimes. The horses were grazing in the meadow nearby.

Hopefully, we'll have fish for dinner, I thought absently, still thinking about the conversation I'd had with Ben. I grabbed a shovel and began mucking out the stalls, giving me time alone to think about our problem with Charlie. Should I simply wait for the law to figure things out? Or should I say something official? I felt a strong need to protect Jesse from the dangers involved in exposing Charlie.

A sudden shriek came from the direction of the creek. I tossed away the shovel and ran outside just in time to see a female moose charging toward Jesse and Liam. Terrified, I screamed and began running down to the creek, hoping I would not be too late to save them.

In the pasture below, Sundance galloped forward and stopped between the moose and the children. He reared up, his hooves cutting the air in front of the moose, trumpeting at her.

The moose skidded to a halt and dashed back into the willows. I could see a smaller shadow following her through the brush. Her young calf? Probably.

Sundance trotted toward the retreating moose, chasing her away. He had saved the children. I always knew he was protective, but this magnificent display was remarkable.

When I reached Sundance, he was still wired for action. I grabbed his halter and stroked his neck. "Oh, Sundance! That was great!" I crooned, leaning my head against him.

The big stallion snorted softly and settled down. He had done his job well, and he knew it.

Ben came over at sundown as the children were roasting marshmallows over the firepit. "What's this? Are you making s'mores?" he demanded.

"Yep. Come on. We've got another stick for you to use," Jesse said.

"Oh, man, you should have seen Sundance today!" Liam burst out. "He saved us from a moose!"

I listened to Liam recite Sundance's actions as I sipped a cup of hot chocolate.

"What a horse!" Ben said, shaking his head. He looked over at me. "So how are you doing, Tara?"

"I'm fine—now. But at the time ..." I took another sip of hot chocolate and changed the subject. "Ben, we're going to need hay this coming winter, aren't we?"

"Yes. We get a lot of snow up here in the mountains. We usually mow the north pasture in early July."

"Okay. I saw a mower in the barn, but not a baler."

"We swap with neighbors during haying season," Ben said. "After we mow, we let the rancher across the highway use our mower, and he loans us his square baler. Then we borrow the round baler from another friend. It works out well for us all. We use the square bales for feeding the horses in the barn and paddocks, and the round ones for the cattle out in the field."

"All right. Will you help me hitch up the mower when it's time? I don't think Jess is big enough to handle that."

"Yes. But, Tara, there are some big rocks out there, some of them aren't visible until you're right on them. You've got to know the pasture's terrain. I'll have to show you what to avoid. We usually mow two hundred acres, some for our livestock and some to sell to others who may run out of hay toward spring. The money comes in handy. I hope you aren't planning to do it all yourself."

"I'm going to try," I said tentatively. "I haven't mowed before, but I've watch Papa. By spring, we'll need the income from that extra hay too."

"Of course," he said. "I'll help mow and bale." Ben said firmly. "We'll manage, Tara. In the meantime, I'll be bringing the cattle over sometime next week, if that's okay with you."

"Sure, Ben." Our eyes met and held for a long moment.

My heart was beating so loudly I was afraid he would hear it. The years of remembering our one summer together had laid the groundwork for more than friendship. But this was no time to complicate my life with a man, no matter how much I liked Ben. I needed to stay focused on my family, this ranch, and the Texas problem. I couldn't afford to make decisions based on my emotions. I jerked my gaze away from Ben and took a deep breath.

Looking back up, I smiled. "See you later, Ben." I turned and walked back into the cabin. I sure wished life were simpler.

CHAPTER 32

Tyrel walked into the sheriff's office the morning of the big press release about Levi's murder. "Sheriff Bradshaw, I'd like to talk with you about Levi Carroll." He pulled out a chair next to the sheriff's desk and sat down. "I talked with Levi this week. He indicated Charlie Webster had been abusive toward Evelyn and the children."

"Now see here, kid." Bradshaw's face turned red. "Charlie is a good guy. Are you saying you think he had something to do with Levi's murder? For Pete's sake, kid. He's not that kind of man."

Tyrel held the sheriff's gaze.

"Do you have any evidence?" the sheriff demanded belligerently.

Tyrel hesitated. Did he dare mention Willie's testimony? If the sheriff were a friend of Charlie's, wouldn't he tell Charlie? In his mind, that would be like signing a death order for Willie. "I just have Levi's words—so far. He had nothing good to say about Charlie at all. He said he saw Charlie hit Evelyn once."

"He *said?* He *said?* What kind of evidence is that? Levi always hated Charlie. He was jealous because of Mary. We can't even ask him because he's dead now."

"Exactly." Tyrel looked grim.

"Look here, kid. You leave Charlie out of this." Bradshaw ordered. "He's a fine, upstanding man. The folks around here love him. And don't you go around saying things like that without proof."

Tyrel tipped his hat, turned, and walked out of the office.

Bradshaw picked up the phone. He'd better let Charlie know what was going on.

Tyrel drove through town, relishing the air-conditioning in his car as he headed toward his parents' house.

Walking up the sidewalk, he barely noticed the periwinkle, evening primroses, and other flowers blooming in his mother's garden and along the walkway. Stepping over the alyssum and bee balm, he walked around the house toward his dad's study, where he knew the judge would be reading his newspaper and doing the crossword puzzle at this hour.

Judge Morgan glanced up as Tyrel stepped into the room through the stately French doors. "I saw this morning's headlines," he said, waving Tyrel to a chair. "Let's talk."

Sinking into a comfortable chair, Tyrel sighed. "I found a witness, Dad. Willie Peterson was in the alley behind Levi's store the evening of the fire. You know he sleeps behind the dumpster there."

"I see. Go on."

"Well, the night of the fire, he saw Charlie go into the back door of the hardware store before Levi left for the evening. I haven't told Sheriff Bradshaw yet. I let him know I think Charlie had something to do with Levi's death. But if I say anything about my witness, I'm afraid Willie might be murdered too."

"Hm. I see the problem." The judge thought for a moment then said reluctantly, "I don't think Willie's testimony is enough to convict Charlie. A good district attorney would shred it." He paused thoughtfully. "Well, maybe you can work on finding those kids. There must be someone who has an idea where they might have gone ... if Charlie hasn't done anything to them."

Tyrel looked up in shock. "You don't think he's killed them too, do you?"

Judge Morgan shook his head slightly. "I doubt it. I think Tara took off with her family because she was afraid of him. But with a killer, one never knows. He might already have gotten to those kids." He looked up at Tyrel. "Be careful."

"I will, Dad."

Sirens broke the quietness of the night as an ambulance rushed Tyrel to the nearest hospital. The rattlesnake in his shower had struck before he'd had a chance to react.

Judge Morgan and his closest friends set up around-the-clock watch on Tyrel. Was this just another accident? The judge didn't think so. But there wasn't enough evidence. Yet.

DEPUTY BITTEN BY RATTLESNAKE!

Sheriff's deputy, Tyrel Morgan, stepped into his shower last night and was bitten by a large rattlesnake that had found its way inside. Sheriff Bradshaw investigated the incident and commented someone had pried open the window above the shower and likely the snake, a sidewinder, had entered there. Deputy Morgan has been investigating the murder of Levi Carroll. There is speculation he must be closing in on the murderer, thus, the rattlesnake in the shower might not be an accident. However, Sheriff Bradshaw said they have no suspect in mind at this time, and he doesn't think the snake was dropped into the shower. He thinks it just crawled inside.

Reading Jenna's Facebook page online the first Friday in May, I shook with fear. Another accident? Another coincidence? The only good news was finding out Tyrel was on the case and not the sheriff. I closed the laptop.

Jesse plopped down into a chair across the table from me. "Anything interesting happening?"

Forcing myself to be calm, I shook my head. "Nothing much."

Jesse sighed. "I miss my friends, Tara."

"I know, honey. I miss mine too. But we have to stay here a while longer. Have you painted anything lately?"

"No, I've been too busy clearing the practice field with you and working in the garden. I'm too tired to paint."

"Well, why don't you take tomorrow off and work on a painting? We're going to Ben's graduation party this evening, and I'm sure you'll meet some new friends there."

Jesse's face lit up. "Great! What should I wear?"

"How about your purple shirt and your best jeans? I'll do your hair in a French braid and thread matching ribbon through it, if you want."

"That sounds good," she said with a smile. "When we get home, I'll go out to the meadow and paint wildflowers for a while."

Back at Ruby Hollow, Jesse showed me sketches she had drawn earlier. Delicate lines and exquisite, soft pastel watercolors showed her remarkable skill.

"Jess, these are gorgeous!"

"I'm thinking of doing an illustrated book about Montana's wildflowers," she said hesitantly.

"You should definitely do that," I said. "You've got talent, Jess."

A beautiful smile lit up her face. "I checked out a book on how to paint watercolors. There were some good tips in it."

I hugged her and she picked up her equipment, heading for the door.

"Can I come too?" Liam begged.

"Sure. Go get your paints and pencils."

Liam rushed to the bedroom and grabbed his art case. Together, they headed for the hall closet.

"Stay this side of the creek. And stay away from the willows." I called.

Jesse and Liam headed for the meadow, leaving me alone with never-ending work. I loaded the week's laundry into the washer and thought about the latest headline in Doran. What could I do? Nothing! Everything was too nebulous. No solid evidence—except for what Jesse had witnessed. I went to the barn, saddled Sundance, and headed out for a short ride in the cool, clean air, but staying close by in case I was needed.

Jess was still drawing wildflowers and Liam was drawing pictures of bugs when Ben drove over in his pickup truck. Riding Sundance, I met him before he reached the house and waved for him to stop.

"What's up, Tara?" he said after he turned off the engine and stepped down from the truck.

I dismounted Sundance. "Ben, the Doran newspaper said Tyrel, the deputy I was telling you about, found a rattlesnake in his bathroom and the snake bit him! *He's* in the hospital now."

"A rattlesnake? How did a rattlesnake get into his bathroom?" Ben stepped out of the truck.

"My friend, Jenna, said the newspaper is saying they think someone put it there because Tyrel was investigating Levi's murder, and the article mentioned he may be closing in on the killer. But the sheriff said the snake crawled in through the window. For the murder case, they have no suspects."

"Tara—" he paused, thinking it through. "It can't be a coincidence this time. There are just too many things happening to the people involved in this. Looks to me like you got out of Texas just in time." He reached out and took my hand. "I can see why you were afraid to stay in Texas."

I sighed. There didn't seem to be a thing I could do to stop Charlie. But I was eternally grateful God had brought Ben along to help me through this nightmare. I closed my fingers around his hand and gave it a quick squeeze then mounted Sundance and cantered back up to the barn while Ben drove up the hill.

Ben came into the barn, lifted the saddle off Sundance's back for me and put it over a rail. "Tara, don't you think it's time you and the kids came to church with me? I think you would all be happier if you had friends around. Especially Jesse. I think she needs to be distracted from the things that are keeping her so quiet."

I nodded. "Yes. I've been thinking the same thing, Ben. We'll go with you on Sunday." I reached for a rag to wipe down the horse.

Ben smiled. "Good! I'll pick you all up at nine-fifteen Sunday morning. But for now, you and the kids need to get ready for my party. I'll come pick you up at five-thirty. We're having a barbecue, so you won't have to fix dinner."

I smiled. "I'm looking forward to it. I've got everything laid out already." I turned to rub Sundance down.

"See you in a couple hours," Ben said as he walked out the barn door.

The younger children were dressed and waiting impatiently on the front lawn by five-fifteen when I finished dressing. I'd brushed my hair and braided it into a coronet on top of my head. Looking in the mirror, I coaxed a few wavy tendrils loose and left them hanging on either side of my face. A dark red knit blouse with long sleeves topped my blue jeans, bringing out the red in my cheeks and the sparkle in my eyes. I chose beaded leather sandals for my feet and hoped it wouldn't get too cold. I gathered our jackets together, stuffed them into a duffel bag, then walked out to the lawn where Jesse and Liam waited.

"Nice," Jesse said, taking in my outfit. "But I think you should wear some jewelry too. How about those gold and red earrings?"

"Great idea. Thanks Jess." I hurried inside to find them just as Ben's truck rumbled up the driveway.

Stepping out of the truck, Ben walked toward me as I fastened on the last earring. He took both my hands and said simply, "Beautiful."

I smiled and looked up into his eyes.

"What about me?" Liam demanded, strutting over, showing off his belt buckle, a prize from Mutton Busting at the rodeo.

"You look all grown up," Ben said, grinning and dropping my hands as he turned toward Liam. "Jess, you too. You clean up real good."

Jesse grinned. "Glad you noticed. For a minute there I thought you could only see Tara."

Ben blushed scarlet. "Well, you have to admit, she is stunning."

Jesse laughed. "For sure."

Ben opened the passenger doors and helped Liam up into the back seat of the truck while I tossed the duffel bag with our jackets onto the floor in the back then climbed into the front passenger seat, my cheeks hot.

"Move over, Tara," Jesse said, sliding onto the seat next to me and pushing me toward the middle.

"Hey! What about me?" Liam complained loudly. "You left me all alone back here."

Ben closed the back door of the truck and stepped up into his seat, glanced at the seating arrangement and grinned. "It's only for a few minutes," he said. "Buck up, cowboy."

"Okay," Liam said lifting his chin.

Ben's attention on Liam gave me a moment to recover my poise. Hopefully, my cheeks weren't too red. I was a little embarrassed, but mostly pleased. As Ben slid into his seat next to me, I could smell faint scent of his aftershave. Nice. He grinned at me, noting the seating arrangement. Jesse smiled smugly.

Ben drove out to the highway and down to his family's drive. A crowd of college friends were already gathered around the barbecue pit enjoying the warmth of the fire.

"Hey, Ben!" one of the men called and waved. "Congrats!"

Liam jumped out of the truck while Ben came around to help Jesse and me down.

Activity around the fire stopped as Ben's friends noticed us.

Ben put his hand on the small of my back and ushered me toward the fire, Jesse and Liam following us closely.

"Hey, do you all remember Evelyn Webster's grandkids?"

"Sure," said a tall young man with red hair.

"Yes. Of course!" a woman with blonde hair said, nodding. "Are you telling me these are her family? My, how they've grown."

"This is Tara, her sister, Jess, and her brother, Liam. They're here for a few months."

"Glad you could come," the tall man said. "I'm Max."

"And I'm Carolyn, Ben's sister," said the blonde woman.

"Liam, Carolyn brought her son, Jake. He's about your age. If you'll look in the backyard, I think you'll find him."

Liam took off running around the house.

"I'm Kate," a brunette girl said, stepping forward and taking my free hand. "Ben's my cousin."

"Nice to meet you."

"Jess?" said a younger girl. "I'm Anna, Max's sister. Come with me and I'll introduce you to some of the others." She led Jesse up to the deck where I could see a group of young teens standing around talking.

Max nudged the man standing next to him with his elbow. "This is Joe, Carolyn's husband. He doesn't talk."

"Sure, I do. But only when necessary." Joe smiled. "I'm glad you could come to the party, Tara. Ben, tell us where you found her."

"You know Dad and I have been watching over Ruby Hollow for Evelyn Webster, don't you?"

Joe nodded.

"Well, Evelyn passed away recently and left the ranch to her granddaughter, Tara. One day I noticed smoke coming from Ruby Hollow and went over to check it out, and that's where I found Tara and her family."

"Is school already out in Texas?" Carolyn asked curiously.

"I'm finishing up the year homeschooling," I said hesitantly.

"How interesting. I homeschool my kids too." Carolyn said with a smile. "Good for you."

As more people arrived, Ben introduced me to them, too, then moved over toward the barbecue. I listened to Carolyn telling me about her children and her most recent homeschool challenge. The other girls peppered me with friendly questions and drew me into their conversation. But after a while I felt overwhelmed by their questions and conversations about events of which I knew nothing.

"Could I borrow Tara?" Ben slipped his arm around my shoulder.

"Sure," Carolyn chirped.

"Come out back with me," Ben said, dropping his arm from my shoulder and taking my hand. "I want to show you something." He led me around the side of the house, across the lawn, and into the trees. "Look up there." He pointed up into the branches of a huge old tree.

"A treehouse?"

"Yes. Come up with me."

"Okay." I followed him up the boards nailed to the tree trunk.

Ben settled with his back against the wall and invited me to sit beside him. "I spent many hours up here as a kid. This was my secret hideout." He looked at me and grinned, his eyes sparkling. "I thought you could use a few minutes away from all those new people."

I sighed. "Thank you."

"No problem, Nature Girl."

"I called Gran's lawyer."

"Good. Is he going to help you?"

"Yes, but I've told him not to tell anyone where we are or what Jess saw. He said he would keep my secret."

"That's a relief."

"I know if he told the sheriff, that would be the same as telling Charlie, and then Charlie would come after us. They're friends. I can't risk it, Ben."

"I understand." Ben frowned.

We sat in comfortable silence for a few minutes, just relaxing.

"Tara?"

"Yes?"

"If the law catches Charlie and puts him away, will you go back to Texas or stay here?"

I sighed. "I don't know yet, Ben. This is my ranch now, and Jess and Liam like it here. But Jess misses her friends. If I decide to stay here, we may have to go back to Texas for a while first."

"Hm. Yes. I see that. Jess will have to testify, won't she?"

I shrugged. "I don't know if it's even going to happen, Ben. The law may never catch Charlie."

"Well, what I wanted to say is—"

"Ben?" Carolyn called. "Barbecue's ready. You coming?"

"Sure. Be right down." Ben called. He stood and held out his hand to help me up. "I'll talk with you about it tomorrow. Let's go eat."

What was Ben going to say? I felt exasperated. Why did Carolyn have to call us right then? I followed Ben back down the tree and around to the barbecue.

Within minutes, I relaxed as Ben's friends helped me feel part of their group around the table.

Max leaned toward Ben. "I see now why you haven't been interested in dating lately. She's a beauty. How long has this been going on?"

"Oh, since the first week in April," Ben said, grinning at Max. "I'm bringing them to church Sunday too."

"Good," Max glanced my way, a wide grin on his face.

The whole evening felt like a whirlwind. By the time Ben drove us home, we were exhausted. Liam fell asleep right away, and Jesse yawned and leaned her head on my shoulder.

Ben carried Liam to bed and removed his shoes. Jess stumbled over to her bed, kicked off her sandals, pulled up the blankets and feel asleep.

"Have a good time, Nature Girl?" Ben asked softly as I walked with him to the front door.

"I did. Thanks for taking us."

Lying in bed later, I wondered what Ben had been about to say in the treehouse when he was interrupted. Tomorrow, I would know. I smiled and closed my eyes.

CHAPTER 33

May had been incredibly busy, with the children finishing their studies during the morning and working around the ranch most of the afternoons. Each night, we fell into bed exhausted. The sunshine warmed us up a little during the day, but nighttime still seemed awfully cold. The meadows were green and lush. Ben said the fields were sub-irrigated by high ground water and fed by springs in the surrounding hills and mountains. They would remain green through the summer months.

The morning after Ben's graduation party, I awoke to the sound of whistling and hooves and cattle running outside my bedroom window. Jumping out of bed, I grabbed my jacket, pulled on my shoes, and hurried out front.

Cattle came trotting past the house, bellowing loudly. Ben followed behind them, swinging his rope coil at the cattle, urging them forward. He drove them quickly past the house and down to the pasture below. He had come through the pass between our ranches, by far the quickest way to move the cattle to our pasture. His dad's house stood opposite ours on the other side of the hill, a mere quarter mile away through the pass. But by the road, the drive was over three miles.

Seeing me on the porch in my nightclothes, my hair tossed from sleep, he grinned and waved. "Hi, Nature Girl! Time to get up!"

I yawned. "Okay. If you say so," I called back.

Down the hill the cattle went, calves trotting alongside their mothers with a bull in the lead.

I turned and hurried back to my room to dress. Looking into the mirror, I moaned at the mess my hair was in. Ben had seen me this way. *Aaaagh!* I ran a brush quickly through my tangled curls and pulled them back into a loose knot at the back of my head. In record time, I'd donned jeans, blouse, socks, and boots. I raced into the bathroom to wash my face and brush my teeth.

The stove in the kitchen was stone cold when I hurried in. I gathered some bark and kindling, set a few larger pieces of wood on top, and lit it. The aroma of burning wood and resin filled the room—a homey, primitive scent. About the time the fire was going, Ben knocked and walked in.

"The cattle are in the south pasture," he said.

"Good. Did you eat breakfast yet?"

"Yes, but I would never turn down a cup of coffee."

"Sure." I filled the water kettle and set it on the stove. "All I've got is instant. I ran out of the other two days ago. Is that okay?"

"If you make it strong, instant will be fine." Ben hung his cowboy hat on a peg by the door.

"I'll get some ground coffee next time I'm in town," I said. "I prefer that too."

Ben stepped closer, put a hand on my back, reached over my shoulder and pulled a mug out of the cupboard. My cheeks flushed, my heart pounded, and I felt a little breathless.

Ben looked down into my eyes and grinned.

I turned and walked over to the refrigerator for milk, eggs, and butter. "Are you sure you won't have some pancakes with us?" *Keep your head, Tara.*

"Pancakes? Well ..."

I laughed. "I make very good pancakes."

"Okay. I'll try them."

A bedroom door opened, and Liam came out yawning. "Mornin', Ben," he said, plopping down into a chair next to him.

"Mornin', cowboy."

By the time coffee was hot, and I had started dropping pancake batter into the skillet, Jesse had joined us, her hair brushed and face washed.

"You're here early," she said, a question in her eyes.

"I just brought the cattle over to pasture them here for the warm months."

"Warm?" Jess shivered. "You call this warm?" Jesse exclaimed.

"Sure," Ben said. "I know—in Texas, this would be freezing. But you'll get used to it here. Give yourself time to adjust."

Jesse pulled her hoodie closed. "Burr!"

"Things are going to start to get busy for me this coming week. I've got to concentrate on getting my business started. But I'll drop in every afternoon and check up on you all." Ben grinned.

He reached over and picked up the Bible sitting on a small table nearby. "So, now that we've had breakfast, let's start the day with something King David wrote in Psalm 139." He flipped skillfully through the pages and read the chapter carefully.

My heart was comforted by the words assuring us God was with us always, no matter what. Closing my eyes, I sat back in my chair and let the words wash over my soul as Ben led us in prayer for the day.

"All right, let's take a break and go for a horseback ride today. Sound good?"

"You bet!" Liam said, jumping up and grabbing his coat. "Can I ride with you, Jesse?"

"Wait," Ben said. "Dishes first."

"Aw," Liam said.

"I'll wash, you dry, Liam. That way the girls can get ready."

"How long will we be gone?" I asked, thinking ahead to lunch.

Ben rolled up his sleeves. "We'll probably be back by noon. But if you want to make some sandwiches, we can stay longer and have a picnic."

"Okay, sounds fun." I pulled a loaf of bread out of the cupboard, whipped together some peanut butter and jelly sandwiches, and put them into a sack with apples, a big bottle of water, and some plastic cups. I went out to the camper and pulled out a spare blanket to tie on behind my saddle.

We mounted up twenty minutes later, bundled up against the cold mountain air. Golly trotted along beside us.

"We're going up to an alpine meadow you own, Tara." Ben pointed to where two hills met. "We'll drive the cattle up there in August. It's a good summer pasture."

"What's the name of those little yellow flowers all over the mountain?" Jesse asked.

"Those are glacier lilies and yellow bells. Soon we'll have white Mayflowers blooming along the creeks. In about a month, the whole mountain will be covered with wildflowers."

"There aren't any in the pastures," Jesse said.

"No. I spray them with weed killer. They aren't good for cattle. But I don't worry about these flowers along the mountain. We don't graze the cattle here. It's too steep."

"Great. Now I know where to find new flowers to draw."

"She's really good at art," I told Ben. "I'm hoping she will do something with it as she gets older."

"I'm painting a book on wildflowers," Jesse said.

"That's awesome, Jess!" Ben said. "If you want to see more wildflowers, I'll take you all up to Seeley Lake later in the summer. They have bear grass. Over in Lincoln, there are wildflowers everywhere too."

Liam sighed in disgust. "Flowers. I want to see wild animals."

"You'll see them." Ben grinned back at him. "But you have to keep looking around while we ride. Wild animals like to hide. They stand real still, like that fox over there." He pointed casually.

"Oh!" Liam breathed, craning his neck as we passed the red fox standing motionless beside a tree.

Golly barked, and the fox fled.

"The trick is to train your eyes to see animal shapes," Ben said. "It's something you will learn if you practice."

Our trek to the top of the mountain didn't take long. Before us lay a wide, green valley, snow still dotting the edges in places.

"This valley belongs to me?" I asked in amazement.

"Yes, Tara." Ben turned, smiling. "We'll bring the cattle up here after we mow the north pasture."

"Wow!" The beauty of this alpine meadow spreading out before me left me speechless.

Ben led us toward a hill on the northeast side of the valley. "It's drier up there. The meadow is still saturated with melted snow. This area around the rocks should be better for exploring."

We rode slowly through the wet meadow, drinking in the beauty, unlike anything I had ever experienced. The air was so pure, and a soft breeze rustled through the trees and grass.

"Look!" Liam pointed into the sky. "What's that?"

"It's an eagle," Ben said. "You should write down the names of all the birds and animals you see today."

"Yeah!" Liam enthused. "I wish I had a camera to take pictures of them."

I laughed with joy. "Ben, coming here was such a good idea."

We dismounted by the rocks.

"Stay close," Ben called as Liam and Golly headed for the trees. "Watch out for bears."

Jesse wandered off toward a bright patch of wildflowers, taking her drawing pad and pencils.

"Tara," Ben said.

"Yes?"

"Tell me about your life in Texas."

"Well, I was finishing up my first year at West Texas A&M University when I had to leave to get the kids away from Charlie."

"What were you studying?"

"I took some business classes because I'll need to know those things when I start up my own ranch. My parents raised and trained barrel racing horses and taught kids how to barrel race too. In Texas, that's a big thing, and there's a lot of money in it. I want to do that too."

"You want to do that here?"

"Yes," I said. "If I stay in Montana, that is."

"I'm pretty sure you will find people here who want to learn barrel racing. I hope you do decide to stay, Tara." His eyes met mine.

"Hm," I said noncommittally, leaning forward to let my hair cover my face. "We'll see."

Ben leaned forward, his hand brushing my hair back. He looked down into my eyes, then at my lips. Tilting his head, Ben leaned closer.

My breath caught for a second, anticipating his kiss.

A spine-chilling scream shattered the peace, and Golly started barking fiercely.

Ben jerked back, ran over to his horse, jumped into the saddle, and raced toward the sound of Golly's barking. I was right behind him on Sundance. In seconds, we had reached Liam.

Golly stood between my little brother and the mountain lion crouching on a boulder. Liam, holding a big stick, was coming up next to Golly.

"Liam! Stop!" Ben shouted. "Let Golly stay in front of you." He whipped out his rifle, dismounted and ran over to Liam. He lifted the gun to take aim at the big cat.

But the lion, seeing the advancing crowd, slipped away into the forest behind the boulder with one final scream.

I jumped from Sundance's back and threw my arms around Liam, my heart pounding.

Ben lowered his rifle. Golly crowded close to Liam, barking excitedly.

Ben tousled Liam's hair. "You'd better stay in the meadow, cowboy. At least there aren't any mountain lions there."

"Aw-w-w," Liam grumbled. "Golly and I could have taken that ol' lion!"

Ben laughed. "I don't think so, Liam. You and I need to have a talk about mountain lions and bears when we get back to your home, okay?"

"Okay," Liam pouted.

I shot a look of thankfulness at Ben. "Come on, Liam. I've got chocolate chip cookies for dessert."

We remounted, Liam behind Ben, and headed back to our picnic area. Jesse, who was running toward us, stopped when she saw us coming.

"What happened?"

"Liam scared up a mountain lion," Ben said. "But we've got it under control now."

The rest of the morning passed without incident, but it was impossible to recapture the moment when Ben had nearly kissed me. My heart relived that moment in the hours and days ahead. Was I ready for this? All I knew was I had wanted Ben to kiss me, and I had felt cheated when we were interrupted.

As we rode back down the mountain with Jess and Liam ahead of us on the trail, Ben came up next to me and leaned over. "I'd like to spend some time on Fridays with just you, Tara. Think we can manage that?" He raised an eyebrow at me and smiled.

Our eyes met in one long look, and my pulse raced. "Yes. I'd like that."

CHAPTER 34

Houston was cooling down after a sweltering day when Charlie walked into Gino's office. "Hi, Gino," he said, forcing a smile. "I've got an installment here for you."

"An installment? How much?" Gino stared at Charlie. The two-month deadline he had given Charlie for repayment of the debt was nearing.

"I've got twenty-five-thousand dollars for you, and I've put my ranch on the market. I've got ads out, and once it sells, I can pay you the full price."

"You still owe me five hundred thousand. I gave you two months, Webster."

Charlie bowed his head and said, "I'm still working on it. I think I can scrape together half of what I owe by the end of the month. But I don't think I can get it all for you that soon, even if I sold the ranch tomorrow. There's escrow, you know. I haven't been able to find my nieces and nephew yet either. Once I've got them, I'll have the profits from the sale of their parents' ranch and can pay in full. I've eliminated a lot of places they could have gone, and it's only a matter of time before the law tracks them down. But I'm searching too. Can you give me another month? Until the end of June?"

Gino stared at him for a long moment. "Okay. But if you don't get the money before then, you'll be losing a finger or two."

"Lose a finger? No! That's barbaric!"

"I mean it, Webster." Gino turned his back and left the room.

Charlie, shaken deeply, headed back to his office. Business was still slow but should pick up in another month. Unfortunately, he needed money fast.

I awoke early Sunday morning. After washing my face and adding a small touch of makeup, I went to the closet and examined my clothes. The church in town was casual, not dressy. But I wanted to look nice on my first day there in years. I pulled out a soft, cream-colored blouse and a pair of tan slacks. A simple necklace designed of tiny turquoise stones hanging from a gold chain, plus matching earrings dressed it up just enough. I pulled the front part of my hair back into a low, half ponytail over the loose waves in the back and fastened it with a simple abalone shell barrette. Slipping on a pair of comfortable sandals, I went into the kitchen to start breakfast. *Bacon, eggs, applesauce, biscuits, and milk should be enough to keep the kids until noon. The oven will warm the room while I bake.*

This time, I used the electric stove for cooking to avoid getting ashes on my good clothes. Jesse heard me moving dishes around and stumbled out of the bedroom yawning. She blinked. "You're dressed up."

"It's Sunday."

"Oh. That's right. We're going to church with Ben today?"

"Yes. Why don't you get ready while I make breakfast? And wake Liam up too."

By nine-fifteen, we were sitting together on the bench outside the front door, watching for his truck.

"Ready?" Ben asked upon his arrival.

I nodded.

Ben glanced me over with a quick appraisal. Leaning close, he said softly, "You are always beautiful."

My cheeks grew warm.

Ben opened the back door to the truck and let the kids in, then walked me around to the front passenger seat. I was nervous. I knew the sheriff would be there. What I didn't know was whether there were any bulletins out on us from Texas or not.

Liam chattered with Ben all the way over the mountain and down into the valley below. I was still awed by the steep drop-offs along the highway. But Jesse and I were silent. I think we both felt nervous about meeting a lot of new people.

Ben pulled into the church parking lot and came around to open the door for me. Jesse and Liam had already climbed out and stood together waiting for us.

"Tara," Ben said softly, "this will be good. You'll find new friends here in Montana." He smiled encouragingly, holding out his hand to help me down.

"You're right." I took a deep breath, took his hand, and stepped out of the truck.

Ben smiled and walked toward the church door with us, pulling my hand through the crook of his arm.

"Hi, Ben!" A young man slapped him on the shoulder and grinned. "Who are your guests?"

"Tara, this is my cousin, Jordan. Jordan, do you remember Tara? She visited a few years ago with her grandma, Evelyn Webster."

Jordan shook his head regretfully. "No, I don't remember. But I'm glad to meet you now."

Once inside the church, Ben introduced me to more of his friends. Max and Kate, I already knew. Alex and Kelly welcomed me warmly.

"Ben, you should bring her to our meeting on Friday," Kate insisted.

"I'll see what I can do," Ben smiled. Leaning over to me, he said, "There's a youth group for Jesse's age on Wednesday, too, if you think she'll want to go."

Ben nodded toward a distinguished, middle-aged man nearby. "That's Sheriff Carlson," he said. "I think he might be helpful, if you decide you'd like to talk with him."

"Okay." I eyed the sheriff carefully.

Being around other young people again felt good. The pastor's message about faith lifted my heart to God. By the time we reached home in the afternoon, I was feeling relaxed and happy. Jess was smiling again. Liam, who chattered about his new friends, was yawning. We all felt thoroughly welcomed. Yes, going to church was just what we had needed.

But deep inside I wondered, would we ever be safe from Charlie? He wasn't the kind to give up hunting for us. There was too much for him to lose. A chill of fear threatened my peace. I must remember to keep my eyes on Jesus, I reminded myself. He will keep us safe.

CHAPTER 35

Monday morning, I awoke earlier than usual. Sunbeams on my face beckoned. Jess and Liam wouldn't be up for at least two hours. I sat up in bed. A quiet hour or so to myself would be nice, along with a cup of tea out on the patio to soak up the sun.

Opening the closet, I searched my meager store of clothing, looking to see if there was something different to wear. A dark red peasant blouse caught my eye. I hadn't worn it since leaving Texas. Though impractical for ranch work, it would expose my shoulders to the sun. The thought of warm sun on my skin was appealing. Besides, I'd been in work clothes now for over a month, except for Ben's party and church. It was time to relax and wear something pretty around the ranch for a change.

As I pulled the blouse over my head and scooped my hair out over the wide ruffle, I wondered what Ben would think. He had been protective from the moment he'd learned of our problem. He'd been kind and thoughtful. But did he see me as anything more than a responsibility? Even though he had almost kissed me, I still wasn't sure about him. His actions said he liked me a lot. But I needed to hear words. Something definite to let me know if he was serious or not.

I sighed, combed my hair, and let it lie loose on my shoulders. I tucked the blouse into my blue jeans and slipped on a pair of flip-flops. Going out to the kitchen, I started a fire in the woodstove. Since the mornings were still cool, a small fire in the stove would warm the cabin up. I put the kettle on the electric range, however, where it would heat more quickly.

A few minutes later, a cup of warm lemon tea in my hand, I went outside, a blanket over my arm to spread on the grass where I could relax and soak up the sun. Below, the valley stretched out still and pleasant. The liquid song of a meadowlark pierced the air with incredible sweetness. A doe with two fawns grazed down near the creek.

I'd been relaxing, shoes off, dozing in the sun for about a half hour when I heard a horse cantering up the road.

I stood and walked down toward the pasture, enjoying the feel of soft, wet grass on my bare feet, and climbed onto a rail of the paddock fence to wave at Ben.

He raised his hand in greeting. A few minutes later, he arrived at the fence, smiling at me. "Hey, Nature Girl," he said, his voice husky. "I need to check the fences in the north pasture and see how the grass is coming along. Want to go with me?"

"Okay." I smiled back. "But I'm barefoot."

"That doesn't matter. We aren't going to do much walking. You'll be fine."

Ben moved the horse up to the fence, took my hand and helped me mount behind him. I wrapped my arms around his waist and laughed. What a beautiful morning. I tucked my feet against the horse's warm flanks.

"Hold on," Ben said, smiling back over his shoulder at me.

"Sure," I said.

Ben turned his horse away from the house at a canter and headed along the mountain slope toward the north pasture. Aspen trees with delicate leaves quivered in the slightest breath of air brushing the track at the foot of the mountain. A gurgling stream rushed alongside the pathway. Soon, we came to a small, grassy meadow at the base of the mountain, where the brook sprang from the mountain slope in a small waterfall and rushed merrily down the hill. Yellow, white, and blue flowers adorned the hidden bower.

"Oh! Look at all the flowers."

"Want to get down and take a closer look?" Ben asked, grinning over his shoulder, and bringing his mare to a stop.

"Yes, please."

Ben pulled one leg up over the saddle horn and jumped down, then turned to help me. My hair, still loose on my shoulders, fell partly across my face as Ben lifted me down from the horse. I brushed it back and laughed.

Ben's hands stayed at my waist. I saw his eyes widen in awareness as he held me.

I caught my breath and turned to look at the cascading water. "How beautiful." The dew on the grass bathed my feet. The air was sweet with the early morning scent of damp grass and wildflowers.

Ben dropped the horse's rein to ground hitch it, and strolled toward me, hands in his pockets. "Yes—beautiful," he said, a twinkle in his eyes.

"Hey, Ben! Let's bring the kids up here later. Jess will love the wildflowers, and Liam can hunt for small animals and bugs. Did he tell you he has a collection?" I turned and looked back.

"Yes, he did."

"What are these?" I knelt and touched some of the blue flowers growing all around me.

"Those are blue camass," he said. He knelt on one knee, broke the stem, brushed my hair behind my left ear and tucked the flowers over it.

"Jess will love these flowers." I was aware I was chattering, but I somehow needed to bring the emotional tension down.

Ben took my hand and brought me up facing him, holding my eyes with his. As he drew me close, butterflies flitted around inside my stomach. His hands shifted to my waist.

"Tara," he breathed looking into my eyes.

"Ben," I said, meeting his eyes steadily, "I'm not looking for a short-term relationship."

"Neither am I," he said. "I love you. I want this to last forever. But I don't want to rush you."

"Oh, Ben. You must know how I feel about you. But I just don't know what I'm supposed to do yet. I have to consider my responsibilities and think about Jess and Liam. Is Montana the best place for them? Or do I need to think about taking them back to Texas eventually?"

I searched his eyes, silently pleading with him to understand.

"Okay," he said, lifting my chin and looking into my eyes. "But know this, Tara Webster, I am seriously in love with you. And I think you know that."

I gazed into his eyes and pondered what he had said.

He leaned down and kissed me gently, his arms holding me close. "You don't think that I have been helping you here at the ranch every spare minute just because my dad had a working deal with your gran, do you?" he breathed against my hair.

"Well," I said, smiling, "I did wonder. But are you sure about this?"

"Yes. I am most definitely sure. I've known it since I saw you that first morning."

I pulled back, searching his eyes, still hesitant, but longing to be free to love him.

"When you are sure what you want, I'll be here." He lifted my hand to his lips, kissed the back of it gently then released me.

I turned and started back toward the horse. "Ben—the kids will be up soon. I don't want them to be frightened if I'm not there. We need to check the north pasture and get back."

"Sure," Ben said, smiling at me. "Come on." He reached for my hand and led me back to the horse. He mounted then reached out his hand. I took it, stepped onto his boot top and he pulled me up behind him.

Once again, I wrapped my arms around his waist as the mare cantered down the pathway. In my heart, I felt sure Ben was my man. But there were too many confusing things needing to be settled before I could make any decisions about the relationship. I had to think of Jess and Liam. What was best for them? I had to figure out what to do about Charlie and Texas. This was no time to let my heart get the best of me. Even so, my rebel heart gave evidence against my practical thoughts. I felt joy pounding on my heart's door, demanding to be let in.

I forced myself to think about other things. I should start entering rodeos soon too. We need the prize money. Most of the Montana rodeos aren't televised nationally. Some will be shown on local TV only, so there's little chance Charlie would see me in news footage down in Texas. But on the other hand, Sundance is a known horse. There might be someone in Montana who would know about his disappearance and contact the sheriff in Texas. The rodeo circuit is a small world. I'll have to wait on the rodeos until the law catches up with Charlie and we are safe again. I can't risk Jesse's and Liam's safety.

I tried to focus on my responsibilities, but my heart drew me back to thoughts of Ben. I found myself leaning against him as we rode. I breathed in the scent of his body—the perfume of his aftershave—the freshly washed smell of his denim shirt.

"The grass looks good," Ben said, pulling up at the entrance to the north pasture. "If all goes well, we should be able to mow in early July."

"Isn't July rodeo time in Helena?" I asked.

"Sure. But we'll get it cut before then. It only takes one person to drive the tractor, and I've done this field before. July is the best time to mow, since it's dry and hot. But it's over a month away. Let's ride around the pasture and check the fence."

Ben turned the horse and we headed around the field at a comfortable canter, circling back toward the cabin afterward. When we reached the ranch yard, I slipped off the horse before Ben could help me down and walked up to the house ahead of him.

Jesse opened the door and stared. "Where have you been?" she demanded.

"Ben and I rode out to check the grass in the north pasture," I said. My cheeks felt hot.

Ben turned his mare into the corral.

"Jess, get out the bacon, eggs, and cheese. I'll be right back and start breakfast," I said.

"Okay," she grinned playfully. "And don't think you're going to get away with not telling me what happened on that ride, Sis."

Ducking into the bathroom, I splashed my burning cheeks with cold water bringing the color back down. Running a brush through my hair and tying it back, I glanced at myself in the mirror. My face was still glowing. Breathing deeply, I ran my hands down my jeans and tried to look nonchalant.

I was mixing pancake batter when Ben came into the kitchen. His eyes danced as they met mine. I looked away and tested a small drop of batter in the frying pan. Satisfied at how it sizzled and rose nicely, I spooned more batter into the pan.

Ben moved up next to me and put bacon into another pan. Our arms brushed as we worked together, sending strong pulses of passion through my veins. Jesse glanced at us and grinned knowingly. My cheeks were still warm, and I knew they were red. By the time Liam came into the room, the air felt electric between Ben and me. I slid a couple of pancakes onto plates and took them over to the table, where Jesse and Liam put butter and syrup on them and began eating.

Gradually, the tension faded as we worked and ate together. But I couldn't look at Ben without my cheeks getting warm, so I focused on the children. My eyes followed Ben when he left after breakfast to tighten some barbed wire around the pasture, taking Liam with him.

"Okay, Tara, spill!" Jess demanded, her face lighting up fully for the first time since we had left Texas.

"Oh, Ben took me to the north pasture, and we saw a beautiful little meadow on the side of the mountain on the way. There are some gorgeous wildflowers. I'm going to take you and Liam up there," I said, trying to divert her.

"Yeah. And?"

"Well, I think you should get used to having Ben around," I hedged.

CHAPTER 36

Eli Farley, now recovered from surgery, had returned home. He came over to Ruby Hollow frequently to help. Quiet and thoughtful, he added another layer of security to our ranch. Liam followed him around peppering him with questions, reminding me of how I used to follow Ben around the same way. I was pleased to see a fast friendship developing between my little brother and Ben's dad.

With school out, Ben, Jess, and I found plenty to do. There was always something needing to be mended on the ranch. Stretching and straightening barbed wire, cutting down dead trees, gathering and chopping firewood for the coming winter. We finished clearing the practice field, raked it, and started training the horses for barrel racing.

Since Ben had told me he loved me, I was giving more thought to whether there was a future for us in Montana. *If Charlie isn't stopped, we'll have to stay here.* I felt good about staying, but not at all happy over the possibility of Charlie remaining on the loose to threaten us.

But what if the law catches up with him? What then? Will I want to go back to Texas where all my friends are? What about Jesse and Liam? Would this be a good place for them too? Would Montana be a good place to raise and train horses? Was there a good income in it here? With others depending on me, there's a lot to consider besides love.

Every day, Ben and I drew closer in little ways. Sometimes, he would bring me a small bouquet of flowers from the field. Other days we would walk through the forest together hand-in-hand, talking about all the little things making up our lives. The work around the ranch kept us busy. But we still found time to talk together at the end of each day.

I was falling a little deeper in love with Ben every time we met, but I kept him at arm's length physically, only allowing him to hold my hand or give me a quick hug, and sometimes a light kiss. I still wasn't sure whether we would return to Texas someday. I could think better if I kept things simple. But Ben didn't make it easy. We often rode horses together with the younger ones, exploring the mountains and meadows, sharing our thoughts and dreams along the way. On Fridays after Ben's work was finished, we'd leave Jesse and Liam with Eli and go into town together, exploring the shops and dining out, or driving over to one of the lakes for a picnic. Sometimes we met some of Ben's college friends along the way. Afterward, we attended the young people's group at church. As the days passed, our understanding of each other grew. I could no longer imagine a world without Ben.

Meanwhile, I had meals to prepare, in addition to training Sundance and Rosie. Always there were Liam and Jesse to care for and nurture. Working together drew us into a tight-knit circle. I was thankful Ben was giving me time to make up my own mind about our future.

May and June passed quickly. I liked attending church with Ben. I was relieved to finally be around other Christians my own age, and the older people were friendly too. Jesse and Liam were making friends as well, and Jesse was beginning to relax and open up a little more every day. She had taken over the greenhouse and the garden, and Liam helped her, freeing me to work with the horses.

One Friday afternoon when I was getting ready for our young people's meeting, Jesse came into my room and plopped down on the bed. She was quiet for a long time.

"Jesse? What's up?"

She fingered the pattern on the quilt covering my bed. "Oh, I was just wondering if Ben has asked you to marry him?"

I smiled. "No, he hasn't. But he's hinted at it enough. I'm just not sure whether we should go back to Texas someday. If the sheriff figures out Charlie murdered Gran, that is. It would be safe for us then." I looked over at her. "I'm trying to figure out what would be best for you and Liam."

Jesse looked up. "Tara, I miss my friends in Texas, but I don't ever want to live there again. It would remind me of Gran's murder and Mama and Papa's deaths. I'd have nightmares for sure." She paused and looked up at me. "Since we've been here, I've been happy. Liam has too. We're making new friends. And we love Ben. He's perfect for you, Tara. I know he loves you. I can see it in his eyes. I want to stay here."

"Thanks for telling me, Jess," I said, sitting on the bed next to her and taking her hand in mine. "You're an awesome sister."

The last week of June arrived. Ben and I were currying the horses in the barn when Ben's cell phone rang.

"Uh-huh. I see. Where do you want me?" Ben frowned as he spoke. "Okay. I'll be there in thirty minutes."

"Who was that?" I asked.

"The volunteer fire department. There's a fire over in the Scratch Gravel Hills. I need to go."

"Oh!" I said, reaching for his hand. "Are there a lot of fires in Montana?"

"Yes. Every summer we have them," he said, putting away the curry brush. Together, we walked quickly out of the barn and headed for Ben's truck. "We usually have rain until the middle of June, then things dry up in July." He looked around at the ranch. "Not here. In this valley, the grass stays green because of the creek and the high ground water level. But there are a lot of places where it gets bone dry up on the mountains. There's also a lot of beetle-killed pine up there. This time of year, we have some serious thunderstorms. Sometimes they are just lightning with no rain. If the lightning strikes a dry area with lots of dead pine, the fire takes off. We've had some big fires around Helena. I've helped fight some of them during the past few years."

"This sounds so dangerous, Ben." I gripped his hand a little tighter.

"Don't worry, honey. Our teams have been doing this for years," he said smiling down at me. Letting go of my hand, he strode quickly toward his truck.

As the truck disappeared in a cloud of dust, I prayed silently for his safety.

After Ben left, we didn't see him for the next three days. When his truck pulled up outside the house, I ran to meet him. "Ben! You're back!" I threw my arms around him, resting my head against his chest.

"What a nice welcome." He teased, holding me close.

I laughed and stepped away.

Hand-in-hand, we walked back to the house where Liam and Jesse plied him with questions about the fire.

Later in the evening, after the the younger ones went to bed, we sat out under the stars and watched the moon rise.

"Do you think we'll have a lot of fires this summer?" I asked.

Ben shrugged. "There's no way of knowing. If we can spot them quickly, we might be able to keep some of them from getting too big, like we did this last one. We just pray and hope for the best."

"I see. How long have you worked with the volunteer fire department?"

"About four years now. Those of us who are younger are really needed during the summer months. The older crew members are starting to retire, and it's hard to find replacements."

"Well, I hope we don't have any more fires this summer," I said. "I worried about you the whole time you were out there."

Ben laughed. "Tara, this is just part of life in Montana. Get used to it, honey."

CHAPTER 37

The town of Doran lay sweltering in the sun. Tyrel, now recovered from the rattlesnake bite, was sitting in the police station filling out reports when Sheriff Bradshaw entered.

"'Morning, Tyrel. How's the leg?"

"Much better, thank you."

"Can you think of anyone who might wish you harm?"

Tyrel looked across the room and met the sheriff's eyes. "Only Charlie Webster," he said firmly.

A red stain started up Sheriff Bradshaw's neck. "Now don't start that again."

"Sheriff, with all due respect, I think you are ignoring the facts. First, Evelyn Webster has an accident. She falls down some stairs and breaks her neck. Then the kids run away. I start asking Levi questions about Charlie Webster. Next thing that happens is his store catches fire and burns down with him inside it, and he barely escapes with his life. Then someone murders Levi. I keep investigating Charlie, and somebody plants a rattlesnake in my shower. Sheriff, that's too many coincidences." Tyrel held Sheriff Bradshaw's eyes.

Dan Bradshaw averted his gaze.

"If it were anyone else, someone you didn't know, you'd be all over him, investigating him from every angle." Tyrel said.

Sheriff Bradshaw flared, "I know Charlie Webster. He's a fine, upstanding man. Tyrel, lay off him!"

Tyrel stared at him for a moment then went back to his paperwork. Trying to talk to Sheriff Bradshaw was pointless once he'd made up his mind.

"My vacation is coming up next week, Tyrel. You will be in charge. I hope you will not get it into your brain to arrest Charlie Webster while I'm away."

"I will not arrest him without good, solid evidence." Tyrel stated firmly.

"Hm. Well, as long as that is understood—but you be darn sure of your facts before you do anything. I don't want you disturbing the peace of this town with false accusations. Charlie has a lot of friends here."

"Dad, I don't know what to do. Bradshaw won't investigate Charlie Webster, and he doesn't want me doing it either. After this rattlesnake situation, I'm not sure what to do." Tyrel shook his head in frustration as he sat in his dad's study, a cold lemonade clasped with both hands.

"At this point, it might be wise to just keep your head down and your eyes and ears open for more information." Judge Morgan poured cream into his coffee and stirred it. "You're going to have to be careful. Maybe you should think about moving home until you catch Charlie. We're here most of the time. That would give you some protection."

"Thanks, Dad," Tyrel said. "Let me think about it. Bradshaw leaves next week for his vacation, and I'll have until September to work on the case."

"Sure. You know we're always here for you, Son."

Jean came into the study, sipping a glass of lemonade. "Ty, I remembered something Tara said once. She mentioned the ranch her gran inherited was in Idaho or Montana. I think. I could be wrong, but that came to mind today."

Tyrel looked up with renewed interest. "Idaho or Montana? That should narrow the search. I'm on it. Thanks, Sis!" He jumped up and headed out the door.

"Jean," her dad said, "I think it would be best if you didn't tell anyone else about the ranch. Word might get to Charlie Webster, and it could create danger for Tara."

"I won't say a thing." Jean promised.

CHAPTER 38

"Tara," Jesse said during breakfast. "I hate to ask, 'cause I know we're short on money, but I seem to have grown a little lately. My jeans are too short and a little tight, and so are my tops."

"Yes, you have grown. Stand up and let me look at you."

Jesse pushed her chair back and walked around the table to me.

"I see what you mean. Okay. We'll go into town after breakfast. We may not be able to afford many new things, but we can at least get a couple tops and some jeans at Country & Ranch. Then we'll go over to Goodwill and see if we can find a few things there."

Jesse sighed in relief. "Thanks, Tara."

We headed for town. Although Ben had pointed out the Country & Ranch store, we hadn't yet been inside. The clothing section wasn't huge, but there was a good display of western wear, so we looked at a few things together.

"This shirt looks nice," Jesse said, holding up a purple shirt with white flowers embroidered on the yoke, and a button-down front. "What do you think, Tara?"

"I like it. Why don't you try it on?"

"Okay." Jesse looked around for the nearest dressing room and headed toward it.

Sorting through the shirts again, I looked for a few more items Jess might like.

"Can I go look at the cowboy hats and boots?" Liam asked.

"Sure. Just don't go where I can't see you." I went back to searching for shirts.

Suddenly, two girls about my age came up to me, one on each side. Both were well-dressed and beautifully made up.

"Isn't she the one we've seen Ben with?" said the girl with light brown hair to my left.

"I think she is," the girl on my right said. "I wonder what she's doing here?"

"I can't imagine what Ben sees in her, can you, Lorene?" said the first girl. She looked straight at me. "Ben is mine, you know."

"That's right. Ben belongs to Nikki. He'd never settle for a squaw."

"What?" I gasped, staring at the girl. I had no idea who those girls were.

"We've been dating for a few months." Nikki's eyebrows arched. "Didn't he tell you?"

"Um, no—"

She shook her beautifully cut hair. "Isn't that just like him. Why, not too long ago, he was dating another girl." She laughed sardonically. "He sure gets around. But now he's mine, and no squaw is going to take him away from me." She bumped into me sideways, shoving me against the clothes rack. "So, keep your hands off him."

"Yeah," Lorene said, rudely bumping me with her hip.

Hurt and embarrassment flooded me. Who were these girls?

Nikki put her face in mine, backing me into the hangers digging into my back. My hair got caught in them as she shoved me again. This time, I fell to the floor.

"Stay away from Ben." she hissed.

Just then a wild bundle of energy hit her. "Leave my sister alone!"

Nikki turned on him and cursed, grabbing him by his thick, black hair. He whipped around and kicked her leg. She let go of his hair and screamed, both hands going to her shin.

"Here! Here!" a man came running over. "What's going on?" The store manager grabbed Liam, who was standing between me and the girl, his hands balled into fists. "What are you doing, young man?"

"That little brat kicked me!" the girl shrieked.

"She attacked my sister!" Liam shouted.

The manager saw me then. I was struggling to untangle my hair so I could stand without the hangers pulling it out.

"Ma'am, did this girl push you?"

I nodded, speechless with shock.

"The lying ..." Nikki hissed. "I didn't lay a hand on her!"

"That's right!" Lorene chimed in, linking her arm with Nikki's.

The manager looked around. "Ma'am?" he said to a girl standing at a nearby clothes rack. "Did you see what happened?"

"Yes," she nodded, walked over, and stood beside me. "This girl was looking at shirts. The girl with the fancy-cut brown hair and her friend came up and started pushing her and saying mean things. When this girl fell, her little brother came over to defend her."

The manager released Liam and turned to me, holding out his hand to help me up. "I'm so sorry, ma'am. Please accept my apologies. Would you like to press charges against these women?"

I eyed them and considered. If I were to press charges, our names would be published online, and our location might get out. I slowly shook my head. "Not this time," I said quietly.

The manager turned to the two girls. "Please leave."

"Well!" Nikki said. "My family is very rich and influential. You'll be sorry, mister."

"No, I don't think so," the manager said firmly.

Nikki's mouth opened in surprise, then cussing and making a worse scene, she and Lorene left the store.

The manager turned back to us. "Please pick out any outfit you like. On the house. Just bring it to me, and I'll see to it you are not charged a cent."

I nodded and looked down, his kindness bringing tears to my eyes. I quickly brushed them away, took a deep breath and looked back up.

"I'm so sorry this happened. Please know you are welcome here anytime," he said.

"Thank you." I nodded gratefully.

Hurt and embarrassment flooded me. Who were those girls? Were they telling the truth about Ben?

The girl who had defended us said, "I'm so sorry you were treated like that. My name is Mariah. What's yours?"

"I—I'm Tara," I said, tears welling up in my eyes. I dashed them away.

"Hi, Tara," she said. "Most people here do not act like that girl. She's a bully. But I think niceness is priceless. I think you'll find a lot of the people here are friendly and feel the same way. Don't give up on us because of one or two who aren't nice."

"Thank you, Mariah."

"What happened?" Jesse asked, coming from the dressing room with the top she had tried on.

I brushed away the tears forming once again. "Oh, some mean girls just hurt my feelings. I'll be okay." But deep inside, I was crushed.

Liam spoke up. "Those girls were mean to Tara. I protected her. Nobody better treat my sisters bad!" He put his arms around my waist. "I love you, Tara. Don't let those girls make you sad."

"Okay. I won't." I said, trying to hide my hurt from the children.

Jesse handed me the shirt. "This one fits, but we don't have to get it now if you don't feel like it."

"No. The manager offered us an entire outfit for free. We can use the help, and I think the manager would feel better if we took him up on his offer too. Find some jeans to go with it, and we'll leave. We can come back another time."

Ten minutes later we exited the store carrying our shopping bags. We saw Nikki and Lorene standing beside a Mustang, glancing at us, and talking. They started toward us, anger written all over their faces.

"Get in the truck," I told the children.

I whipped the cell phone out of my pocket and punched in 9-1-1. "Stop where you are," I said. "If you take one step closer, I'll call the police."

"Wait!" The second girl, Lorene, stopped and grabbed the first girl. "I don't want to get in trouble."

The lead girl stopped, glaring at me across the space between us. "You're lucky my friend doesn't want to get involved. Next time, I will punch you out!"

My thumb hit the dial as I lifted it to my ear. I knew I needed to protect our family from those girls. I had to take the risk. This was a small town. Chances were, we'd see them again.

"9-1-1. Do you have an emergency?"

"Yes," I said. "My name is Tara Webster. Two complete strangers—two girls—just attacked me in the Country & Ranch store. When the manager made them leave, they waited for me in the parking lot. One of them just threatened to punch me out next time she sees me."

"An officer will be there in a moment. Please stay on the line until the officer arrives."

The two girls turned and hurried back to their car. I leaned into the truck and said, "Jess, write down their license plate number."

Jess reached into the glove compartment and pulled out a paper and pen.

The two girls pulled away with a screech of tires.

"I got their number," Jess said.

A police car pulled into the parking lot from another entrance. I waved them over. I told them briefly what had happened, and Jess handed him the license number.

"What kind of car was it?" one of the officers asked.

"A red Mustang. The girls' names were Nikki and Lorene. I didn't hear any last names. The manager of the store can identify the girls and tell you what happened inside," I said. "There was a witness too. Her name was Mariah. The manager may know her last name."

Another ten minutes passed before we were free to go.

"Ma'am," the officer said, "when we stop the girls who attacked you, would you like to press charges?"

I sighed. "Could you just give them a warning?"

"We can do that, if you wish."

"Yes. I'd prefer you to warn them and let them know you are watching them," I said. "It might be enough."

The officer nodded. "That works well sometimes. Let me have your contact information for our records." He handed me a notepad then radioed to the other police in the area and to explain what happened.

After writing down our address and phone number, we headed back to my truck. "Let's go home. Those girls are gone, and I don't think they'll be bothering us again."

"Good riddance!" Jesse said vehemently. "I hope the police find them."

"Yeah!" Liam echoed.

I sighed. "I know how you feel, but we need to remember people like them need Jesus. Mama used to tell me there would always be mean people in this life, but we must not treat them like they treat us. If we act like them, we will become like them. She told me, 'As we grow older, we become more of what we are,' and to choose wisely what we wish to become."

"What do you want to be when you're older?" Jesse asked.

"Kind," I said firmly. "I want to be kind. Always."

I didn't feel like shopping any longer, but I didn't want the children to dwell on what had happened. "Would you like some ice cream?" I asked.

"Yes!" they chorused.

"Okay. Let's go over to Dairy Queen."

The ice cream served as a momentary distraction. But later, when we were home, I saddled up Sundance and went for a ride in the warm, afternoon air. Only then did I allow myself a real cry. My mind whirled in confusion. *Is Ben dating that awful girl? Has he been leading me on? Do I really belong here in Montana?*

The tears came. "God, please show me what to do," I prayed, "I've never allowed myself to get close to any man before. I'm new at this relationship thing. I want to trust Ben, but I just don't know what to think."

A Bible verse popped into my mind. "Be still in the presence of the Lord and wait patiently for him to act. Don't worry about evil people who prosper or fret about their wicked schemes."

"Thank you for answering me, Father," I whispered. I said the words he had put in my heart again. Yes. I must wait patiently for God to straighten this out and not let my emotions run away with me. God would show me what was true and what was false. If Ben had been playing with my heart, God would show me. But if Ben's love were true, I would know it once we talked.

The familiar scents of leather and sweet-smelling horse sweat brought some peace and comfort to my aching heart as I rode through the meadow.

After dinner that evening, Ben frowned and walked out onto the porch. But I stayed inside and cleaned the kitchen. He'd tried to draw me out during the meal, but I wasn't ready to talk yet. I felt hurt and confused.

Liam followed Ben outside. I heard him say, "Today when we were in town, two girls were mean to Tara."

"What? Who were they?"

"Their names were Nikki and Lorene. We never saw them before. But they pushed Tara into the clothes rack and onto the floor, and they said mean things to her." He paused and said with satisfaction. "I kicked Nikki, the meanest one, in the leg."

"You did? Wow! Thanks for telling me, Liam. I'd better get in there and see how Tara is holding up," Ben said, turning on his heel and heading back into the kitchen.

"Tara?"

I still didn't know what to say, so I said nothing.

"What happened today?"

I sighed. "Well—um—we went shopping at Country & Ranch."

"Is Liam right? Did Nikki and Lorene hurt you?"

I nodded.

"What exactly happened," he demanded softly, coming up behind me and putting his hands on my shoulders.

I stiffened against his touch. "One of the girls said you were dating her and that you belonged to her. She told me to stay away from you. Then she pushed me down."

"What?" Ben was angry. I could hear it in his voice.

"Are you dating her?" I asked.

"No. Definitely not. I went to lunch with her and Lorene a couple of times during the school year after class. But when she became possessive, I had Max and Kate join us for lunch, and I pretended I liked Kate so Nikki would back off."

"You pretended you liked your *cousin?*"

"Yes. She is good at helping us guys in the family fend off aggressive girls."

I could hear the smile in his voice. "I see. Then Kate must be the other girl she mentioned."

"What other girl?"

"She said you were dating some other girl recently."

"Oh. Right. She must have meant Kate," Ben said, turning me to face him. "Tara, you are the only woman in my life. My intentions are serious and honorable. I love you. I'm just waiting for you to be ready."

His arms came around me. I leaned my head against his chest and stood there, letting his love wash over me, washing away those ugly words Nikki had said. Tears of relief flowed down my face. "I am so sorry this happened to you, Tara."

I felt his lips on my hair. "There was another girl at the store who spoke up for me. Her name was Mariah."

"Mariah? Did she have kind of long, dark hair? Soft-spoken?"

"Yes. Do you know her?"

"Yes. She's one of God's bright stars in Helena. I'm glad she was there for you, Tara. Jesus must have sent her to help you."

I nodded against his chest. "That would be just like Jesus."

Ben lifted my chin, saw the tears, and wiped them away. "Tara, you and I have shared our hearts. We have a lot in common. And we both follow Jesus. I would never consider dating a girl like Nikki. She isn't a believer. I'm not one for missionary dating."

"What's that?"

"It's when a Christian dates a non-Christian and tries to get them to become a believer. It doesn't usually work. Some people have managed to make it work for them, but it's rare. I don't think it's a good idea to date someone hoping to change them. That's God's job. I prefer to date a woman who already belongs to Jesus and shares my beliefs."

"I see. That makes sense."

Ben held me close and stroked my hair. "After I met you, Tara, I completely forgot about every other girl around. No other girl can hold a candle to you. I'm a one-woman man—and I am yours." He dropped a kiss on my hair.

The hurt in my heart faded away as we stood with our arms around each other there in the kitchen. With my head against Ben's chest, I could hear his heartbeat. Gradually, the hurt and the tension faded away, and I was comforted.

CHAPTER 39

July's heat descended on our mountain home. "Ben? Tara?" Jesse called as Ben and I walked toward the house. "Do you want some lemonade? Levi and I made some for you." She held out two cold glasses of juice.

"Thank you, Jess, honey," I said, gratefully accepting the juice and drinking half of it thirstily. "Tastes great." I was pleased at how helpful Jesse was becoming in this time of crisis, when we didn't know from day to day if we would be safe.

"Sure hits the spot," Ben said, draining his glass.

Jesse beamed at the praise.

I was exhausted. The heat, though not nearly as hot as Texas, was still hot enough to drain me. Ben and I had spent the day taking turns mowing hay in the north pasture. He helped me hook the equipment to the tractor and showed me where there were boulders rising from the earth in the pasture so I could avoid them. By the time we were finished, we were both hot and sweaty from the heat and hard work. We'd bale the hay in the early hours of morning on the third day, which would give the hay time to dry, but keep it moist enough to hold together well.

Later, after showering, I felt refreshed and relaxed. My nineteenth birthday was just a couple of days away now, but I already felt older. The responsibilities of the past few months had been challenging. I still felt nervous about Uncle Charlie, but maybe he wouldn't find us here. I could only hope. Every night before falling asleep, I asked the Lord to protect us and keep us safe. I knew he heard me, for he gave me peace whenever I was afraid.

Ben had gone home to clean up, but he was back now, playing a board game with Jesse and Liam in the living room while I finished putting the week's laundry away.

I knelt to put a pile of fresh socks on the lower shelf of my closet when I noticed a slight metal gleam on the wall which I hadn't noticed before. Moving the socks to the floor, I studied the metal disk. Was there a safe built into the wall? I traced the edges of a door, tightly fitted into the wall, with my fingers. But where would the key to the lock be? Remembering the keys we had found in the tractor in April, I backed out of the closet and went over to the dresser where I had casually tossed them.

Inserting the smallest key into the lock, the safe's door swung open, revealing some papers, a bundle of neatly bound money, and an envelope.

Snapping off a rubber band, I counted the money. *A thousand dollars! We can sure use it. We're running short on cash.* Reaching into the manilla envelope again, I pulled out a letter to Uncle George in Gran's handwriting.

Dear George,

I hope you are well. I miss you. We are working hard down here on our ranch. Since Mark and Nora died, I've been raising the grandchildren. Tara is a great help, and she's a natural at barrel racing. She's been winning almost every contest she enters. The prize money helps pay for her needs at school, and she has a good scholarship. Which means her inheritance from the sale of Mark and Nora's ranch and the horses will be intact when she's old enough to start her own horse ranch, as she plans to do when she finishes college.

I've willed everything I have to Tara. I've named her as guardian for the children when I'm gone. The doctor said I'm doing well, but you know how it is with this illness. Tara is very responsible and has a lot of good sense. She'll take good care of the younger children. I can count on her. She has been practically running my ranch since she and the youngsters came to live here. She manages money well too. Anyone who knows her is aware she is capable and responsible, more so than many adults.

I'm worried about Charlie. He is so violent! I am afraid he will get out of control one of these days. He lives in Houston, but he comes here sometimes. He has hit me several times now. But I don't want to say anything. It's a family problem. I don't want the town gossiping about it.

Once Charlie was yelling at Tara, holding her by the shoulders, and Tara's dog ran up and bit his leg. Charlie turned and kicked the dog hard. Then he went into the house, got a shotgun, and shot the poor dog right there in front of Tara! He must be a little bit insane. He is certainly not safe. I would never trust the children to him.

Charlie has always been a bully. Mark once told me Charlie keeps a box of trophies from people he has hurt. He showed it to Mark once. Mark said it spooked him. Something is seriously wrong with Charlie, and I don't know what to do. He hated Mark, his own half-brother. So, keep us in your prayers, George. We hope to see you soon.

Love,
Evelyn

I sat on the bed shaking with emotion. Gran's words made me feel closer to her, even though she was gone. I remembered the day Charlie had killed my dog as though it were yesterday. Once again, the shock hit me. Gran's warning about Charlie sent shivers up and down my spine. I jumped up from the bed in desperate need of fresh air.

Placing Gran's letter on my nightstand, I walked quickly out of my room toward the front door. Ben, Jesse, and Liam looked up, startled. "I'm going for a ride," I said as I headed outside into the starlight.

I walked quickly to the barn. Sundance raised his head and looked at me when I opened the side door and hurried in. I picked up a bridle and slipped it over Sundance's velvety nose. "Come on, boy. Let's go for a ride under the stars. I need to think."

Sundance snorted, sensing my emotional turmoil. I rubbed his neck and leaned my head against him for a moment, breathing in the horsey scent.

I tossed a blanket and saddle over his back, led him toward the barn's main door and mounted up. Down the hill we went, into the starry night, gaining speed over the smooth, open road, the wind flowing like water over us, the moon lighting our path.

Gradually, I felt the tension ease. Slowing Sundance to a walk, I turned him homeward. As I reached the barn and slid off the horse's back, Ben stepped out of the shadows into the moonlight.

"Tara? What's wrong?"

Dropping the horse's reins, I turned and walked straight into his arms. Tears flowed down my face, soaking his shirt. He wrapped his arms around me, stroking my hair. "It's okay, honey. It's okay."

When the tears subsided, I leaned against Ben, feeling safe in his arms.

"Want to tell me what's wrong?" Ben asked softly, fishing in his shirt pocket for a fresh, folded handkerchief. Gently, he wiped the tears from my face.

"I found a letter from Gran. I'll show it to you, and you can tell me what you think." I pressed my head against his chest, absorbing strength from him.

Ben lifted my chin, bringing my lips up to his. The kiss in the moonlight was wild and sweet.

Texas suddenly seemed far, far away.

"Let's go look at that letter now," Ben said shakily a little later, releasing me from his embrace but keeping possession of my hand.

"I need to rub Sundance down first," I said picking up the reins.

We walked toward the barn, not speaking while we cared for the horse. Walking around Sundance and out of the stall, Ben put his arm across my shoulder. We walked up to the house together, my heart at peace. *I know I belong to Ben now. He has guarded us and kept us safe since we arrived in Ruby Hollow. I trust him. I will love him forever.*

Ben waited in the living room with Jesse and Liam while I went to get Gran's letter. I silently handed the letter to him and watched him read it.

"Tara, you need to send a copy of this letter to that deputy who is investigating the murder back in Texas," Ben said handing it off to Jesse. We all sat down at the table to talk things over. "You should have Jess write down what she saw and include it with this letter too."

"But Ben," I protested. "That would put her in danger."

"No, it won't if we do this right." He shook his head briefly. "I have a friend who drives trucks. I can give him your letter and ask him to mail it far from Montana. That will keep Jesse safe. This information will help the deputy gather evidence against Charlie. Once Charlie's locked up, you will all be safe."

"Tara, I want to help," Jesse said, her face determined. "I don't want Charlie to get away with this."

"Yeah!" said Liam, pumping his fist.

I reached over and placed my hand in Ben's. "You're probably right. But I want to think about it first."

Liam yawned and rubbed his eyes.

"Come on, Liam. Time for bed," Jesse said, hauling Liam to his feet.

Ben led me over to the couch and pulled me down next to him. I felt his lips on my hair. He sighed. "Tara, you can't let Charlie keep on hurting people. First it was your Gran, then it was Levi, and now the deputy sheriff is in danger. You need to speak up, honey."

"I know, Ben." I sighed. "I'm just so scared."

"Yes. I understand. But if your letter is mailed from another state, you will be okay."

"That sounds safe," I said after a moment. "I'll—I'll think about it tomorrow."

"I'd better head home and get some sleep," Ben said finally. "You too, Tara." He leaned down and kissed me lightly. "Good night, Nature Girl."

"Good night, Ben." I watched him cross the room and step out into the night.

Lying in bed watching the stars, my thoughts were wrapped up in Ben—and our wild, sweet kiss out under the stars. I knew now we would be staying in Montana. There was no way I was going to walk away from Ben's love.

When the sun's rays woke me the next morning, I knew Ben was right.

CHAPTER 40

Tyrel sorted the mail, weeding out junk and finding only a few relevant letters to read. Sheriff Bradshaw had left on his vacation, and Tyrel was now in charge of law enforcement in their small town, supervising a small staff of three deputies and a dispatcher. He tossed the letters onto his desk and headed for the coffee maker.

Braced with coffee, Tyrel leafed through the letters. Most of them were junk, which he tossed. But there among the envelopes was a hand-addressed envelope with his name on it. Although there was no return address, it had a Jefferson City, Missouri postmark. Slitting it open, he glanced down at the signature. What? Tara Webster!

Dear Tyrel,

I heard you are working on the Levi Carroll murder investigation, so I am sending you the letter I just found among my grandma's papers. But first, you should know my sister, Jesse, saw Uncle Charlie push Gran down the stairs of our ranch house and kill her, which is why I took Jesse and Liam and left town. I must keep them safe. If Charlie knew Jesse saw him kill Gran, he would kill her for sure too.

For now, just know we are okay. If you can get enough evidence to arrest Charlie and put him in jail, I will contact you. I will hear about it once it is in the newspaper. We have friends looking out for us here, so do not worry about us. With the information in this letter I found from my grandmother, you may be able to find evidence to arrest Charlie without Jesse's testimony, I think. But Charlie must not know where we are or that Jesse saw him.

Sincerely,

Tara Webster

P. S. I'm enclosing Gran's and Jesse's letters. I hope this is enough evidence for you to stop Charlie from hurting anyone else. I think he killed Levi too. Levi knew how wicked Charlie is.

Jesse's letter was next:

Hi, Tyrel,

Two days before we left Texas, our Uncle Charlie came to the ranch and tried to make Gran give him Tara's horse, Sundance, He had run up a lot of gambling debts and said if he couldn't sell Sundance, he would be killed, But Gran said he would have to find another way to get the money, because the horse belonged to Tara, They were upstairs on the landing,

Charlie got mad and shoved Gran down the stairs, He went down to check to make sure she was dead, Then he took her wedding ring off and put it in his pocket, I don't know why he took the ring, but it creeped me out, He didn't see me because I was hiding behind the lilac bush,

Jesse Webster

Tyrel's pulse raced. At last. Something solid. He jumped up from his office chair and let out a whoop. He reached for his cell phone and dialed. "Dad! I've got to show you something. Do you have time? Okay. I'll be right over."

Grabbing the letters and his keys, Tyrel dashed out the office door, pausing only long enough to lock up. Taking every shortcut he knew, he made it to his parents' home in record time.

Judge Morgan had coffee ready at the kitchen table, and Tyrel's mom had added some cinnamon rolls, fresh from the oven. "What happened, Ty?"

The deputy strode up to his dad holding out the letters. "This came in the mail this morning."

The two men sat down at the table while Ty's mother, Dottie, poured coffee and slid rolls in front of her son and husband before sitting down.

"Hm. This does help legally." Judge Morgan passed the letter over to his wife. "But without Jesse here to testify, you still don't have a witness, except for Willie," he said. "Where did Tara mail this letter?"

"The envelope says Jefferson City, Missouri." Tyrel held out the envelope.

"*Missouri?* Who do those kids know in Missouri?"

Dottie Morgan reached out for the envelope, holding it for a moment, considering the postmark evidence. She set the envelope down, smiled and shook her head thoughtfully.

"What is it, Mom?" Tyrel asked.

"Well, Ty, if it were me, I would try misdirection. I wouldn't mail something that would give away my location. Tara's smart. I think she would find someone else to mail this for her in a different place. I don't think she's in Missouri at all."

Judge Morgan nodded his head. "You're probably right, Dottie."

"So, I should keep looking toward Montana or Idaho for answers?" Tyrel asked.

"Yes," his dad said. "It's what I'd do. But here's another thing to keep in mind. If this is an interstate investigation—and this envelope indicates it should be—you can call in the FBI. In fact, I think you must." Judge Morgan stood and walked over to the house telephone and opened a drawer, pulling out a black book from its interior. He flipped through the pages and handed the open address book to Tyrel. "Here's the number."

Tyrel hesitated. "Dad? Won't Sheriff Bradshaw be angry if I do this?"

"Maybe. But we'll cross that bridge when we come to it. The sheriff won't be back until September, and the FBI may have this case all wrapped up by then."

CHAPTER 41

Ben timed me while I put Sundance through his paces around the barrels. "I'd say you'd win everything in sight, Tara," he said, looking at the stopwatch in amazement. "That's a sixteen-second course. You just did it in 13.9!"

"Whoo-hoo!" I yelled, pumping my fists above my head. "You did it, Sundance." I patted the big horse excitedly. "Good job."

Sundance seemed to know exactly what I said, raising his head, neighing, and prancing a little.

"I wish I could ride in the Helena rodeo. I doubt anyone in Doran would be watching. They will all be focused on the Cheyenne Frontier Days event the same weekend. That's the biggest show around. But the judges here in Helena might recognize Sundance and know he's missing. Word travels fast in the rodeo circuit. I can't risk it."

July's heat had settled down over the Helena region. In Ruby Hollow, the apple trees around the house were covered with small green fruit. Walking beneath the trees the next morning, I sank into a lawn chair and nibbled on a piece of toast. I loved eating breakfast outside in the sweet-scented air. Jesse and Liam sat at the picnic table. Ben and I had finished baling the hay and had started moving it to the barns. There was a tall stack of thirty-five-pound bales stacked next to the smaller barn near the house. *We'll have to move it inside before the autumn rains, but we can wait for cooler weather to do that chore.* I looked over the neatly stacked bales with satisfaction. *There's plenty here for winter.*

"I'm going to bake you a cake for your birthday, Tara," Jess said. "What flavor do you want?"

"Is there really any flavor that counts besides chocolate?"

"Okay, okay! But I wanted to make sure," Jesse said, laughing at me.

Tomorrow would be my nineteenth birthday. Would the courts allow me to be the guardian for my sister and brother? I felt nervous. Even if they would, we would not be safe with Charlie still out there. I hadn't seen anything in the newspaper about his being arrested, though I'd sent the papers off to Tyrel Morgan. *It's probably too early for him to act on the information.*

A shadow crossed the lawn and moved over me. Looking up, my eyes surveyed the graying sky and clouds moving in. A severe thunderstorm could ruin Jesse's garden. But even worse, the dry lightning could spark more forest fires.

"Let's put the horses in the barn," I told Jess. "I don't like leaving them out with an electrical storm coming."

Ben came over as we led Sundance, Rosie, and her colt into the barn. Gathering me into his arms he looked into my eyes. "Jesse told me it's your birthday tomorrow."

"Yes." I lifted my face and welcomed his kiss.

As thunder rumbled in the distance, Ben looked up at the sky and released me. "Jesse, Liam, run for the house," he commanded. "Tara and I will be right in, just as soon as we finish with the horses."

Jesse and Liam ran up to the cabin, reaching the door just as the sky let loose with a bolt of lightning followed quickly by a loud thunderclap. By the time we had the horses in their stalls, the wind was whipping through the trees. Another flash of lightening, a roar of thunder, and the storm was overhead. Ben and I paused at the barn door, waiting until the lightning paused before we raced toward the house.

For the next half hour, Jesse and Liam clung to me as we huddled together on the couch. Ben paced the room, anxiously glancing out the windows to see where the lightning bolts were landing. Eventually, he came over to where we sat, picked up his guitar, and began singing "Awesome God," a song about God's power. A power far greater than the storm around us, reminding us of the One who was watching over us. Gradually, we relaxed.

After the storm moved over the mountains toward Helena, Ben went over to his dad's place to check for damages and to help clean up. Our place was relatively untouched. Great Uncle George had done an excellent job building the house in a protected nook in the mountainside, and the high peaks around us blunted the wind a lot. But the Farley house was more exposed to the elements.

I made some hot chocolate, and we walked onto the porch, enjoying the stillness of the evening before we went to bed.

"I hope it won't rain for your birthday," Jesse said, yawning and giving me a big hug. "I baked your cake and frosted it. Every bit of it is chocolate," she said, a satisfied smile on her face.

"It doesn't matter. Rain or no rain, I'll love eating your delicious cake." I said. I hugged Jess and Liam as we headed inside and went to bed.

The sudden ringing of my cell phone awoke me in the early hours of the morning. I answered it to hear Ben's anxious voice, the sound of wind in the background.

"Tara, the dry lightning sparked a fire just over the mountain and across the road from Ruby Hollow. The wind is blowing it your way. You'll have to get out of there before your road is blocked. Get the horses out. Take them to the fairgrounds. I'm sure the staff will let you wait out the fire there. They'll let you put the horses in the stables too."

"Okay. What about the cattle?" I asked, suddenly wide awake.

"I already put them in the northwest pasture on the other side of the hill yesterday. The way the wind is blowing, the fire probably won't go there. Dad is already moving our horses to the fairgrounds. I'm close to the fire line now. I've got to go. I'll call you when I can. I love you!"

"I love you too! Be careful!"

The line went dead.

I jumped out of bed and rushed into the other bedroom. "Jess, Liam, wake up."

"What?" Jesse mumbled, lifting a tousled head from her pillow.

Liam opened his eyes and blinked.

"Ben just called. He said we have to get the horses and leave Ruby Hollow," I said, trying to be calm. "There's a fire coming our way. Let's go."

Both children rolled out of bed and started dressing rapidly. I ran back to my room and did the same. I grabbed a change of clothes, stuffed them into a duffel bag then ran out to the truck. Driving over to the horse trailer, I called. "Come help me with this, Jess!"

Working together, it took us another fifteen minutes to hook up the trailer and load extra hay for the horses. Liam was already in the barn putting a lead on his colt by then.

Jesse and I ran back into the house. "You grab a change of clothes for Liam and you, and I'll get some food."

"The cake!" Jesse shouted. "It's in the springhouse!" She darted for the springhouse door.

I grabbed our sleeping bags. When Jesse came in from rescuing the cake, she helped me gather cereal, milk, bowls, and silverware and took them out to the living quarters of the trailer. The kids would be hungry. I packed a loaf of bread, a jar of peanut butter, a jar of jam—I looked out the kitchen window. Another cloud of smoke poured into the valley. We needed to get out before the smoke grew worse.

"Jess, I'll load the colt into the trailer. You put Rosie into the stall next to him, and I'll load Sundance.

"Okay."

The horses went into the trailer readily. I closed the back doors and climbed up behind the steering wheel. As we headed down the road. the smoke grew thicker. At the highway, we could see the fire coming over the mountains. Ben was up there. I gasped and nearly froze.

Carefully turning onto the highway, I drove away from the billowing clouds of smoke and headed over the pass toward Helena.

"God, keep Ben safe." I prayed aloud.

"Amen." Jesse said.

"Yes. Amen." Liam echoed.

Overhead, I heard the roar of a helicopter. The water it dumped from its huge bucket seemed like a small drop compared to the leaping flames.

Stopping near the business office at the fairgrounds, we could see the smoke darkening the dawn over the mountains. Glancing over my shoulder, I noticed Eli Farley already in the parking area with his horse trailer.

"Are they letting you and the horses stay here?" I asked, pulling up next to him.

"I'm sure they will when they get here," he said with a nod. "I'm sure they'll let you stay too. But it's too early for anyone to be at the office."

The kids were restless. They kept looking over at the mountains where the smoke rose in a great mass. Once the horses were settled in the fairground barn, I got out cereal for Jesse and Liam, but I couldn't eat a bite, knowing Ben was out there fighting the inferno. Instead, I sipped on a hot cup of tea to settle my nerves.

Questions hammered at my brain. Would Ben be okay? Would the fire burn our ranch? Would the cattle escape the flames? By noon, I was emotionally exhausted. Jesse made me eat a peanut butter sandwich and drink some milk.

"God is with Ben," she reminded me. "Have faith, Tara."

We spent the next couple of days alternately caring for the horses and peering through the smoke filling the valley, seeing the flames at night. Relief washed over me when my phone rang on the evening of the third day.

"Tara," Ben said, his voice tired. "We did it. We caught the fire in time, and the wind shifted, blowing the fire back on itself. We were able to contain it before it reached the ranch."

"Oh, Ben!" I gasped. "I'm so glad to hear your voice. Are you okay?"

"Yes, honey. I'm fine. Where are you?"

"We're at the fairgrounds. Your dad's here too."

"I'll be staying here at our camp until the fire is completely out. We still need to do mop up work."

"Okay. We are praying for you."

"Thanks, honey. Gotta go."

Jesse leaned against me. "Is he okay?"

"Yes. Thank the Lord. They have the fire under control, but he will be gone for a few more days."

Eli, who had been talking with some other evacuees, came over. "We'll have to stay in town until we are allowed to return home. I picked up some food at the store. Do you have enough? Are you doing okay in the trailer?"

"Sure. I'm okay for now, but later I need to unhitch the trailer and go to the store too."

Eli nodded. "Good. I'm calling for some pizza. Do you want some?"

"Yes. Thanks, Eli."

Jesse piped up. "And I've got birthday cake for dessert."

"It was Tara's birthday Tuesday, and we forgot!" Liam shook his head.

We camped at the fairgrounds for the next two days. Late on the fifth afternoon of our evacuation, Ben called with an update.

"I'm going home to shower, then I'm going to get some rest. It's okay for you to round up the horses and go home."

"I'm glad the fire's out and you're safe, Ben."

"Me too, honey. See you tomorrow."

I turned to my sister. "Jess, the fire is out."

We hugged each other while Liam galloped around shouting, "Yes! Yes! It's over!"

CHAPTER 42

We drove back over the pass an hour later and saw how close the fire had come to our ranch. The flames had reached the edge of the property across the road from us before the winds had shifted and blown the fire back on itself. On the mountain below, we could see a wide swath of burned conifer trees blackened on the slopes.

When we arrived at Ruby Hollow, we unloaded the horses and checked on the cattle. Smoke still lingered in the air, but we were grateful to be back home.

Ben came over the next afternoon. Liam was full of questions about the fire, but Jess and I were content just to listen. Later that evening, as Ben and I sat outside under the stars together, he asked, "Tara, are you going back to Texas after the rodeo next week?"

"Not yet," I admitted, my head against Ben's shoulder. "Charlie is still a danger, and I cannot risk going back until I know the law has arrested him. But once I know it's safe for us, I do need to go back and take care of some things. For one, I need to make sure the court gives me guardianship of Jess and Liam. I'm not sure how long it will take."

"I don't like the idea of you going back to Texas alone."

"I don't either," I admitted.

"Tara, have you made up your mind about what you want?"

"Yes, Ben," I said turning and looking up into his eyes. "I'm coming back to Montana once everything is settled. Texas isn't my home anymore. *You* are."

Ben lowered his head and kissed my lips, my eyelids, my hair. I was swept away with love for this man.

Ben released me and stood. "Wait here. I'll be right back." He got up and walked rapidly into the house. A moment later, he was back, this time with his guitar.

He sat down on the grass next to me. "I wrote something for you."

"You did?"

"Yes. You inspire me, Tara."

"Oh." My heart pounded faster inside my chest.

His eyes held mine as he settled the guitar under his arm. He strummed a few chords, got a good country rhythm going and began to sing.

There's a feeling in my soul—whenever we're together,
Warm, sunny days or cold, stormy weather,
And my heart sings 'cause I know it's forever,
Take my hand, oh baby, it's love—
Oh, honey, it's a love song—Big enough to last a life long
Take my hand and we will go along
Just you and me.
Turn it loose and let it fly, like an eagle in the blue, blue sky,
Come to me and we will dance a while,
Oh, honey, you'll see ... It's a love song.

"Ben." I gasped. "It's beautiful."

"It's for you, Tara honey."

"Sing it again." I demanded. This time, I hummed along with him in harmony.

Ben set the guitar down and reached for my hand. "Shall we dance?" He stood, pulled me to my feet and into his arms. Softly singing our love song together, we waltzed around the lawn, so much in love we were in a world of our own. The problems we faced just faded away as we danced. I didn't want the moment to end. I rested my head against his chest and smiled.

"Marry me, Tara," Ben said softly.

"Yes." I could hear his heart pounding in his chest. I turned my face up to him, and he kissed me, a kiss of promise for a future of love and joy.

We danced together under the stars while the moon drifted across the sky, wrapped up in love, dreaming, hoping, laughing.

The next morning at breakfast, I told Liam and Jesse, "Ben said he will fly to Texas if we need him, when it's safe to go back and settle things with the law. Then, if all goes well, it looks like we'll be coming back here to stay."

Jesse nudged Liam in the ribs and grinned. "Told you so." she said.

Liam tossed his back in laughter.

"And by the way, Ben and I are getting married."

Liam shouted, "Yes!"

Jesse jumped up and threw her arms around me. "I knew it. I knew it. He loves you."

I hugged Jesse and laughed. "Yes, I believe he does."

CHAPTER 43

The winds across the Rocky Mountains soon blew the smoke away from the ranch. Ben and I made a good team moving the smaller hay bales to the barn next to the house, and the round bales over to the big red barn across the valley.

"We've got plenty for our cattle and horses through the winter now, plus hay to sell later," Ben said. "It's good to have extra for other ranchers who might run short on it in the spring. Especially for those in the valley who lost their hay to the fire. In fact, we might want to mow another hundred acres or so."

"Are we keeping the cattle in our pasture through the winter? Or are we taking them over to your place?" I asked.

"I think it's more sheltered here," Ben said. "We have fierce, subzero winds in the winter, and this place has more natural windbreaks where the cattle can get away from it."

"Then let's keep them here," I said. "It makes more sense."

"We need to think about building an addition to this house too," Ben said, a secret smile on his lips.

"Why?" Liam asked.

Jesse said, "When Ben and Tara get married, Ben will move in here. We'll need more room."

Liam looked up at Ben, his eyes bright. "Having another man around the house will be awesome."

We all laughed as Ben ruffled Liam's hair and looked over at me. "We could build an add-on at the back of the house. I know a place where Dad and I can buy seasoned logs."

"That would be great. Let's do it," I said.

"I'd like to add a propane heater too," Ben said. "With a bigger house, we'll need more heat than the woodstove gives off. A second source of heat is a good idea out here in the mountains. How about looking at some designs tomorrow after work?"

"I like this one," Ben said the next evening, tapping one drawing. We were sitting at the kitchen table, house plans spread out before us. "It's got a main bedroom and a bath downstairs, and a couple of smaller bedrooms above them. The staircase on one end could go down into the pantry and open at the corner into the main room. What do you think, Tara?"

"I like it too. When we start a family of our own, we would have plenty of room for everyone."

Ben smiled. "A family of our own. That sounds nice."

"Ben! Ben! Come help! Golly's foot is bleeding!" Liam called from the yard.

Ben and I rushed outside.

"What happened, boy?" Ben asked, kneeling, and gently lifting a bloody paw. "It looks like he stepped on something sharp. We should take him to the vet to get this checked out."

Ben and Liam spent the rest of the morning at the vet's and came home without Golly.

"What happened?" Jesse demanded.

"The vet cleaned out the wound and put in about three stitches. We took Golly over to our place. Dad's going to keep an eye on him for a couple of weeks and make sure the wound heals. So, until the stitches are out, Golly will stay there."

"He'll be okay, Liam. He'll be back before you know it." I said, giving Liam a hug.

"I miss him already," Liam declared.

Despite the dog's absence, we were all feeling more relaxed now. Life in Montana was looking better each day. I felt safe again for the first time since March.

"No. Please. I have an offer on the house. I'll have the money to you in three months." Charlie screamed.

"It's too late, Charlie," Dino said. "Get him, boys."

Two large men standing by the door moved in and grabbed Charlie.

"Hold him down," Gino demanded, turning toward his desk. He pulled out a knife and advanced on Charlie.

"No!" Charlie screamed again.

The next morning, Charlie Webster staggered out of the kitchen in his Houston apartment holding a small bag of ice against his cheek where Gino Vincenti's man had slugged him. One of his front teeth felt loose. He hoped it wouldn't be a permanent problem. His hand, however, would never be the same. He glanced at the gauze bandage around his left hand. The little finger was gone. Gino said he'd keep cutting fingers off until Charlie paid up. He had given Charlie three more weeks to produce the full payment. If he didn't have it by then, Gino would take off the next finger.

Throwing his clothes into a suitcase, Charlie headed for the airport. He knew time was running out for him. Gino was growing impatient. Charlie desperately needed to find those kids and the horses.

Arriving at the Amarillo airport, he went straight to Evelyn's old, battered car which he'd left in the parking lot, tossed his things into it, and drove back to the ranch. There must be a clue someplace in Evelyn's files.

His hand throbbed abominably. He wished he had never met Gino or run up such a huge debt to the loan shark.

The house was stuffy from sitting without air conditioning in the summer sun. He flipped on a switch and opened the doors. The air outside was hot, but it was fresh.

He opened the fridge. Yes, there were a couple of beers sitting on the back of the top shelf. He pulled one out, popped it open and poured it into a beer mug. Taking a few swallows, he headed upstairs to search Evelyn's office again.

One by one, Charlie searched every piece of paper, every letter, every bill, looking for a clue.

He looked around Evelyn's bedroom. The dresser—wasn't it an antique? Yes. He remembered Evelyn talking about inheriting her grandmother's antique furniture. He emptied the drawers onto the bed and pulled the dresser out from the wall. He'd call the antique dealer in town. There were probably more antique pieces around too. He could raise some serious money this way.

Moving the heavy dresser out into the room, he saw an envelope stuck in the baseboard. *What is this? It's addressed to Evelyn from a G. Marten in Elliston, Montana. Who is G. Marten? Wait. Didn't Evelyn come from Montana? Was G. Marten a relative? Huh. This is a post office box. Better open it and see what this is.*

Curious, he slid the letter out. Wasn't Marten Evelyn's last name? Wait. She had a brother—one who died recently.

He skimmed the letter until halfway down the page he stopped and backed up to reread part of it.

My neighbor, Eli, is helping me with the ranch now. I'm getting too weak to do all the work myself. You remember Eli? He has a son about four years older than Tara. He's a good boy. Sometimes he comes over to help me too. When my time comes, Ruby Hollow Ranch will be yours. The doctor said I have about two months left.

Checking the date on the letter, he found it matched the date when Evelyn had gone north somewhere to her brother's funeral. "That's it!" he shouted, jumping up, excited by this new information. Evelyn had inherited a ranch—and that ranch must now belong to Tara. The kids must have gone to Montana. He looked again at the address—the Elliston post office. Where in Montana was Elliston?

He looked up the information online. There it was—close to Helena, the capitol.

He glanced back at the letter, simply signed, "George." He lived someplace called Ruby Hollow Ranch.

Charlie thought for a minute. He'd better check to see if there was a rodeo in Helena—maybe, just maybe—he found the rodeo number online and called. No, there was nobody named Tara Webster registered to ride in the July rodeo. If he didn't find her at the ranch, surely Tara would attend the rodeo, even if she wasn't performing. If she wasn't at the ranch, he could just take the horse. She probably had the papers in whatever house was on the property. He'd get those too. He had a friend who could fake ownership papers. The next rodeo was only a week away.

Swallowing the last of his beer, Charlie packed a bag, raced downstairs, closed the house, and jumped into the car. Montana would be quite a drive, but he would need a car once he got there, and he couldn't afford to fly or to get a car rental once he was there. If he could not find Sundance, he knew Gino would show him no mercy.

CHAPTER 44

FBI agents Brad Hanley and Kristine Noble arrived at the sheriff's office two days after Charlie Webster had headed north. Together, with Deputy Sheriff Morgan, their goal became three-fold—find the missing children, gather enough evidence to convict Charlie Webster of murder, then arrest him. They had no way of knowing Charlie had already left Texas in pursuit of the children.

First, they swept Willie Peterson away to a safe place until he would be needed to testify.

Agents Hanley and Noble, following Tyrel's tip, began a property title search, starting with Idaho and Montana, and quickly located Ruby Hollow Ranch, listed as belonging to Evelyn Webster.

"That must be where those children are," Tyrel said.

"It's a good possibility." Agent Noble agreed.

"Here's the letter Tara Webster sent me, the one her grandmother wrote." Tyrel handed it over to Kristine Noble. Agent Hanley looked over her shoulder.

"Hm," Brad Hanley mused. "Says here he keeps a trophy box. Quite common for serial killers. We could search Charlie Webster's apartment for the box. This could provide some good evidence … if we find it."

"Okay. I'll get us reservations on the next flight to Houston," Kristine said.

Five hours later, warrant in hand, they entered Charlie Webster's vacant apartment in Houston.

"I found it," Brad called from the bedroom.

Kristine joined him from another room to look at the box of trophies from Charlie's victims which had been hidden in a dark corner of the closet. Not the most original hiding place.

"Look. Here's a woman's wedding band and a medical alert necklace with Levi's name on it. There are a number of other personal items in the box too."

"The kid's letter said that Charlie took her Gran's wedding ring," Brad said, fingering the ring. "I'll bet the ring is hers. I think we've got him. This, plus the letters, plus Jesse Webster's and Willie Peterson's testimony, is enough to go to trial."

"I wonder who these other things belonged to?" Kristine said. "Looks like he may indeed be a serial killer. Well, he can't escape prosecution now. Let's go get him."

"We can check some other cold cases after we find him," Brad said. "Now that we know what we're looking for, we may be able to add to the charges."

The agents put out an all-points bulletin on Charlie before questioning the landlord.

"No, I ain't seen him around the last couple days." The man shrugged, his eyes bright with curiosity. "What'd he do? Rob a bank? Kill someone?"

"Can't say," Hanley said.

"He had a fat lip and a black eye last time I saw him. His hand was bandaged too."

"Hm. Interesting. Thanks for your help, sir."

"No problem." The landlord watched the agents head back to the apartment.

"He works at Gorman's Real Estate. That's just a few blocks north of here," the landlord called.

"Thanks." Kristine Noble turned and smiled briefly.

Back inside Charlie's apartment, the agents searched for clues as to where he might be.

"Here's his bank records," she called from the spare bedroom.

"Hm. Looks like he was being paid regularly by this real estate business," Brad said, scanning the pages. "They might know something."

Within an hour they managed to find Charlie's boss. "No, Charlie hasn't been in this week. He said he had to take some time off. Something about family business. You know he lost his mother lately, don't you?"

"Stepmother," Kristine corrected.

"Oh. I didn't know," she said with a shrug. "Anyway, I'm not expecting him back for another week or so."

"Do you know where he went?"

The boss shook her head. "No. He said something about a family ranch. That's all I heard."

"Thank you. If you hear from him, please contact us immediately," Brad replied, handing her a business card. As the office door closed behind him, Brad muttered, "We'd better find those kids before Webster does."

Hopping a commuter flight back to Amarillo and driving back to Doran, the agents reached the sheriff's office by evening. Tyrel was waiting in the office, ready to be useful.

"We'd better figure out where that ranch is and get up there." Kristine rubbed her neck.

"I'm printing it out now."

"Would you like some coffee?" Tyrel asked. "There's a fresh brew here."

"Sure. Thanks." Kristine said.

"That would be great," Brad said, grabbing the printed map.

"Tara might be doing rodeos this summer. She usually does several a year," Ty chipped in.

"Do you think she would try riding in a rodeo if it would alert her uncle?" Kristine asked Tyrel between sips of the strong brew.

"The kids must be getting low on cash by now. Yes. I think she might try doing a rodeo. It's a quick way to bring in some money—especially with a horse like Sundance."

"Okay. Then I'll start checking the rodeo circuit between Colorado, Idaho, and Montana. She might be registered to ride some place away from Ruby Hollow."

"Where's the nearest airport?" Tyrel asked, looking over Brad's shoulder.

"There's no airport in Elliston, but there's one in Helena."

"Let me see how soon we can fly out of here to Helena," Kristine said.

"I don't suppose you'd let me come along?" Tyrel asked, glancing at Kristine. "After all, I know Tara. If Charlie's already looking for her, we're running out of time. Horses are involved in this case too. I'd recognize Sundance easily. Plus, I'm good with horses. You may need me. I could be your CI."

Kristine exchanged glances with Brad. "Sure," she said. "We're working against the clock on this one. You would be quite handy to have along."

"I'm worried about Charlie Webster," said Brad in agreement. "If he shows up, it would be nice to be able to spot him before he finds those kids. I've never seen him other than in the one photo."

"Thanks." Tyrel nodded.

"Hey! Don't get in the way," Brad cautioned.

"I am a police officer, you know," Ty said dryly. "I know the rules." Walking over to the lunchroom, he said, "Malone, the FBI needs my help in Montana, so I'll be flying north with them immediately. Would you take over while I'm away?

The other deputy nodded between bites. "Sure thing, Ty."

"Thanks. I'll trade you a couple of days work next week."

"I need to put a call in to the sheriff in Helena before we leave. It's the closest police department to the airport and to that rodeo we need to check out." Kristine found the phone number. "Sheriff Carlson? This is Agent Noble with the FBI. We are going to be in your area tomorrow looking for some missing children and a probable murderer. The kids are Tara, Jesse, and Liam Webster. The murderer's name is Charlie Webster. He's about forty-five, six-foot-two, has brown hair flecked with gray, and green eyes. He may already be in Helena. I'll text you his photo. We'll be flying in tomorrow morning from Amarillo, Texas. Pass it around to your deputies just in case they see him. It's possible the kids will be at the rodeo. We'll be bringing the sheriff's deputy from Doran, Texas, with us. He knows the kids and Charlie."

"I'll meet your flight," Sheriff Carlson said. "I've seen the children and know where they live."

Sheriff Carlson, a distinguished, middle-aged man with gray hair, shook hands with Hanley, Noble, and Morgan. "Thanks for the photos. Let me know if you'll need me. Here's my card. Otherwise, I'll stay out of your way."

"Thanks, Sheriff," Agent Hanley said, "but this may be an emergency, and we'll need your help." He held out the photo of Charlie Webster. "This is the guy we're looking for. If you see him, call me at this number. We'll take it from there." He handed his card to the sheriff. "The three Webster kids ran away from Texas to get away from their uncle, Charlie Webster. One of the kids saw him kill their grandmother. So, I'm guessing they are running scared. Tara is a pro-rodeo competitor. We didn't see her name among the performers for your rodeo, but she'll probably be there today, I'm thinking. If we don't find her sooner."

"Those kids go to my church. I know where they live too. Their place is just across the line in Powell County. I'll call the sheriff there and let him know what's going on. Do you want me to go up there while you hit the rodeo? It may take a while for the other sheriff to get to the ranch."

"No, thanks. You are familiar with the rodeo. You cover it while we head out to their ranch."

"Okay. I'll post some deputies at the fairgrounds," Sheriff Carlson said. "Thanks for the fliers."

Turning to Tyrel, Noble introduced him. "This is the Deputy Tyrel Morgan from Doran, Texas. He's been working the case and knows the kids and the man in this picture. If you find Charlie Webster, arrest him. He's dangerous. We believe he has already killed at least two people. Maybe more."

Sheriff Carlson nodded. "Thanks for the information. I'll pass it along."

"Could you point us in the direction of Ruby Hollow?" said Agent Nobel.

"Sure." Sheriff Carlson drew directions on his notepad and handed the paper to them. "If you get lost, just give me a call."

"Thanks." The FBI agents nodded and left with Tyrel.

An hour later, Agent Hanley called Sheriff Carlson. "Sheriff, we had trouble finding Ruby Hollow. Could you guide us there?"

"Sure. Where are you?"

"We're at the gas station in Elliston."

"Okay. I'll meet you there in twenty minutes." While Sheriff Carlson remembered seeing the Webster kids at church, he had not guessed that they were in trouble, though he had picked up fear in Tara's voice when Ben had introduced her.

"Lord, please help us to find these kids before Charlie Webster does. Keep them safe. In Jesus's name, amen."

He turned on his lights and siren and headed toward Elliston.

CHAPTER 45

Twenty minutes before the FBI agents arrived in Elliston, Charlie Webster had walked into the Elliston post office and looked around. This is barely a town, he thought. A convenience store, a small motel, a school, and a few houses scattered around. Charlie gave his most charming smile to the postmistress, who was closing the customer window. A sign above the counter indicated the post office was only open until noon.

"Yes? May I help you?" She paused, her hand on the window.

"Yes. I'm looking for a ranch around here that used to be owned by a man named George Marten. My nieces and nephew came up here for a visit, and I need to get in touch with them. Their grandmother died. I'm having a tough time finding the ranch."

The woman examined him. "Well, there *was* a rancher here named George Marten. He died about a year ago. I believe he left the property to his sister who lives in Texas."

"That's the one." Charlie laughed, flashing a beautiful smile at her. "Where can I find the ranch?"

Sliding a piece of paper with directions on it to him she said, "The ranch is called Ruby Hollow."

"Thank you so much. You've been quite helpful." Ruby Hollow was close. His excitement mounting, he climbed into Evelyn's car, and drove back onto the highway. The directions took him right to the turnoff.

Carefully, he drove down the long drive searching for a place to hide his car. He could see the house now in the distance, through the trees. Ah. A dim track lead down to the creek. He could follow the path and park out of sight of the road.

Parking behind some willow trees near the creek, Charlie made his way toward the log cabin. Through the trees, he saw a girl riding a horse. Sundance. Yes!

I was alone. A meadowlark's song filled the air. Wildflowers bloomed in a profuse explosion of delicate colors on the hillside. The sun's warmth felt good on my shoulders.

Earlier that morning, Ben had stopped by the house.

"Hi, Tara," he said, kissing me firmly and wrapping his arms around my waist. "Want to go to the rodeo today?"

"I'll go this afternoon." I smiled up into his eyes. "We have tickets to see the roping and bull riding later. I have a few things I need to do here first."

"Aww!" Liam whined. "I wanna go now!"

Ben saw Liam's disappointed expression. "I could take Jess and Liam now and bring them back for a late lunch, if you want."

"That sounds good," I said. "I'll look for you about one o'clock. Okay?"

"Yay!" Liam shouted.

"Okay. Kids, get in the truck!" Ben said, laughing.

"Thanks, Ben. I know the kids really wanted to go this morning."

Ben gave me a quick kiss and headed for the truck. "See you in a few hours," he called over his shoulder.

I waved as they drove away. Back inside the cabin, I finished cleaning the kitchen and started the laundry. Wanting to spend some time alone with Jesus, I took my Bible and settled into a corner of the couch to read and pray. This quiet time alone with God had proven to be my strength during these long days since Gran's murder.

Around eleven o'clock, I headed for the pasture to saddle Rosie. I needed to practice with both horses for a while before leaving for the rodeo. I was hoping we could be in the first rodeo available after Tyrel and the law caught up with Charlie.

I put Rosie through her paces first. She wasn't as fast as Sundance, but she was almost as good as he was at barrel racing. Patting her neck, I rode her back to the barn and put her saddle away. After brushing her down, I turned her loose in the pasture again with her colt, standing for a moment to watch the colt trot happily to his mother and thrust his nose below her belly to nurse.

"Come on, Sundance," I said, leading the big stallion up toward the barn where I saddled him. "We've got a workout ahead of us."

Sundance, who had been waiting impatiently at the fence while I exercised Rosie, nuzzled my shoulder, and pricked up his ears. He loved our daily routine.

Across the valley, hidden by the willows, Charlie Webster watched. As far as he could tell, Tara was at the ranch alone. He'd waited patiently while she worked with Rosie. This might be the best time to act, he thought, watching her work with Sundance, the horse he just had to have—the horse that could eliminate his debt and save his life. He moved stealthily through the trees toward the house.

CHAPTER 46

The July sun beat down on me as I worked with the big stallion. He went through the paces like the pro he was. Fifteen minutes into our workout, I heard the first roll of thunder and glanced up. I hadn't noticed the clouds coming in from the east. A distant flash lit the sky followed a few seconds later by thunder, this time louder.

"Whoa, Sundance," I said, drawing him up short. "We'd better head for cover." I turned the horse and nudged him into a trot. As we approached the barn, the horse became skittish. Strange, I thought, he's never been afraid of lightning before. I reined him in and dismounted as lightning flashed more closely this time and big drops of rain landed in the dust with a thud.

I led Sundance toward the barn to unsaddle him and brush him down.

But Sundance was restless. He tried to pull away, his ears laid back, nickering nervously.

"What's wrong, boy?" I asked, rubbing his neck reassuringly.

As we were passing the hay bales stacked next to the small barn, Sundance neighed and pulled sharply back, dragging me with him. As I struggled with the horse, a bale of hay crashed to the ground right where I would have been the next second! Only Sundance's quick jerk had saved me.

An instant later, I heard a harsh shout of rage. Uncle Charlie dropped from the top of the hay bales to the ground right in front of me. In his right hand, he held a fat stick. Raising his arm, he swung the club down at me.

I fell back against Sundance's shoulder, still holding onto the reins, a scream of fear rising in my throat. I heard the whistle of the stick slice down through the air and felt a stab of pain as it landed on the edge of my shoulder and slid down my arm. I let go of the reins.

Charlie, furious, whipped the stick back up above his head and took aim again.

He's going to kill me! Panicking, I turned to run, tripped, and landed hard on the ground next to the horse.

Sundance saw the stick descending and smelled his old nemesis. Giving a high, wild scream, he reared up. His flashing hooves caught Charlie across the chest and knocked him to the ground. Before Charlie could roll out of the way, Sundance came down on him, his right front hoof crushing Charlie's chest. The horse pushed away to get off the man, crushing the bones even deeper into Charlie's chest, and jerked away.

I laid still, rain pouring over and around me, stunned at what had happened in a matter of seconds.

Seeing Charlie's face pale with shock, I pushed myself up from the ground. He could barely breathe, for the weight of the horse had driven his ribs into his lungs. Lying in the dust, Charlie stared up at me, his eyes huge. "You're ... just ... shot with ... luck!" he gasped. With that, he died, his eyes still fixed on me, blood spilling out of his mouth.

Holding my bruised shoulder and crying hysterically, I didn't hear the cars coming up the drive or the sirens or the slam of the car doors. I was in a world of shock. But I did hear Tyrel Morgan's voice when he said, "Tara? Are you okay?" He put one hand on my good shoulder.

"Tyrel!" I gasped. "What are you doing here?"

"I got your letter and figured out where you were. Let me see your shoulder," he demanded.

I pulled the neckline of my knit blouse down over my wounded shoulder and exposed the throbbing flesh.

"Whew! Looks painful," Ty said, raindrop rivulets chasing each other down his face. "We'll have to get that taken care of."

I pulled the blouse back up, still too traumatized to speak.

Tyrel turned me away from Charlie's body and walked me toward the bench in front of the house where the roof extended overhead. "Let's get you under shelter. You should sit down. You've had a shock."

I gratefully sank down on the bench, holding my arm close, and gasped, "He tried to kill me."

"Yes, I know. But you are safe now, Tara." He put his arm around my uninjured shoulder. "It looks like we got here just a little late. Thank God for Sundance."

I continued to shiver as I worked to calm down.

A black SUV and a patrol car were parked in the ranch yard.

"Here. Let me put a blanket around you, Tara," Sheriff Carlson said kindly, coming from his patrol car and draping a blanket around my shoulders.

A man and a woman wearing FBI jackets took pictures of Charlie. The man fetched a tarp to toss over the body. Together, they turned and headed my way.

"Miss Tara Webster?" the woman asked, wiping the rain from her face as she stepped under the roof next to me.

"Yes," I said, looking up blankly.

"I'm Agent Noble of the FBI. This is Agent Hanley. Deputy Morgan called us in on the case when he got your letter."

"Thank you for coming," I said, a sudden shiver shaking me. "We have been afraid of Charlie for a long time."

Sheriff Carlson walked back over to his patrol car and radioed back to the police station. "I need you to send an ambulance and a photo crew up to Ruby Hollow Ranch west of MacDonald Pass. The case started in Lewis & Clark County, but now it's over the county line. Contact the sheriff for Powell County. Let him know the case took me here. He may already be on his way. It's the ranch formerly owned by George Marten."

Tyrel soothed Sundance and led him into the corral, returning quickly to make sure I was okay.

Sheriff Carlson came over and sat down next to me on the bench. "Tara, the Lord was looking out for you today," he said. "You are safe now. The FBI may need you to answer some questions. I know I do too. Do you want to tell us the whole story of what happened?"

For the next half hour, the FBI agents and Sheriff Carlson listened and took notes, throwing in questions along the way. Finally, the sheriff said, "Do you have anyone you could call to come out here to be with you?"

I nodded and with shaking hands reached into my pocket for my phone just as Ben's truck came roaring up the road. A moment later, he jumped out and, with long strides, ran over to me, Jesse and Liam right behind him.

"Tara! Are you okay?" he called. Rushing forward, he gathered me in his arms. "What's going on?"

I winced. "Watch out for my shoulder," I gasped.

He quickly loosened his grip. "You're hurt?"

Jesse and Liam stared at the long figure covered with a tarp.

"Charlie tried to kill me, but Sundance stopped him."

Ben gasped and drew me gently to his chest, then turned to look at the stallion standing at the corral fence, one of his hooves still bloody from the encounter.

Jesse and Liam stared at me with wide eyes. "Who's that under the tarp?" Jesse asked.

"Charlie," I said, turning toward the children. "He's dead. You don't need to worry about him killing anyone ever again." I held out my arms and gathered Jess and Liam close.

Agent Noble said, "Our job was to arrest Charlie Webster and to take you and your brother and sister back to Texas so Jesse could testify at his murder trial. But there won't be any trial now. Your uncle had the sheriff in Doran issue a local alert for you in your home county. But now that we know the whole story, you are free to work this out with the authorities in Texas yourself. I don't think you will have any problems. We'll be submitting our report to the FBI and the sheriff there." She turned to Tyrel. "We'll wait for you to be finished here. Afterward, how about doing dinner in Helena before flying back to Texas?

Tyrel grinned. "Sounds good to me, Kristine."

He turned to me. "I think you will need to come back to Doran to settle a few things, Tara. Your lawyer said your grandmother left everything to you, and she appointed you guardian of your brother and sister. Now that Charlie is gone, the Texas ranch will be yours. You'll need to work out the legal paperwork for custody of your sister and brother. But I don't think that's going to be a problem."

I breathed a sigh of relief and buried my head against Ben's strong shoulder.

"I appreciated you sending me those letters, Tara," Tyrel continued. "After I received them, I was able to call in the FBI. Looks like Charlie killed more than a few people. Anyway, you are safe now, and that's what matters."

"Thank you for helping me, Ty," I said. "I've been following the case online. When I saw that you were in charge, I knew I could trust you. Sheriff Bradshaw—not so much. He was Charlie's friend."

"I appreciate your confidence," he said, nodding. "Your letters were what opened up this case."

An ambulance made its way up the drive. Sheriff Carlson directed them to the body. Ben stood between the children and the medics, his arms across their shoulders facing them away from the broken body so they wouldn't see it being moved into the ambulance.

Sheriff Carlson spoke to one of the medics. "I'd like you to look at Tara's shoulder before you leave. The dead man tried to kill her with that stick laying over there," he said, pointing to the hefty rod lying on the ground. "He missed her head, but he managed to hit her shoulder pretty hard."

The medic came over to me while the other medic strapped Charlie's body into the ambulance. "Could you show me where he hit you, miss?"

I pulled the neckline of my blouse down to show my shoulder to the medic.

Ben gasped. "That was close, Tara!"

"I know." I glanced up and saw the shock on his face. "But I'm okay, Ben. Don't worry."

The medic gently examined it. "I think you'll have quite a bruise there," she said. "But I don't think anything is broken. Here. Let me put some ointment and a light bandage on it." She efficiently proceeded to patch me up with Ben, Liam, and Jesse watching intently. The soothing medicine took the burning sensation out of the wound.

"Would you like us to take you to the hospital and let a doctor examine you?" she asked, taping down the bandage efficiently.

I shook my head. "No, thanks. I will put some ice on it. If it doesn't feel better later today, I'll have Ben take me to one of the Urgent Care places."

"Okay. But let me give you some Tylenol, a tube of this ointment and a few bandages to use in the next day or so. It's going to hurt pretty bad."

I pulled my blouse back up. "Thank you for helping me," I said.

She smiled, handed me some packets of Tylenol and bandages. "You take care now."

Ben's arm came around me gently.

Tyrel grinned. "Tara, I can see you are in good hands."

"Ty, this is Ben Farley—my fiancé."

Tyrel's eyebrows shot up. He chuckled and held out his hand. "Congratulations, Ben. You are getting one very brave girl for a wife."

Ben smiled and took the young deputy's hand, keeping one arm around me. "Tara told me you were one person she could trust in Doran. She mentioned your dad too. So, thank you. I'm sure glad to meet you, Tyrel."

"Likewise." Looking at me, Tyrel asked, "When do you think you'll be coming back to Texas, Tara?"

"As soon as we can arrange it. I'd say we can be there in a couple of weeks."

"See you then," Tyrel said, turning to walk back to the SUV through the rain.

"Are you planning on driving back to Texas with the children?" Ben asked.

I nodded. "Yes." I could see he was uncomfortable with the idea. "We'll be okay, Ben."

He sighed and scratched the back of his head, a troubled look on his face. "How long do you think you'll be gone?"

"I'm not sure. Maybe a month. I doubt it will take longer to take care of things."

"I see." Ben looked down and scuffed the toe of one boot on the lawn. "Listen, Tara. If you have any problems at all, call me. I'll fly down and help you."

"Okay." I gazed up into his eyes. "Don't worry, Ben. I'll be back. I promise to call you every night. If I have any problems about getting custody of the children, Tyrel can testify that he's met you and can confirm that we're getting married. That should settle any doubts the court might have about our security here."

"All right. But if you need me, just let me know, and I'll be there," Ben said, pulling me back into his arms. "Dad can take care of the livestock until we get back."

Jesse, who had ducked inside the house for a moment, returned with a bag of frozen peas and handed it to me. "Put this on your shoulder," she demanded.

"Thank you, Jess," I said. Gingerly, I put the frozen bag over the bruise.

After the FBI, the ambulance, the sheriff, and Tyrel finally left, Ben and I walked into the house with Jesse and Liam. We had all started to calm down a little by then, and Liam was hungry.

"I don't think I could eat a bite, Ben," I said. Outside, the thunder had ceased but light rain still made a pleasant, homey sound on the roof.

"Just sit down in the big chair, Tara. I'm gonna make some ham and cheese sandwiches for us all. When you're ready, you can eat. A few minutes later, he set a sandwich and a glass of milk on the small coffee table next to me and put the remaining sandwiches and milk on the table.

"Come," he told the kids, coaxing them over to the table but moving his own chair up close to mine. He reached out for my hand, and the younger children joined hands too.

Ben prayed, "Father in heaven, we are full of thanks today. Thank you for watching out for Tara, Liam, and Jesse today. Thank you for removing all danger from them. Thank you for providing all their needs, according to your riches. Thank you for the food that you have provided. Continue blessing us this day we ask in Jesus's name. Amen."

Later that evening, with the rain past and stars twinkling above us in the cool, night sky and the moon glowing softly, Ben and I walked hand in hand, breathing in the fresh, Montana air.

"It seems unbelievable we're finally free!" I said, leaning against Ben's shoulder.

"Um." Ben nuzzled my hair. "God has a way of working things out, I've noticed. You know, Tara, I might never have met you if you hadn't left Texas."

"Yes, you would have," I said. "God had a plan for us. Some things are just meant to be."

EPILOGUE

In June of the following year, I stood once again in my Texas bedroom, in front of the full-length mirror, wearing a delicate, off the shoulder, white wedding dress.

On the lawn below my bedroom window stood a For Sale sign with a diagonal "Sold" sticker pasted over it. The ranch had been handed down to me, and I had sold it. A small moving van was parked behind the barn ready for Eli to take some of Gran's furniture and other items we would need back to Montana after the wedding. Liam and Jess would go with him while Ben and I went on our honeymoon.

My hair was pulled back in a chignon, a long, tulle veil fastened just above it with a spray of miniature red roses. My friend, Jenna, dressed in pink satin and lace, looked me over to make sure everything was in place, then handed me the bridal bouquet of red roses and baby's breath.

"You look beautiful, Tara. Who would have thought you'd have to run away to Montana to find your sweetheart? Weren't there enough cowboys here in Texas?"

I laughed. "Jenna, I have loved Ben since I was twelve years old. He is the only cowboy I have ever dreamed about."

Music floated up from the shady lawn. Jesse and Liam, of whom I now had custody, awaited me at the foot of the stairs, ready to precede me down the aisle. The shadows were long, and the air was cooling off as the last rays of the sun disappeared behind the trees.

Walking ahead of me, Jenna led the way down the staircase and out the sliding glass door, stepping onto the long, white runner. Fireflies twinkled in the evening air. Tiki torches lined the perimeter where our guests sat. Fairy lights glowed on the latticework arch where Ben waited, his eyes fixed on me, a warm smile on his face.

The string quartet paused then began playing *Pachelbel's Canon in D*, signaling the small audience of friends and family to stand.

But I had eyes only for the tall Montanan, standing at the other end of the aisle.

My eyes met Ben's, and I walked forward to take his hand. He was my life, my love, my true home.

ABOUT THE AUTHOR

Sheri Schofield is a Bible teacher and award–winning author/illustrator, serving God in the Rocky Mountains of Montana. Colorado Christian Writers' Conference named her Writer of the Year in 2018.

Sheri began teaching the Bible as a young teenager with Child Evangelism Fellowship. By the time she was fifteen, she was teaching her own Sunday school class of second–grade girls. During college, she studied theology and Christian education of children at Prairie Bible College and Biola University in preparation for her lifework.

After many years of teaching children about Jesus through her classes and books, Sheri now writes for adults as well. She is a member of Advanced Writers & Speakers Association (AWSA). Along with a great team of other writers at Arise,

AWSA named her Arise Daily Devotions Writer of the Year in 2020.

Sheri is the president of Faithwind 4 Kids ministry, serving alongside Tim, her husband. The ministry's focus is to put her books about salvation into the hands of children, teens, and their parents.

"I see myself as a planter, throwing seeds out into a field. The books are the seeds. The people around me are the field. God waters the seeds, which grow in people's hearts and eventually become his harvest. My job is to plant the seeds of the gospel, then pray for God to work," Sheri says. "I want to do my part in helping others meet Jesus. In Daily Devotions (arisedailydevos.wordpress.com), Sheri offers insights about God's work in our lives. She often brings her life among the wild creatures of Montana into her writing.

If you've enjoyed *Before You Find Me*, please write a line or two about the book on Amazon, Goodreads, or Barnes & Noble. Reviews mean the world to us authors—they're what keep us writing!

Contact me at https://sherischofield-faithwind4kids. com. I'd love to hear from you.

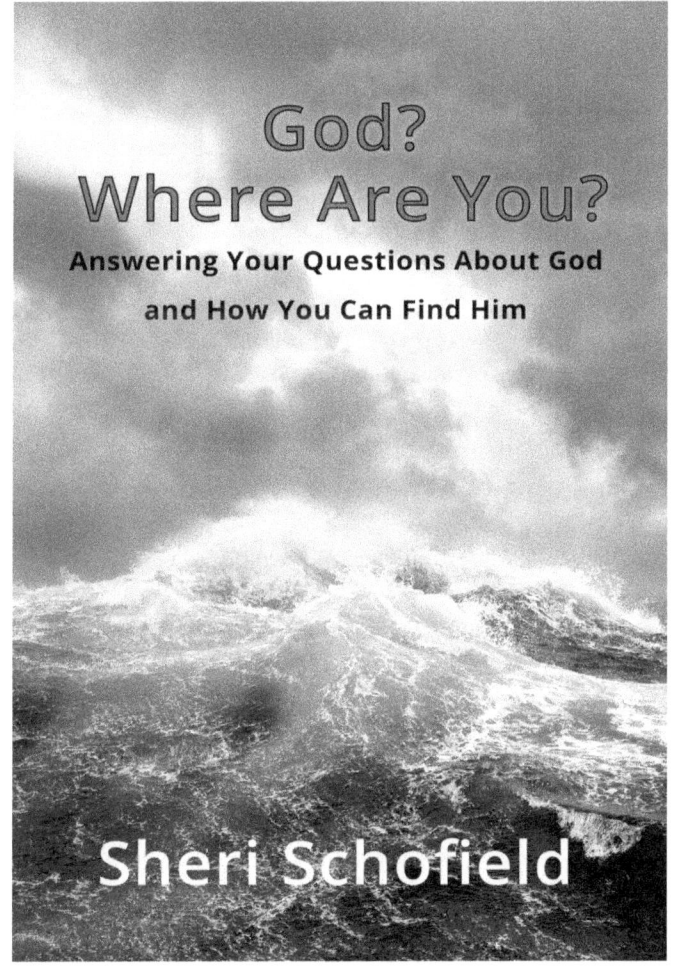

God?
Where Are You?

Answering Your Questions About God
and How You Can Find Him

Sheri Schofield

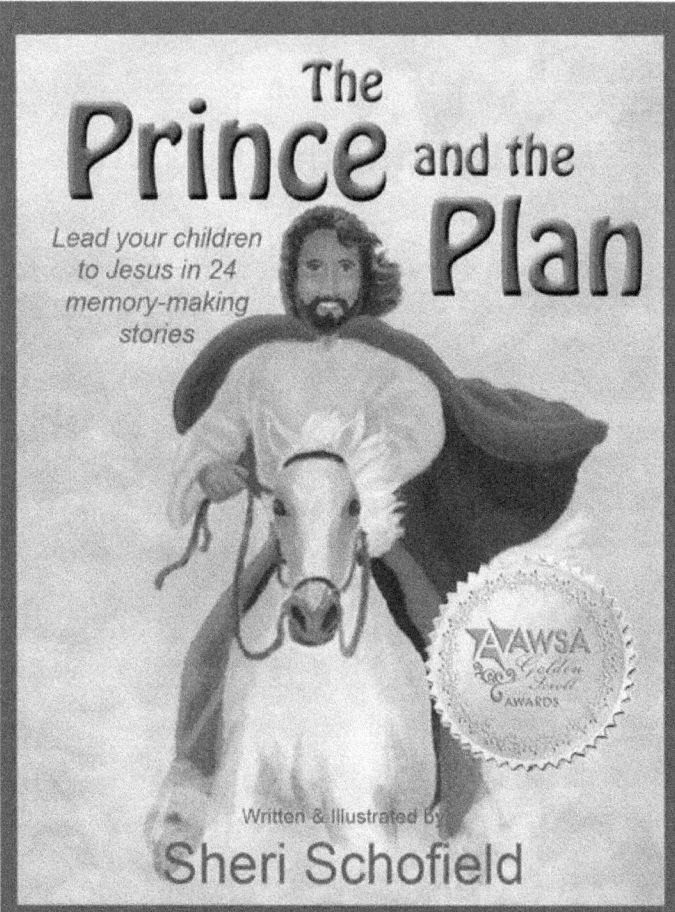

The
Prince and the
Plan

*Lead your children
to Jesus in 24
memory-making
stories*

Written & Illustrated by
Sheri Schofield

AWSA
*Golden
Scroll*
AWARDS

S.M. HAUSEN

Based on True Events

ONE STEP AHEAD *of* *the* DEVIL

A STORY OF HONOR AND BETRAYAL